The S
Salva

by the same author

VOICES UNDER THE WINDOW

JOHN HEARNE

The Sure Salvation

faber and faber

LONDON · BOSTON

First published in 1981
by Faber and Faber Limited
3 Queen Square, London WC1N 3AU
First published in this edition in 1985
Reprinted in 1986

Printed in Great Britain by
Redwood Burn Ltd., Trowbridge, Wiltshire
All rights reserved

British Library Cataloguing in Publication Data

Hearne, John
The sure salvation.
I. Title
813[F]   PR9265.9.H4
ISBN 0–571–13452–1

for
SHIVAUN ALISON HEARNE
and
LEETA MARY HEARNE
in custom and in ceremony

Part One

THE POOP

CHAPTER ONE

1

By the tenth day, the barque was ringed by the unbroken crust of its own garbage. And the refuse itself had discharged a contour of dully iridescent grease which seemed to have been painted onto the sea with one stroke of a broad brush.

By the fifteenth day, even the most insensitive of the five hundred and sixteen souls aboard tried not to see this clinging evidence of their corruption, which the water would not swallow and the sun could not burn. Occasionally a small shark rushed avidly from the depths, seized a jettisoned fragment and vanished on a turn. Otherwise the ship was the still centre of a huge stillness: pasted to the middle of a glazed plate that was the sea, exactly under the dome of a gigantic and impenetrable cover-lid.

It was now, as the calm entered its third week, that a vague and debilitating panic began to gnaw at the crew. A curious sense of expectancy attended any group of seated men. Abrupt and unnecessary labour was invented by the sailors before any direction from the officers. And these bursts of activity were succeeded by periods of quiet, mournful tenseness, as if each man were trying to fashion for himself some memory of the world's tumult.

In this prison of unyielding silence and immobility their only proofs of being were the writhing edge of the sun and the nightly fattening of the moon. They were tantalized by the conviction that immediately beyond the walls of opaque blue—on the horizon's edge, if only they could get there—they would find waves running before the wind, curling at their crests with a hiss of spray, and a sky loud with swooping birds that shrieked beautiful and reassuring discords.

In the cabin behind the wheel on the poop deck, Hogarth raised his eyes from the meticulous copperplate of his noon entry: at a distance, the words and figures could have been mistaken for print.

For a little while, etching them with such precision, Hogarth had been happy. It was not often at sea that he could experience the dutiful pleasure of fashioning letters as he had been taught. Too often the shudder of the barque as it lunged into a wave would mar the smooth hook that should have completed an *a*, or the bows would toss briskly, forcing the table up against his hand and squashing the perfect curve at the top of the 9. Now, in this calm, the deck steady as the floor of a room, his fist returned effortlessly to its first lessons. Almost as if that other, loving hand in the long-ago rectory of his boyhood had closed around his and guided the pen.

He shut his eyes and drew a deep, quick breath, as though the thick air of the little cabin had become suddenly suffocating. The memory of that hand enfolding his as it rested on the glossy surface of the yet unmarked page had surprised him cruelly. And with it, the excitement of the new adventure, the anticipation of the inevitable approval that would be his, both from the slight, lilac-scented woman, who leaned over the back of his chair as he sat squarely to the table before his first copy book, and from the stout, clumsily assembled man with two strands of lank, greying hair always caught between his temples and the arms of his spectacles.

"Oh William! That was *splendid*. The whole alphabet at your first attempt."

"Can I show father?"

" 'May I show father', dear. Of course."

Scampering ahead of her, buoyantly carried on the waves of her loving pride, he bounced into the large study where the few books, the small desk, the worn little rug were overwhelmed, incongruous, like peasants occupying a corner of an abandoned palace.

"Father, father! Look, I've made the alphabet."

"Well, well ... let me see ... so you have. But this deserves a reward. Hannah, my dear, are you sure this is not your work? I scent deceit here. Oh yes! Conspiracy to defraud a poor father. The whole alphabet. Such work must be worth at least . . . What would you say, William? What is a fair return against so mighty a labour?"

Awkwardly histrionic, he was doomed to these ponderous declarations of his great love, as his inept body was fated always to stumble over the one obtrusive stone in a smooth path, to brush the fragile ornament to the floor, to jolt the table when he rose as the ladies retired.

Hogarth had seen none of this for a long time. The child's barbaric mind has a great capacity for acknowledging essentials only: the glow in the weak eyes behind the thick spectacles, the six pennies' worth of reward for his aptitude that represented—he was later to realize—a week without tobacco for a man who had no indulgence but that.

These were the essentials. These and the silent exchange of astonished pleasure he had surprised between the two who had, so improbably, fashioned five years before his vibrant body with its little bull's neck, deep chest, wide flat back and chubby tireless legs.

He was the one triumph of their failed, exhausted lives. His happiness and radiant security compensated for the sullen parishioners who responded to their shy, clumsy offerings of care with contempt, and who spoke with servile nostalgia of their brusque, patronizing predecessors.

They had known themselves to be dull, timid and irritating; accepted their irrelevancy without bitterness: when they first discovered each other it had been difficult for either to believe that the world did not intend to forbid a consummation. And when they realized that the world would not because the world did not care, they had eloped. Eloped and matched for two weeks, the two sleeping animals within them. At first they had been appalled, then astonished, then utterly confounded by joy at how quickly the two untended, uncertain beasts grew fierce and sleek with abandon.

They had returned, penitential after the marvelling whispers and the new laughter and the long nearly unbearable shudders that visited the bodies they had learned to tangle so expertly.

9

And when they discovered that repentance was not needed (her parents had been glad to consign her to the shambling diffident thief of a curate who carried his poverty with such gross meekness), they withdrew, finally, into the obscure shelter of a love into which nobody would ever take the trouble to pry.

It was as if they had spent all their capacity for adventure in finding each other; and they were grateful, really, when her father pulled a lesser string and they were offered the declining agricultural parish—long since drained of its young people by the great town to the east— which nobody else could be persuaded to take except as a temporary posting: they simply sailed, without complaint, into this early harbour that was neither commodious nor hospitable.

The birth of their son, long after they had any right to expect it, had nearly frightened them. It had seemed almost like theft; for months after he was born they were both tormented by a vague, irrational panic that they would be somehow "discovered" in possession of happiness.

And neither dared admit this to the other. Not for fear of arousing laughter or impatience—they were both accustomed to these—but because admission might let their guilty secret abroad: start the hue and cry.

One night in the confessional dark of the old rectory's master bedroom (for which they could never afford sufficient coal in winter, which was always dank with the winter's chill in summer) little Mrs Hogarth had begun to sob raggedly into the hollow between her husband's neck and shoulder.

Promise me, should I die first, that you will not let them take him away.

Take him away! Woman, are you mad? What? ... They'd have a business, I assure you.

His growl was such a ludicrous assumption of ferocity that she began to giggle. And then he too had begun to laugh. At himself as much as with her. And in their laughter, and in their subsequent slow, infinitely tender coupling, the fantasy about losing the child was laid. After that night, they were never again afraid of anything. They ceased, even, to be embarrassed by surly or ungracious manners. They had too much to do.

In the confidence born of this release, they had the temerity to become ambitious.

Not for themselves, to be sure, but for the small, vigorous flame of life they had kindled when it was nearly too late; when their own gentle fires had become scarcely more than hands clasped or a back hugged on a cold night. In the many-roomed old rectory—built on a manorial scale during an age when wool tithes had supported two curates and an impressive stable—the underfed, ageing couple dreamed of conquests for their son, performing miracles of deprivation on themselves against the rewards of his future.

Here, at last, they proved themselves competent, indeed cunning. The boy was almost fourteen before he realized the other cargo that freighted the heavy box of fine linen, stout boots and expensive books he took to school each term.

It happened, as do all the discoveries that are going to determine a life, in a moment: the landfall at the end of a voyage without charts. But for the child, landfall had been shipwreck in the dark. He had foundered on pity and guilt without a warning, although afterwards it seemed to him that he should have realized the portents earlier. The unreplaced teeth, the dress washed to drabness, the boots drying on the rack above the stove with cardboard cutouts lining the inner soles, the grey potato-nourished faces which were the price of the glutinous delicacies in a boy's tuck box. These had been there all the time: warning rocks exposing themselves at intervals above the waves of a lee shore. The two old people who loved him beyond discretion had acted out, with consummate and pathetic skill, a pretence of well-being; but they could not protect him from the confusion that pity and guilt bring to those who nourish them too early.

Animal attachment to those who care for them, sympathy and simple acts of contrition are all that should be demanded of children. The greater emotions, in their hands, become purely destructive.

Hogarth leaned back in his chair. Now that his entry was complete, he could feel the impotent quiet of the ship settle on him again like a useless burden to be shouldered up a hill. There was no comfort now in the disciplined achievement of

11

the two lines of writing that headed the fresh page of the log. Behind them were fourteen, no fifteen, nearly identical entries. With each entry he recorded the progress of a battle that must end in his defeat. For a moment he tensed in his chair, as if gathering his energy to hurl it against the bright stillness beyond the cabin. Then, slowly, he relaxed and closed his log on the lines that read:

Noon, May 17, 1860—Lat 1° 14' S, Long 32° 16' W. No distance. Calm continues. Full sails set. Cargo in prime condition because of our special care.

On the table before him was a desk-set of heavy silver: two inkwells, one covered, sunk into a broad slab, the raised rim of the open well curved over and in so that the pen was dipped into the trapped ink through the small end of an inverted cone; the pens themselves, in their solid exactness of quill shape, might have been selected from the feathers of some large, enchanted silver goose.

Hogarth removed the pens, laying them on a square of chamois spread on the right of the dense slab. He picked up the cover of one well from the same square of stained leather and began to screw it on slowly, lifting his hand after each turn and gripping again with the same concentration until, in mid-turn, the threads of rim and cover made final engagement. His scrupulous, slow and methodical movements gave an incongruous significance to the mechanical exercise, as though he were salvaging a fragile artifact from the chaos of a midden. He lifted the desk-set and put it into the bottom compartment of the pigskin secretary which stood on the table one foot in front and one foot to the side of his right hand. The two objects —the massy silver desk-set and the handsome secretary—stood out against the frugal neatness of the little cabin like two patricians strayed into a suburb of anxious, genteel appearances. They belonged in a setting of large confident gestures.

Hogarth said, "Well, that's finished, my dear," in the bright, false voice of one visiting a bed of incurable and petulant sickness. Abruptly he took up the long, thick-stemmed silver pen

12

from beside the log and began to clean the steel nib with a little square of black-stained green felt.

Across the cabin, the woman reading on the small settee under the port window raised her head. Grey, small eyes flatly met Hogarth's tentative smile. Her full, round-chinned face was pale with heat and a few threads of fading yellow hair had stuck to the film of grease on her broad forehead.

"What did you say, Captain Hogarth?" she asked, and closed the book on her forefinger.

"It was nothing, Eliza," Hogarth said carefully. It was in these moments of banal domestic exchange that she so often sprang her quiet, merciless reminders of the past, tearing at the shell he had been able to grow around himself during a week's respite. Any chance remark might serve to start these bitter, righteous reproaches. Anything at all. And they would continue —low-pitched, corrosive, unforgiving—until his harsh appeal for silence burst out like an animal plunging from a trap. Then the drab and furtive expectancy would flicker out in the depths of her eyes and her face become almost sleek with an arid fulfilment.

Sometimes, in those moments, it seemed to Hogarth that she enjoyed opening her injury as once she had enjoyed exposing, with a sort of demure wantonness, her deep-breasted, broad-hipped country body to his desire.

Now he repeated: "It was nothing, my dear. Nothing of importance. I merely remarked that I had completed my noon entry."

"Yes," she said, and Hogarth felt a cautious stir of gratitude as he recognized the distance in her tone. Indifference was a signal promising another ration of peace. He was comforted by her withdrawals as another husband would be by a sudden hug in passing, or a kiss on the top of the head. Even in estrangement, two people living together formed intimacies that no one else could share: the human instinct to make something unique out of any relationship, however cruel or sordid, was oddly consoling.

He said almost cheerfully, inspired by his reprieve, "Our position is serious, my dear. Another two days of this and we shall have to broach our reserves."

13

Suddenly, and irrationally, he felt hope stir within him. As if in the distress that impartially threatened them both they could only come together in understanding and reconciliation. He gave her an appealing smile. She looked back at him with impersonal attention, her interest caught, but unmoved by his offer. Hope dissipated like smoke in the little cabin.

"And then?" she asked.

"We wait for a fair wind," Hogarth said. He struck the table with the flat of his hand: a controlled tap of a blow, stiff with frustration. "I had allowed for everything. Everything. And then this . . ." His furious gesture seemed to take in the steady bulkheads, the white glare beyond the open port, the still, oven heat, as if they were the justifying evidence in a case he was presenting to an invisible jury.

"Is there no likelihood of the calm ending soon?"

"It must, Eliza. It must." He gestured again, but wearily, like a man on the ground conceding defeat. "But in these latitudes, at this season . . ." He seemed to reach in the air for the next commonplace, fell silent. "Who can tell? Who can tell? I had allowed for everything but this."

The woman nodded once and bent her head over her book; Hogarth picked up the pen he had laid aside. For a moment, he gazed at the fading yellow of the bent head with an air of bewilderment, his eyebrows squeezed against the high, knobbed bridge of his nose in a frown: the same frown, at once irascible and sad, that knits the brow of an ape faced with some experience just beyond its grasp. Then he shook his head decisively, removed the steel nib from its fat silver holder and slid it, point first, back into the slot before placing the pen in the rack built onto the right inside wall of the secretary. Another, identically fashioned silver pen, nib reversed, rested in the rack. He folded the little square of felt with which he had cleaned the nib and placed it in the secretary precisely on top of another folded felt square stained with wipings of red ink. From the right-hand pocket of the white linen jacket hung over the back of the chair, he took a bunch of keys and looking down, pulled one free. Briskly he closed the little twin doors of the secretary, fitted the extended key into the lock and turned it. He palmed the bunch of keys with a quick snapping movement like a conjuror's, returned them to the pocket, pushed the chair back from the table and rose. Standing, he seemed to fill the little cabin with a tense and distressing vigour. As if the matter and muscle of his thick, wide-shouldered body had been fashioned to fill a much larger man and was barely contained by his taut skin. His closely scissored, springy dark hair curled exuberantly —like a wig assumed for a youthful role and forgotten—above the weather-cured face with its flat, hard cheeks and the two rigid furrows that held his full lips in parenthesis.

He took his jacket from the chair and put it on. Immediately, the extra layer of cloth, light as it was, made the sweat start on his body. He wiped his face carefully with a large silk handkerchief laundered to transparency, its colours faded. From the peg on the bulkhead by the opened, latched back door, he took a wide-brimmed straw hat of the sort worn by the Portuguese on the African coast.

"I shall be back within an hour, my dear," he said, "for luncheon. If you need me, you have only to send one of the watch."

"Very well, Captain Hogarth."

She did not lift her head as he went from the cabin.

CHAPTER TWO

The glare off the sea as Hogarth stepped onto the deck was like the explosion of a huge mirror bursting against his face, lancing his eyes with unbearable bright slivers. Heat stabbed through the awning. It was as if the ship had sailed into the core of the sun.

And yet it was more tolerable than in the cabin. The pure sky and the great ring of still water gave an illusion of freshness. Hogarth drew a deep breath and stretched before he walked towards the man who stood at the wheel just aft of the poop rail. Here, for a little, he could pretend that he was free. *Was* free. Four feet of open deck and a thin bulkhead separated him from the world within the cabin. But these were enough. One of the unspoken agreements between them was that beyond the cabin door, he was no longer the betrayer—only the captain. He left the past on the threshold like a penitential shroud, to be picked up and assumed again when he returned to her. Even when she came out for exercise, she acknowledged his different role, looked at him with a different recognition. Sometimes she would take his arm and they would pace up and down the port side of the poop in decorous complicity, like two travellers in a foreign port, bound by that common citizenship with which even the worst marriage invests the two who endure it.

The helmsman was one of the Portuguese. His hands (dark as an African's except where the old scars of fishing-line and sieve-rope cuts made a hatching of fine white seams) rested on the wheel. In this calm, he was useless, and he stood to his post wrapped in the dense, organic stolidity of an oak. As Hogarth came up, he lifted his right hand and touched his forehead with a finger; his dark face bunched around a wide, sweet smile.

Hogarth nodded absently and glanced, from habit, at the compass in its box before the wheel. It registered South-South-

West instead of their course, West-North-West. At some time in the hour since he had last checked, the ship must have turned with the turning world: part of a movement too vast and slow to be felt.

"Bring her head round," he was about to say, and checked the mechanical words. There was nothing the man could do. Nothing that any man aboard could do. The barque lay in the dead sea like a needle caught in a bowl of molten silver. "Steady as she goes," he said instead, and gave a sketchy, ironical grimace. The man stared back at him, frowning a polite inquiry. Like the other Portuguese of the crew, he had learned the functional English of the commands and exchanges that kept a ship handled. Out of context, a phrase was disconcerting. Then he seemed to realize the joke that was intended. Again the wide sweet smile split his face as if a strip had been peeled suddenly across the bark of an old tree. He ducked his head in delighted, courteous appreciation. "Oh yes, captain. Oh yes. I keep her steady as she goes." He chuckled.

But Hogarth already had dismissed the little sardonic pleasantry. For a moment it had given him a perverse relief, like sucking a stab of agony from the nagging discomfort of a decayed tooth; but now as he stared down the length of his command, he could feel again the dull throb of defeat.

Its signs were all about him to be read: the unruffled edges of the awning rigged between the poop and the foremast; the spread sails hanging like flags of surrender; the thickening crust of waste at the waterline.

Failure had been waiting for him like an uncharted sargasso here in the open ocean, and he had sailed his life into the clutch of its invisible tendrils.

On the decks below him, the routine of the ship continued. Little knots of activity either too energetic or too languid, like the pulsations of blood in a body that has rested too long. Three of the Portuguese were mending sail by the open forecastle door, their dark hands moving with almost feminine deftness as they plunged the great curved needles into the canvas. But they were doing it with the genteel leisureliness of ladies gathered for a Dorcas, at which the real purpose is to exchange the gossip of the parish. Astride the bowsprit a man, his face shadowed

17

by the limp inner-jib, sandstoned a patch of worn varnish with a kind of frenzy for a minute, then rested with his back humped, staring over the spar's unmoving tip at the horizon. A red-haired boy carrying a bucket came from the midshiphouse. He put the bucket down when he reached the bulwarks and straightening began to undo two of the knots that lashed a five-foot-high wall of netting to the rail. Raising the section of freed netting with one hand, with the other he lifted the bucket, balanced it on the rail and emptied its contained slops onto the skin of refuse below. Then he leaned slackly against the bulwarks, the bucket still resting on the rail, the loosened section of net shawling his shoulders, and gazed down at the clinging filth as if bemused. The man on the bowsprit seemed to be riding a huge lance thrust into the sky. A new intensity of heat fell upon the ship— as though the sun's rays had accumulated like a downpour in the awning above until the canvas had given way under the load. Beside him, Hogarth heard the Portuguese helmsman give a gasp, unconstrained yet resigned, like an animal's. When he turned, the man's dark eyes met his without complaint, with trust.

"This," the man said. "This hot, captain. Bad. Very bad."

"Yes," Hogarth said, and turned away uneasily. He found it difficult to accept the affable casualness of the Portuguese. They seemed to lack all sense of rank, of the attentive silence owed the higher by the lower until the higher indicated that it might be broken. It was not that they lacked respect. The oldest of the thirty-two who had signed on at Setubal—a huge grand-father with a wild white thatch, his leather wineskin face scored by sixty years exposure in the sardine boats—treated him with a filial deference. It was simply that they offered themselves too prodigally: to him, to his officers, to each other. As if by the act of commiting themselves to the same service, they had all become members of the same family. They all seemed to have an enormous capacity for laughter and enjoyment of others; an effortless, tolerant accommodation of life. Sometimes, when their voices were filtered back to him from the forecastle head at night, or rose on fountains of sound as they fell to on a job, he would be conscious of a sour, irrepressible resentment. It was like having to share quarters with a group of thoughtless

18

aristocrats who gambled away unearned fortunes of contentment, security and easy affection. He remembered the Portuguese schooner lying alongside his ship in New Orleans
twenty-five years ago, when he was second officer: the gaudy
splashes of decoration on the poop, the plump, stubble-jowled
captain darning a sock, with what looked to be a steward or one
of the ordinary seamen sprawled snoring on the deck at his feet
—until the captain, grinning indulgently, had put a slippered
foot on the man's ribs and rolled him onto his stomach. The
man had raised his head from the warm deck, his face petu-
lantly questioning, seen his captain's reassuring grin and had
slumped back into sleep with the captain's foot gently and
absently rocking his body as though it were in a cradle.

Hogarth rested his hands on the poop rail.

"Mister Bullen!" he called, his voice carrying the length of
the ship with the pent force of a jet from a hose. "Mister Bullen.
A word here, if you please."

A thin, pale wedge of flesh appeared round the forward
starboard corner of the midshiphouse; a face topped by a limp
and faded officer's cap pushed back on dark brown hair, fine as
thistledown, straight as thread. The body that followed the face
onto the open deck was like some immensely elongated, knobbly
and tasteless vegetable grown in the dark, pathetically and
pallidly striving towards the light.

"Aye, sir," Bullen said, and stepped aft with an energy, a
manly purpose, as spurious as the *bonhomie* of a racecourse
tout.

Hogarth watched him stride towards the poop, thudding his
heels with fraudulent resolution into the old teak, and thought:
*A man like that! Five years ago, I would not have signed him
on as cook's boy, let alone my first officer. At least, I had that
left. My reputation.*

As Bullen came nearer, he repeated silently, opening his lips:
My reputation. In those days, three voyages as chief officer
under Hogarth, and his laconic recommendation, could mean
the offer of your own command. Owners poached with flattering
ruthlessness for a "Hogarth man"—scarcely bothering to read
the body of the note which the man would bring, looking only
for the large, heavily pressed, up-sloping signature.

19

This introduces Mr Charles Doyle, the note might read, *I earnestly recommend him to your attention,* or *This introduces Mr Angus Livingstone. I recommend him for your consideration.* The only differences between the notes—*earnestly recommend* and *attention* in the first, unadorned *recommend* and *consideration* in the second—was Hogarth's distinction between the completely proved and the man waiting for the ship on which to prove himself—under a last-voyage captain, perhaps, or one known for demanding too much of his first officers. The bearer of the first note was invariably given his own ship. The bearer of the second seldom failed to find his appointment waiting for him in Falmouth on the return journey from Hong Kong or Sydney.

It was in those days, at presentation ceremonies in the City (the curtains drawn against the fog, the light from the seacoal fires glinting in old mahogany and on fine crystal), that rich men whom he had made richer drank Hogarth's health with flushed admiration, almost with a proprietorial intimacy. Soon he would be one of them. The gifts, increasingly expensive, were tokens of admission. The final gift would not be expensive at all: the document for him to sign his agreement to join those who studied the great markets and ordered the great clippers to the intricate, degenerating and hapless empire of China or to the raw, ancient and near-empty continent, where the son of a man who might have gone out in leg shackles now raised wheat enough to feed all England.

Bullen clattered up the ladder from the quarterdeck. On his pallid face the sweat looked like the drops wrung from a fever, and he was panting a little from his brisk, decisive stride aft. His chisel jaw was thrust out with the effort of asserting an alert and competent attention, but the small, diluted blue eyes were troubled as they always were: as though at any moment he might find himself out. He carried his authority apprehensively, like a man flourishing an empty revolver in the face of a hostile crowd.

"Yes, sir," he said, and his long, shallow face seemed to hang, bobbing gently like a celluloid mask on strings, above Hogarth.

Hogarth said irritably, "Mister Bullen," and paused. More than anything else about Bullen, he had grown to dislike the conspiratorial intimacy the man assumed, as though they alone in the world of their ship understood the exacting scope of command and its austere rewards. "Mister Bullen," Hogarth repeated, with careful formality: one could not afford irritation in the third week of an equatorial calm; it could run suddenly through a man, like a fire started in dry grass by the embers from a pipe. "Your watch, I believe."

"It is indeed, sir. My watch it is. I'm on deck as you might say."

His face swayed towards Hogarth as if blown on the wind of his specious boom.

"Very good, Mister Bullen." Hogarth turned away; it was easier to avoid the spark of irritation if one did not look at Bullen. "I think you had better call the hands under cover." He pointed over the rail to the man on the bowsprit who had resumed his sandstorming lethargically. "Isn't that Dunn yonder on the boom?"

"Yes, sir . . . By God, look at him. As if we had all eternity between here and Brazil to make the ship smart. I'll . . ."

"Order him in, Mister Bullen," Hogarth said wearily. "It is too hot. In these latitudes, without a wind, white men cannot trust the sun. And I cannot afford sickness. Who have you aloft?"

"Calder, sir. And Dolan. Along with three of the dagoes. They're lacing tops'ls to the jackyards as you ordered."

"Bring 'em down. It's too hot even for the Portuguese and they can endure it better than our lads. No exposure between now and eight bells, Mister Bullen, except it become necessary."

"Aye, sir. I understand. Understand fully." Bullen wiped the sweat from his forehead and mopped again as fresh drops sprang out. He braced his legs, put his hand behind his back and squinted up under the edge of the poop awning at the burning sky. "Have you ever known anything like this, sir?" His tone was deferential yet comfortable, like that of a junior engaging an older member before the fireplace in their club. "I haven't, by God, and they're not many waters I don't know. I remember one run between Foochow and Sydney. That was a time, sir, believe me. Ten days, still as a flat-iron, with the

21

equator straight across the keel like grocer's twine on a pound of cheese. We ..."

"Mister Bullen," Hogarth could taste his small dry anger, refreshing as an iced drink, "it does not grow any cooler while you talk. I feel sure you'll wish to see to your duties."

"Eh ... oh ... yes, sir. Certainly. I'll see to it immediately. Immediately."

Bullen fell back, his eyes stricken and jerky as his words; but curiously grateful, devoted, as if Hogarth's rebuke had confirmed once again their common dedication to the inexorable service of the sea. He saluted with a flourish, turned and plunged down the short ladder to the quarter deck. Hurrying forward, he passed the small red-haired boy still gazing vacantly over the side. With a convulsive, tangled leap, Bullen broke stride, turned to the boy's drooping back and, with a galvanic thrust of a large, pale hand under the netting, grasped the slender neck.

The child squeaked once as he was snatched from the bulwark, and then allowed himself to hang from Bullen's grasp with the passivity of a loosely articulated puppet, the bucket in turn attached to rather than held in his small, freckled paw as though tied to it by string.

"You there, Joshua!" Bullen cried. "You there, I say. What do you think you're up to, eh? Eh?" He shook the boy as if trying to stuff him into an upright box. The child flopped obediently, his red curls shifting from side to side on his round head, his eyes and face expressionless. "Now, sir," Bullen continued, "answer me. What are you doing there, eh? Idling. Yes, *idling*. I've had my eye on you." His fine roar began to trail uncertainly, as if he were groping for the next words of a badly prepared speech. "Idling," he concluded on a wistful shout, and flung the boy towards the open midshiphouse door. The boy staggered forward in the same loose, boneless fashion, the bucket dancing in his hand, until he heard the exaggerated tattoo of Bullen's heels beating forward. Then he straightened, seemed to shake his scattered limbs into one firmly knit package, and sauntered into the midshiphouse, grinning.

Feet spread and arms akimbo, Bullen called from the bows to the man on the bowsprit. "Dunn!" he barked. The man's back continued to rock to the slow, even rhythm of his sand-stoning. "Dunn!" Bullen moved up, three quick and irresolute steps. "Dunn, I say! Are you deaf?"

On the bowsprit, the man brought his sandstoning to a halt, examined a spot and gave it a final scrape before swinging his leg over the spar with the casual deftness of a circus rider clearing the pommel of a saddle. Sitting sideways, his bare feet curled in on the netting below, he turned his head slowly to Bullen. The neat, sallow face and large-boned yet compact body gave an effect of faceted hardness, as though they had been fashioned under tremendous pressures, squeezed at vol-canic heat until everything malleable had spurted out leaving only the irreducible substance. Dark eyes, all surface like smooth stones, examined Bullen with a remote and speculative hatred; the straight, bitter lips seemed to part reluctantly, as if, one by one, old surgical stitches were being removed from a healed wound.

"No, mister," Dunn said, "I ain't deaf."

"Then answer, damme, when I speak to you," Bullen pleaded with petulant fury. "We have a ship to run, don't you realize? I can't be calling you all day, can I? All day?" He paused, studied the bleak, unyielding profile between him and the sky, and added, "Now look here, Dunn ... Lively now ... Take shelter under awnings until further orders."

He pivoted on his heel and bustled aft from the forecastle head. Leaning back out over the bulwark on the port side just aft of the mainmast, he shouted aloft, "Calder! You up there! Calder!"

"Aye, aye, sir."

"Bring your lads down. Immediately."

"Aye, sir."

The mellow, deferential voice from its invisible source above seemed to fall on Bullen like rain on a thirsty plant. He straigh-tened, glared triumphantly at Dunn, and came aft again.

He took his stand just under the break of the poop; beside the small brass culverin which, mounted on a swivel, pointed its muzzle at the grating of the after hatch. Two canisters of grapeshot stood on the deck beside the culverin. By each canister was a small keg, and a trickle of black powder had spilled through the imperceptible, heat-warped fissure between the staves of one. A charcoal brazier glowed redly a yard behind the canisters, and laid on the deck beside it were a linkstock—a plug of frayed, oil-soaked hemp on an iron stick—a cleaning rod, and a ramrod.

Through the grating of the hatch there came an acrid, heavy smell: a smell that pervaded the whole ship, sticking to the wood like paint, and no more noticed by those aboard until they stood directly above the source.

As Bullen took his position behind the culverin, the murmur deepened, became a chorus of moans that rose and burst wetly on the deck like the fat and sticky bubbles on the skin of a sulphur pit; and then subsided, leaving a few individual voices that still persisted, insubstantial as puffs of steam, on the still air.

Bullen looked down at the hatch cover and then questioningly up to where Hogarth stood beside the helmsman.

"Yes, Mister Bullen," Hogarth said, "we'll bring them up soon. But see all hands fed first. Anything may happen at this stage and I want every man ready, not thinking of his dinner."

As though his words had been a signal, the drawn-out, sodden moans once more seeped through the grating. They sank again, to quick shallow murmurs that were almost inaudible; as if some great, docile animal lay dying of its wounds in the hold, bubbling its last breaths through torn lungs. The murmurs were punctuated by the faint clink and scrape of iron against iron, and the rank smell seemed to thicken between the awning and the deck like tobacco smoke in a crowded room.

Hogarth turned, passed behind the motionless helmsman, and began to pace off his accustomed walk between the break of the poop and the taffrail. He felt drained by helplessness. The dry equation between time and the resources he had left whirled in his brain like a stone on a string. Pausing at the taffrail, he stared out over the flat, dazzling water to the arc of the horizon. Somewhere beyond that rim, the patrol ships of three navies steamed across calms as dead as the one in which he was trapped, or butted effortlessly into adverse winds. They were a factor too: a risk he had calculated and set aside, not as insignificant but as mathematically small enough not to endanger the other equation of success. Here in the great Atlantic corridor that stretched its thirty millions of square miles from pole to pole without any landfall larger than a whaleboat, there were too many horizons over which a man could slip: the surfaces of the great ocean could swallow the frail splinters it carried as effectively as could the deeps.

He felt no resentment for the solemn and reliable men who would bring him before an outraged court if they took him or who would coldly hang him if he resisted capture. The next day they might as dutifully pound some obscure village on a jungled coast into ruins with their guns. They served a cruel and cynical necessity of which they understood nothing. As they would come to serve and protect him if he won through. As everyone and everything served the ruthless few who farmed the world between them. His own body jerking madly on the end of a rope sixty feet above a deck, the uncomprehending villagers torn to pieces by flying, white hot steel, the two gentle and un-complaining old people fading from neglect in a half-forgotten country parish were tokens on the page of a ledger. All were condemned to die or permitted to live, dispassionately, according to the contribution they had made when the ledgers were being balanced.

"I have come too far", Hogarth said suddenly, aloud, "to lose *now*."

It was like a promise.

He turned and walked rapidly back to the break of the poop. And for the third time, as if acknowledging his appearance above the grated hatch cover, the undulating and animal moans of bewildered protest rose from the hold in which, stacked and stowed with the greatest care, lay the four hundred and seventy-five bodies he had discriminately culled along the coast from the Congo to Angola for sale to the Brazilian plantations.

CHAPTER THREE

1

Dunn gazed at the smoke as Calder exhaled past the stem of
the old briar that jutted from his mouth like a blackened ex-
tension of his teeth. The smoke crawled up Calder's nose and
forehead, wreathed his bald head like mist around a plateau,
thinned and dissipated imperceptibly without a swirl.

"Look at that," Dunn said. "Not enough wind to stir the
smoke from a man's pipe ... An' it's been fifteen days." He
cupped his hand above Calder's damp, shining dome and repeated, with a child's excitement at discovery, "Look at that I
tell you," as a little grey cloud gathered in the hollow of his
palm. "You ever seen the like of this, John? Fifteen days of it?"

Careful thought began to disturb the wooden benevolence
of old Calder's face, as though he were methodically peeling
his experience like an artichoke: each memory removed,
chewed and neatly laid aside.

"Aye," he said finally, "once." His vacant blue eyes brightened
with satisfaction. "Once, Ned. That were forty, no forty-five
years ago. Ten days out of Callao bound for the Friendlies an'
we was caught for near a month. Three weeks an' four day, an'
then we gets a little piece of a sou'easter could hardly bend the
topgallants an' it pushed us into some rain. We was grateful to
the Lord for that, Ned. I can tell you. For by that time we was
down to a cup of water a day each soul, an' we was that weak
we couldn't hardly trim the yards. Yes, toward the end there,
Ned, it was ..." He paused, took the pipe from his mouth and
stared profoundly into the bowl "... bad." He nodded as if to
emphasize the gravity of remembered stress that justified so
extravagant a claim.

"*Bad!*" Dunn said explosively, and grinned at Calder with
a sort of respectful patronage. "Then what d'you call *this*, you
old image?"

"This, Ned?" Calder gave a slow blink and consulted the pipe bowl again. His squat body (naked to the waist, with one tattoo of a gaudy, insipid mermaid sprawled coyly across a bicep the size and consistency of a cannon ball), his heavy serene face and his naked scalp were burnt a uniform, polished copper. Squatting on the foredeck beside Dunn, his legs tucked under him, he gave the impression of having been hacked patiently, with ritual purpose, by a dull knife out of some ancient, reddish wood. His heavy face seemed to be going back into time; so that the two tufts of grey hair on his cheekbones gave him the appearance of a whiskered foetus. His lips moved soundlessly to ponderous discriminations. "Now this, Ned," he said after a minute, with a large yet modest finality, "*this* ain't bad. Not yet. Troublesome more like. Yes. Troublesome is what I call it. But not *bad*." He nodded again, with benign and imbecile sagacity, put his pipe between his teeth and squinted indifferently into the wall of excruciating glare between the awning and the bulwark.

Dunn laughed briefly like a man compelled to use a phrase in a foreign language.

"Well, if you don't beat all," he said. "If you don't beat the band . . . You heard that, Boyo?" His voice took on a tone of bullying affection as he addressed the slight figure lying flat across the deck before them, with a wide-brimmed straw hat over its face. "Boyo! Did you hear old John's contribution? 'We ain't badly off', he says. 'Only troublesome'."

A protesting grunt and drowsy oath came through the straw. Old Calder smiled indulgently, and continued to gaze at the brilliant sky as if contemplating in the blue furnace of its depths mysteries incommunicable to the young and hasty.

"Yes, Ned." The melodious voice droned with implacable mildness. "That were a bad time there in the Pacific. That were when I were foretopman on the old *Omnipotent*. Under Cap'n Colinton . . . We had the boats out trying to pull us into a capful of wind, an' Cap'n Colinton himself took the long boat. *Now, lads*, he says, *bend to it with a will. Come, lads, you can do better'n that. If you can't pull for yourselves, pull for me an' old England*. Then he whistles a spell, like a bird, to raise a wind, though he'd no more spit left in his gob to whistle with

27

than any of us. *Lads, lads,* he says, *Call that pulling. A company of bloodybacks would pull better. Or a file of marines. You show 'em, Calder. Pull till your hearts burst. It's a wide ocean, lads, an' there's a wind out there somewhere—"*

"An' to hell with your bloody Cap'n Colinton," Dunn said suddenly. "I'll wager he don't remember *you.*"

"Now he couldn't could he, Ned?" Calder gently chided him. "Seeing as how Yellow Jack carried him off four years later when we was lyin' in the Port-of-Spain roads."

Dunn twitched impatiently on the deck, his face austere and vivid with the fervour of bitter certitudes.

"You an' your bloody Cap'n Colinton," he repeated. "An' all the other bloody Cap'ns you're always on about. As if they ever cared a rat's fart whether you lived or died."

"He were the best cap'n I ever served under, Ned, an' would never see a good hand abused."

"Ah!" Dunn slapped the air between them furiously. "You're no better than *them,* Calder." He jerked his thumb back over his shoulder to where, ten feet away, the Portuguese hands sat or sprawled on the deck around the forecastle entrance. One of them mistook the gesture for a casual affirmation of fellowship and grinned back, shrugging and grimacing in wry dumbshow as he spread expressive hands to indicate the stillness in which they lay. Dunn turned his head away and gripped Calder's shoulder, his face still set in that dark, gaunt anger.

"The likes of you never learn, d'you? No more than them ignorant dagoes. No more than Boyo Dolan here. You never learn how the owners an' the officers use an' use a working sailor an' throw him away when he's not able no more."

He shook Calder fiercely, with confused longing; trying to convey in the little act of violence, the passion of hatred they must both share like love. He felt, suddenly, a wide and thrilling sense of brotherhood, of unity, with the old man who rocked stolidly under the thrust of his hand, with the somnolent figure at his feet, with the faceless men in all the cramped, dark forecastles of the sea, with the bent and wasted figures at the looms of his childhood; even with the Portuguese chattering on the deck behind him.

"My", Calder said, "but you're hard agin officers, Ned. There's
28

good 'uns an' bad uns' as in everything else on land or sea an'—"

"Oh, stow it." Dunn shook his head, regarding Calder with drained and sombre eyes. "You're an old donkey, John, that the masters of this world use to haul for 'em, an' you'll never be anything else."

A loud sigh came from beneath the hat covering Boyo Dolan's face. A square, stubby-fingered hand, its back thickly pelted with dark hair, rose limply and removed the hat.

"Faith," Dolan murmured, "a fellah might as well try to grow grass on the floor av a salon as try to sleep when you get started on the wrongs av mankind, Ned." He yawned, sat up, scratched his bushy, tousled head and looked at Dunn with an avuncular amusement. He had the liquid black eyes glinting under an overhang of brow, the wide, very thin lips and the crumpled face of a sardonic chimpanzee.

"Go back to sleep," Dunn grunted sourly. "I'll wake you when Joshua brings the grub."

"*Sleep!*" Dolan pulled a face of gaping amazement and winked at Calder, "How d'you expect a poor devil av a sailor-man to sleep wid you shoutin' mutiny an' treason into his ear an' trying to heave old John overboard in your fury?" He grinned, yawned again and fell back to the deck, his hands clasped behind his head. "Mother av God," he said mournfully, "but this still heat has me destroyed. If you let go a feather from the masthead it ud drop to the deck like a stone."

2

"There he is," Dunn said suddenly. "You could set a bloody watch by him."

"Who?" Dolan asked lazily, flat on his back with forearms crossed over his eyes, "Joshua wid the grub?"

"No, you stupid Mick. Hogarth, I mean. Up there on the poop. Looking us over to see we ain't sitting too hard on his bloody deck an' wearin' it out."

"Oh, he's all right," Dolan said. "He don't work us out av cover when the sun goes straight above, an' that's more than you can say for a lot av them I've sailed under."

29

"Not because he cares about your precious health, Boyo. I can tell you that. It's because he knows we sail short-handed an' he can't afford any sick. Especially one of us three. If the close-fisted swine thought he could squeeze another shilling of profit out of it, you could wager he'd have us frying on the yards."

"Now, Ned," Calder said with mild, comfortable reproof, "Cap'n Hogarth ain't so bad. I've known lots as was worse. Any road. I gives you he sails short-handed, but you knows why an—"

"An' what about the bloody swill we'll be eating when that black high an' mighty bastard in the galley condescends to throw it to us? What about that, eh? There's farmers in England would think twice before givin' it to their pigs."

"Food don't keep well in a dead heat like this, Ned. You knows that. A calm turns food quick."

"It were only fit for burning when he laid it on at São Tomé. You know *that*. An' you don't see no stinkin' rotten meat going up to the poop for Hogarth an' his bitch. Nor into the officers' cabin neither."

"But they's officers, Ned," Calder protested in faintly scandalized tones. "Now I ain't sayin' as how the grub's *good*, mark you. But you can't call it bad, all things considered."

At their feet, Dolan began to laugh, drawing his legs up to his chest and flinging them out as he heaved into a sitting position again.

"You two," he said, "you're an entertainment. It's worth losin' me sleep just to hear you. You're better'n the dagoes."

He looked wistfully across to the knot of Portuguese. The huge white-haired grandfather, his back propped against the bulkhead, had just finished a joke and the others were laughing in a gaudy tossing and shaking of dark heads, brown, oiled faces, white teeth and glinting earrings. One of them, a boy of about seventeen with a lean-hipped gypsy body and a big red mouth, caught up the joke, adding to it in a high, miming voice, and new laughter rose, the old man's sonorous roar overwhelming the others as he appreciatively pounded his great palm on the pale deck.

Dolan grinned as he watched them.

"Ah, sure an' I wish I could understand what they're sayin'," he said enviously. "It's as hard to get an exchange av dacint English on this tub as in the jungles av Africa. If it wasn't for you an' John, I'd be goin' ashore wid me tongue crippled from disuse."

Of the three British seamen abroad, Dolan suffered most in the prison of extraordinary calm. He could not retire, like old Calder, to a pasture of ponderous ruminations. Nor, like Dunn, could he console himself with dreams of revenge.

3

A few minutes after three bells, the boy Joshua came out of the midshiphouse. In one hand, he carried a large billy of stew and a ladle; in the other, a wide, shallow tin dish of ship's biscuits; slung over his shoulder there was a long rope of purple onions. He placed the billy and the dish on the deck and began to break the onions from the string, dropping them one by one into the dish among the biscuits. Then, as the men began to scramble to their feet, gathering their plates and spoons, he stood over the billy holding the ladle ready. His fat ginger curls were wet and flattened darkly on his round head; his face and the milky skin of his chest and stomach were brilliant with sweat.

"Well, you've taken your time about it, haven't you, you young scut?" Dunn said roughly as he held his plate out for a dollop of the grey, stringy meat, yellow grease and soggy flour balls. "Or did you reckon if we was hungry enough we'd never take no mind of the muck you an' the cook serve us?"

"It's good stew today, Mister Dunn. I tasted it myself afore I brings it out. An' Mister Alex seasoned it special in case the meat wasn't quite right."

He seemed quite unmoved by Dunn's growl and the wide, brown gaze he lifted to the man's frown was shrewd and cheerful. Early in the voyage, a mind honed like a razor on thirteen years of life in a Bristol slum had told him that for some reason, on this ship, he was privileged. He could not have said why. Could not have understood the obscure or unadmitted appeasement of corroding guilt they found in him. He accepted the

31

awkward rough spoiling without gratitude—as he would have accepted unkindness without surprise or much resentment. The deprivations, the cruelties, the sordid usages of the warrens in which he had survived rather than been raised had given him an appalling tolerance of situation. The meretricious beauty, from which all adults aboard salvaged illusions of their innocence, would coarsen in a year or two into foxy, flash good looks —as all that he had seen, or had committed on him, but to which his child's mind could not yet give true meaning, would suddenly become knowledge. Now, all that he had was an ancient, candid appreciation, like a cat's, of every movement and mood of those among whom he had to live. He watched Dunn as the man stooped to take a biscuit (flat, straw-coloured, heavy as a paving stone) and an onion from the tin dish and added quickly another fragment of stew to the yellow-grey mass on the plate. His pearl-skinned, heart-shaped face bunched in a sweet, careful smile.

"You young devil," Dunn said. An expression like pain or bewilderment shadowed his face. "You young devil," he repeated, with an elaborate, hoarse casualness, "I'll wager you an' that big, ugly buck in the midshiphouse eats like lords after you've finished dishin' this slop out to us."

"Oh no, Mister Dunn, sir." The golden-brown eyes widened in well practised, hurt surprise: appealing, cool and pitiless. "We eats the same as you, sir . . . when you're all finished."

"Ah!" Dunn said confusedly. "So you say." The bitter mouth twitched in a lopsided smile. "Well see that you do. I've got my eye on you same as I would on a monkey." He lifted his hand suddenly and tweaked the boy's ear, uncertainly, like a man practising a new game. The child stiffened and his eyes darkened with the pain of the inept caress.

"Oh yes, sir," he said. "Thank you, sir."

"An' don't you be callin' me 'sir' all the time, Josh. Nor anyways 'Mister'. Plain 'Ned' is good enough 'tween you an' me. I'm a workin' lad like yourself an' don't need none of your officers' titles. Come a day there won't be no titles, an' no officers neither."

"Yes, sir—I mean Ned," Joshua said mechanically. He had already transferred his attention to the old Portuguese who stood patiently behind Dunn waiting his turn at the stew. The boy had long ago decided that he preferred the company of the Portuguese to that of the Englishmen. Already he had learned his way through enough of their language to suit his needs: as a cat learns and appropriates the warmest and most comfortable corners of a new house. Each advance in his vocabulary aroused their delight and pride, especially in the huge old man, who would reward him with a dark sweet of a strange but delicious flavour, dug from a little oak barrel on the point of a knife. As the old Portuguese thrust his plate over the billy, he paddled carefully in the stew so that several of the better chunks of meat were carried into the ladle on a tide of yellow gravy.

Dunn moved to where Calder and Dolan had seated themselves. Old Calder had almost finished, the plate held under his chin as he shovelled the mess into his methodically champing jaws. Dolan hunched over his ration, examining it with an air of faintly hilarious suspicion.

"Holy God!" he said as Dunn lowered himself to the planks beside him. "What would you call *this* now?" He spooned up a fragment of meat in a smear of grease and nibbled fastidiously. "I could dip a sieve, be Christ, into any sewer in Dublin an' extract a better dinner than this. You know, Ned, I tapped me biscuit on the deck a minute ago an' even the poor craythurs that fell outa it were wrigglin' wid the feebleness av starvation."

Dunn looked at him with cold pensiveness from under a frown, breathed once and continued his slow eating.

"You're a great one for jokes, aren't you, Boyo?" he said a few seconds later; he filled his spoon from the plate resting on his crossed ankles but did not lift the food to his mouth. "Nothin's too rotten for you to pull a joke out of it. It saves you thinkin' I expect, you poor bloody fool."

"An' you've got no call to be so bloody solemn about it," Dolan said sulkily. "It's not everyone who don't squeeze his lips tighter'n an Orangeman's arse-hole who ain't thinkin'. An' when I say that, Mister Dunn, I'm makin' reference to a certain gentleman who's restin' his buttock not a hundred miles from where I'm sittin' an' who's a damn sight too quick wid his insults."

"Meanin'?" Dunn muttered. Sometimes the brimming charge of vigilant hatred he carried within him like his blood seemed to spill over onto those whom he wanted only to cherish, to join in the great brotherhood where there was no injustice, no indignity, no obeisance. Always, afterwards, he wanted to atone, but he never knew how.

"Meanin' *you*, you great thick," Dolan told him affably.

"I don't get you." Dunn's tone was cautious now. Dolan's passages from comic temper to quick anger and back to amiable teasing again always disconcerted him. As did the darting flights of the little Irishman's mind, lighting unpredictably on some point far ahead in any conversation. "How d'you mean me?"

"Can't y'see, Ned," Dolan said impatiently, "that every penny Hogarth's saved on the victuallin' av this tub adds a mite to our shares when we fetches into Brazil. This meat, now, that I'm attemptin' to smuggle past me throat an' into me stomach before me better judgement raises the alarm, represents anoder twenty poun's at least in Boyo Dolan's pocket."

"Y'mean if he didn't get his full profit out of us one way, he'd get it another. An' as for our shares in the venture—they're small enough when you stand them agin his an' the officers'. We take the same risk an' will hang as high as any of the gentlemen if a patrol lays aboard us."

'You're not questionin' the justice av that are you, Ned?" Dolan asked. He paused, his spoon halfway to his mouth and glanced back along the deck to the grated hatch cover. "Jaysus", he said sadly, "the things a man can learn to live wid. That sad stink, now, comin' up from the poor craythurs we're carrying into captivity. If any man had tol' me once that Boyo Dolan woulda had a hand in that, I'd have taken his hide off him for a portmanteau. An' now it don't mean no more to me than the smell av a fo'cs'le when I come off watch."

"Ah to hell, Boyo," Dunn said quickly. "They're only niggers. They'll live easier an' safer on the plantations than they ever would in Africa."

"You've consulted them on the subject av that now?" Dolan said drily. "I'm glad to hear it. It'll be a sad weight off me conscience, Ned . . . Christ, this bloody swill!" He flung the plate and spoon to the planks before him. "It don't go down any easier for the sauce we have to eat it wid." He glared at Calder and Dunn with absurd, angry challenge.

"Leave it!" Dunn said roughly, looking at his plate. "You didn't start the dirty trade. If the likes of Hogarth didn't have you to work it for them, they'd have another. Leave it!"

"An' if they couldn't find another, Ned, they'd have no one at all, an' the trade ud have to stop. No . . . It's a dirty, dishonourable business we signed for, an' it deserves a dirty, dishonourable end if we're caught at it."

"Leave it, I tell you! The bastards who'd hang us an' preach over us do worse'n what we're doin'. In England. To white men. You think any of 'em would care for one of his workin' men the way we coddle them niggers below?"

Calder said, with heavy suddenness like a weight dropping, "Aye, you're right, Boyo. This be no following for a Christian man. It's like . . . like . . ." He paused as if fishing in the turbid deeps of his mind for the one right comparison ". . . like piracy. It were the money tempted me into it. For when I'm old. But I feels shame of it, an' always will I reckon." He bit thoughtfully on the biscuit he had soaked in the remains of his gravy. "It were the money, Boyo." In awed tones he added, "Five hunnerd poun'! Five hunnerd! Why, I'll get more for my share than the senior lieutenant of the *Renown* got as prize money when we took the *Belle Marie* . . . She were a fine ship, that *Belle Marie*, but couldn't sail close-hauled an' so we took her. Chock full of brandy she were an' we took her off Nova Scotia. Cap'n Foster commanded the *Renown* that time. He were a good cap'n, Cap'n Foster. They Turks killed 'ee at Navarino . . ."

Dunn pulled a sly face at Dolan and gravely asked Calder, "What was the senior lieutenant's prize money, John? For that business with the *Belle Marie* an' her brandy?"

"I never heard for sure, Ned, but they did say it were three hunnerd poun'."

"An' yours?"

"Five shillin'."

Dunn flung himself back on the warm, scrubbed wood with a bark of helpless and sardonic laughter.

"Well, if you don't beat all," he was saying, "if you don't beat the band . . ." as Price, the boatswain, stepped from his quarters under the poop deck and began to call for all hands to muster aft.

35

CHAPTER FOUR

1

Price, the boatswain, turned the key in the second of the two padlocks which, passed through stout rings, secured the grating to the hatchway. He opened the clasp, slid it out of the ring screwed into the grating, clicked it shut again around the ring sunk into the lip of the hatchway, straightened and nodded as he stepped back. Short and fair and thick, with cut-off bandy legs, he had an oblong torso that gave the appearance of being the same width from his hips to his shoulders, and a slab of dough-coloured face that seemed to begin, without the bridge of a neck, immediately above his thorax.

On his nod, Dunn, Calder and the old Portuguese bent and heaved on the portside of the hatch cover. Fore and aft of the cover, six to an end, twelve more of the Portuguese heaved in unison. The grating lifted from the hatchway, was swung across the opening and laid flat on the deck. The smells of sweat and heavy sleep, like a coma, of faeces, menstrual blood, baby's vomit, of closely packed flesh thickened in the air above the hold, diffused slowly about the decks, sharpened by the ammoniac scent of stale urine. And with the smells came a sudden babble of voices, the sounds of untidy movement, and the dull, brutal notes of iron on iron.

"By God," Bullen said complacently to Reynolds, the second officer, "they make a right stench, don't they?"

"They do indeed, Mister Bullen," Reynolds replied. "Filthy brutes. And when you consider how commodiously we house them. D'you think anything will ever civilize the animals?"

Bullen glanced sharply, with unhappy suspicion, into a face as rosy, round and pure as a choirboy's; into deep gentian eyes as calculating and cynical as a gambler's.

"Uh . . . what," Bullen said, "what . . . how d'you mean?"

Reynolds smirked and stretched his plump body luxuriously. He gazed with infinite candour up into Bullen's puzzled face.

"You're laughing at me", Bullen accused him sadly, "again."

"Laughing, Mister Bullen? No, no! You made an observation and I concurred. Concurred most fervently, I assure you." He bent forward slightly and inhaled deeply of what was rising from the hold. "How they do stink!" he cried happily. "Like prime game. Each day they smell richer." Straightening, he rubbed his hands briskly; the clear blue gaze he turned again on Bullen was not quite sane. "What a problem, eh, Mister Bullen? What a problem for the world's digestion."

"You . . . you," Bullen stuttered. His lugubrious eyes followed every movement of the little man beside him with helpless fascination, until Reynolds, suddenly, with the gratuitous sensuality of a cat fleshing its paws, poked him in the ribs and laughed at his awkward scramble away from the probing finger.

Around the hatch, the men were still; staring with a discreet, sidelong curiosity, from under lowered brows, with amused incomprehension at the two officers.

Abruptly, Reynolds ceased his gurgle of enigmatic laughter; his eyebrows, yellow and downy as breast feathers from a day-old chick, climbed his pink forehead in derisive question; his wide, brilliant gaze passed slowly from face to face, pausing until each man dropped his eyes and shifted uncomfortably. For perhaps five seconds, Dunn, alone of all the men, tried to challenge the blithe, unwinking menace which seemed to rise, of itself, at some ancient and inaccessible source of cruelty, of which the little sleek man poised on the balls of his dancing master's feet was only the debonair celebrant. Then Dunn gave a shrug, like the twitch along the flank of a puzzled animal, and looked away. Reynolds grinned, without mirth, with bright pleasure, at the ragged half-circle of bent or turned-away heads.

From the poop above them, Hogarth said harshly: "Mister Bullen! Mister Reynolds! Bring the blacks on deck, if you please."

Bullen jumped as Hogarth's rasp snatched him from his mesmerized contemplation of Reynold's antic display. He glared at the little grinning man with the glum fury of a child caught in the consequences of another's mischief.

"Immediately, sir," Reynolds answered with precise mimicry, drew the American Navy Colt .44 thrust into his belt, cocked it, said over his shoulder to the boatswain, "Ready, Price?" and dived into the shadows of the hold like a ferret. For a moment those on deck could hear only the frisky clatter of his boots on the ladder, and then his voice, lilting with that private savage hilarity, as he addressed the ship's unseen burden.

"Well, well, my black friends! Good day to you again. The calm continues, I am afraid. But put your trust in me. Reynolds will see you come to no harm..."

Price jerked his great blunt head in silent comand to the waiting men and moved to the open hatch, his thick, top-heavy body wallowing stolidly on the truncated legs, a ring of keys dangling from his fist.

Dunn, Calder, the old Portuguese and three of the others followed him. On the deck beside the hatch was a large box, its lid flung back; and from this each man as he passed on his way to the hold drew a stubby-handled whip, a cat-o'-nine-tails, with tightly shrunken knots beading the thongs. And each man's face as he was swallowed by the dark yawn of the hold seemed to assume, suddenly, the blank snout of a visor: a parody, at once diminished and absurd, of the subtle features beneath.

The confused and babbling commentary within the hold, which had stilled at Reynold's descent, began again—as if the slaves comprehended instinctively that those who now came among them were, even if captors, men from the same dimensions of appetite and understanding as themselves.

Bullen moved to a position directly beneath Hogarth's on the poop. Behind the culverin, Dolan knelt with his forearms resting on the breech, his crumpled, monkey face bleak, with all its vivid lines now like creases, the lustrous dark eyes dulled with a sombre alertness. Beside him, one of the Portuguese stood, holding the linkstock, the brown hide of his chest oily with a film of sweat as the brazier of charcoal threw up hard waves of heat. The boy with the slim, flamenco dancer's body and the happily sensual mouth stood behind the grapeshot canisters. Along the starboard bulwark, eight of the Portuguese were ranged, carrying the Springfield carbines issued on mustering by Bullen and Reynolds. Four others, armed like them, were spaced along the forward lip of the hatch. They held themselves with the relaxed yet practised attention of sportsmen in their stands waiting for flushed birds.

Above them on the poop, Hogarth stood with widely planted feet, his hands resting in sculptured rigidity on the rail, his gaze absorbed and remote, as if the life that throbbed in those he commanded or had purchased was only the necessary but ignorant nourishment to the vibrant and superior purpose he represented.

Now from the dark square held in the frame of the hatch there began to filter decisive and functional sounds: the snapping of opened padlocks; the scrape of drawn bolts; the jangle and clash of shackles on wood; tense, harsh voices giving commands; an occasional astounded cry of pain; and a low melancholy buzz. A new wave of stinking air stirred by the moving bodies below rose sluggishly: the smells it carried seemed to catch in the nostrils like the droplets suspended in a warm mist. Among the concerted noise of pain, iron, despair and curt orders, Reynold's jocular and authoritative voice hammered with the insistence of an untended pianola.

Well, my friends, are we ready for our promenade? A walk, I always say, is the best aperitif ... Dunn, you fool, don't push that man. Can't you see his shackle burn's beginning to fester? How much d'you think we'll raise for a buck of his quality if we land him crippled with gangrene ... Never mind, my dear fellow, my fellow Argonaut, old Reynolds will see to you on deck. Liniment, you bounder, to soothe the flesh, and a song to lift the soul ... Price! Tell that half-witted Portuguese to hold the bucks steady until you get the women and the picanins up the ladder ... Patience, patience, Sambo, you black dog! Don't you understand we're at sea, and that it's women and children first? Tradition y'know, but a noble one, a necessary one ... Oh, I'll civilize you yet. You wait and see ... Price! Get those bloody women and their brats stepping lively. We'll be in Brazil and halfway up the Amazon before you get 'em on deck ... Calder, you old bishop, you look pale. What! Don't

*you like the smell? Inhale it, Calder. Fill your lungs. Wallow in
it. It's your fortune you're sniffing, you blockhead.*

The slaves came from the hold and into the light slowly. The
women and fourteen children between five and twelve emerged
singly, unfettered, but the men were shackled left ankle to right
in pairs. Each pair, as they put their heads above the lip of the
hatchway, turned from side to side with dazed caution, blinking
against the first glare, gave a listless heave onto the deck, and
shambled a few paces in lock step before dragging to a halt
like a grotesque music-hall team that had forgotten the routine.
Four of the Portuguese moved among the pairs prodding them
into motion again with the handles of their cat-o'-nines, moving
them down the deck away from the hatch, uttering cries at once
encouraging and peremptory, as a band of drovers might gentle
into order the lurching confusion of an unwatered herd. Like
the men, the women were naked, with shaven heads on which
the first stubble was beginning to grow again : twenty-three of
them were carrying babies, and sixteen were varyingly great
with child.

"They look well, sir," said Bullen.

"So they should, Mister Bullen," Hogarth said flatly, not
glancing down at at Bullen. "I feed them well."

On the deck below, the melancholy protocol of seating was
being completed : the women and children forward of the midshiphouse; the men in ranks three deep, port and starboard of
the quarterdeck, under the culverin and the muzzles of the
Springfields held by the eight sailors now spaced, four to each
side, along the bulwarks. The male slaves squatted with thighs
drawn up to their chest, arms round their shins, with foreheads
sunk on their knees, or vacantly gazing across the narrow strip
of open deck between the two front ranks. Among the women
and children amidships, the sounds of one baby, then another,
wailing, the smack of a hand on flesh and the soprano yelp of
a small boy were followed by a rattle of intense, feminine voices
raised in charge, countercharge and opinion.

And for Dolan, behind his culverin, this ancient and universal

40

exchange was suddenly so unbearable that he stiffened, bent forward with the grunt of a man whose stomach has suddenly begun to bite its own walls. For a moment he could smell the damp grass and the sweet, dank hides of the milch cows, and see the plumes of chimney smoke pale blue against the low purple hills and pewter sky and imagine himself scampering from the cold grey-green of a November afternoon into the assurances of a red-hearted peat fire and the warmth of a tweed-covered lap.

"Jaysus," he said, and for a moment rested his forehead on his crossed forearms, muttering into the breech of the culverin, "Jaysus, I shoulda taken the measure av this . . . I should never . . . I should never . . ."

"Dolan!" Hogarth said tonelessly above him, "Look to your charge!"

Dolan turned his head and met the large eyes that were steady and dully gleaming as chips of dark stone, that seemed to reflect impersonally, from no depth, the scene below them, registering movement only on their surfaces.

"Aye, sir," Dolan said tiredly, and turned again to his careful, bleak observation of the shackled ranks under the mouth of the culverin. The little piece was loaded with grapeshot to a point, calculated with exuberant discrimination by Reynolds four months previous, just short of what would burst it on discharge. Dolan and the Portuguese with the linkstock behind him could, by now, because of natural deftness and rehearsal, fire and reload with a speed and skill that was nearly automatic. "Aye, sir," he repeated softly, "it's my charge an' I'll look to it." From the corner of his vision he saw the first sailor come from the hold.

It was Dunn. The sallow, harsh-boned face that never tanned was paler now and the sweat was running from under the lank, black hair which was plastered to the compact skull in wisps and threads that could not cover the scalp entirely. Below the broad belt, his trousers were stuck in wet patches to his buttocks and groin and the tops of his thighs; and as he stepped from the top of the ladder to the deck, sweat dropped from his legs and was absorbed in small, quickly fading stains on the warm wood. He breathed deeply and rapidly, exhaling with an

41

opened mouth as he strode forward, kicking with absent fury at the extended foot of a slave who had stretched his unshackled leg. The foot was drawn back slowly, seeming to crawl by reflex—like an organism so primitive in nervous structure that it could do no more than recoil vaguely from an uncomfortable stimulus. Dunn was already dipping a ladle of water from the cask lashed to the mainmast before that foot had come to the end of movement.

The huge old Portuguese came next, his shoulders seeming not so much to emerge as to force a passage through the yielding edges of the hatchway. He was followed by Calder, the skin of his face glistening and blanched under the copper varnish. After him, came the three other Portuguese, tumbling from the square of dark with a curious anxiety, like thieves in the night scurrying from a church. As had Dunn, Calder and the old man, the three Portuguese made straight for the water cask as soon as they were clear of the hatch, passing between the cargo they had driven up for airing without glancing left or right.

When Price climbed from the hold and stood on the deck, he turned and thrust his wide, thick hand above the opening for Mister Reynolds to grasp. But Reynolds, already on the ladder behind him, ignored the dutiful offering. He bounded rather than climbed from the hatchway with the festive energy of a cork popping from a bottle of champagne. His pink face had taken on a boiled glaze; his blue cotton jacket and white nankeen trousers were mottled with smudges of bursting sweat: he gave the impression of some merry eccentric who had just emerged fully clothed from a warm bath. In his right hand, he held a broad wooden spatula on which rested a small lump of yellow excrement grained with dark streaks.

A stir, a repercussive tremor, travelled along the columns of slaves as he appeared. For a moment, the voided eyes flickered with the life of something between fear and fascinated bewilderment. He flourished cordially his cat-o'-nine-tails at the black, grey-scurfed faces that had turned to him as though on word of command, spun on his heel and bounced across the deck past the culverin to the starboard companionway leading up to the poop. Before him, at arm's length, he carried the spatula and its burden of faeces with happy concentration of a small boy leading in an egg and spoon race.

"I'll want your opinion on this, sir," he was calling to Hogarth before he had reached the head of the steps. "I don't think we need feel alarm, but you ought to see it."

The clear, light voice was almost soprano, yet without effeminacy. It was easy to imagine it being flung effortlessly from the deck to the cross-trees sixty feet up, above the howling competition of a gale. It was easy to imagine it gurgling with the cool insistence of a mountain stream into the heat of a woman's need.

Hogarth had turned from the rail. His bright lips were drawn suddenly into thin, dulled rictus. The two grooves bracketing his mouth were suddenly much deeper.

"Let me see!"

The words sounded in the hot stillness like three nails being hammered into tough wood; the two faces bent over the spatula and its load of yellow waste ringed by pale yellow gravy.

The wide brim of Hogarth's hat darkened the pale yellow of Reynolds' flossy and buoyant curls. Without looking up, with a regal casualness, Reynolds thrust the whip he held in his left hand at Bullen who had followed him up the companionway and who now swayed uneasily, in exile, one yard from his fellow officers. Reynolds had released his grip on the handle of the cat-o'-nine before Bullen was aware that he was being offered it. Neither Hogarth nor Reynolds turned their heads as the heavy instrument thudded on the deck, nor as Bullen folded jerkily, in sections, to retrieve it: to stand clutching it to his stomach with an air of embarrassed sulkiness, like that of a man with a large bunch of flowers and no one to give it to.

Reynolds, his eyebrows contracted over contemplative slits of blue, felt in the left-hand shirt pocket of his jacket and brought out a bent, rusted six-inch nail. Delicately, with a relaxed and sunny deliberation, he used the point to unravel the squashy coils of stool. He lifted a short, viscous thread of blood-darkened matter and quizzed Hogarth with lifted eyebrows and creased forehead. Hogarth bent closer and sniffed; took the nail with its clinging filament from Reynolds's hand; held it close;

43

dropped it back onto the small pudding of shit; asked, in his turn, a silent question. Reynolds shook his head.

"No, sir," he said, "I don't believe its the flux. It's only haemorrhoids. D'you agree?"

"Yes, Mister Reynolds. That is my belief too. Only haemorrhoids, thank God. But we must make certain. Men's section or the women's?"

"Men's, sir. I've noted the pair. After we have hosed them down, Mister Bullen and I will examine them . . . eh, Mister Bullen? What? You and I will play doctor, eh!" He swung away from Hogarth on the words, and thrust the spatula with its load of filth under Bullen's long nose: a movement begun and completed with a feline insolence of speed almost before the eye could register it.

Bullen reared back in two hysteric steps, his long face twitching with protest and alarm, as if the fingers of some invisible not very talented child were absently fashioning and refashioning his rudimentary features.

"Now, now, Mister Reynolds," he said. "Now—I mean, sir . . ."

But Reynolds had already turned. He looked at Hogarth, his lips parting in a silent laugh like a yawn. Hogarth's mouth twitched briefly with the grin he could not permit himself, and he stepped aside as Reynolds strode to the rail to flick the specimen over the side into the waste below.

And then, turning from the rail, his mouth already open to make some further remark to Hogarth, Reynolds was possessed by an arbitrary and Gadarene madness. So that to those who saw him, his neat, chubby figure moving casually back to his fellow officers, his glance along the deck below, his sudden, wordless howl of rage, his leap over the rail were all like furiously shuffled pictures of a single action. He had landed on his toes, six inches beside the gape of the hatchway, and was hurling himself along the deck to the mainmast while the sound of that extraordinary cough of fury seemed still to linger in the air above the poop where he had uttered it. Dense, amazing, unstoppable as a charging pig, he flung himself among the men who had come from the hold and gathered around the water cask. His well-fleshed shoulder took the huge old Portuguese under the breastbone and slammed the man's fifteen stone

44

against the bulkhead of the midshiphouse as if he had been caught on the outer wave of a detonation. His left flank and pumping arm spun the rooted Calder into a preposterous tangle-footed pirouette. His thrusting head made an opening between two gaping, stocky young Portuguese with the force of a rico-cheting boulder. And as he reached the water cask, his arm swept up and across his pink face, and the edge of his plump hand descending caught the Portuguese who had come last from the hold a terrific axe blow between the hinge of jaw and ear. The man seemed to dive straight into the deck; the ladle from which he had been drinking soared up, struck the awning and clattered on the planks. Straddling the still figure, Reynolds once more raised that constricted, raging snarl, and then, with a barely perceptible transition to a voice as slim and bright as a dagger, said, "I'll flog the next fool I catch gargling his water and spitting it out instead of swallowing it down where it'll do him good. I'll flog him raw, you understand?" He pointed to the deck before him where the unconscious man between his feet had spat after rinsing out his mouth and throat.

"There's a good half pint of water there," Reynolds continued, his voice lightly and mockingly sanctimonious now. "Half a pint at least. Not allowing for what the careless dog spilled when I corrected him . . . And if he feels thirsty before to-morrow morning he can suck his ration from the deck."

The feral, crazy eyes seemed to register simultaneously with each of the staring men, who were still caught, as if shocked into immobility by a thunderclap from a cloudless sky, in the attitudes and postures left by his stupefying passage. A crouch-ing, delicately balanced readiness tautened his small frame as Dunn, his face askew with incredulous anger, made a half step forward, sounding the beginnings of protest that never passed his lips. Then, as suddenly, all the gathered challenge seemed to drain from Dunn, leaving him stiller than the others. The wheezing of the old Portuguese slumped against the midship-house as he dragged air into his violently emptied lungs was the only noise in the silence Reynolds had created.

"Well done, Mister Reynolds," Hogarth called from the poop. "I hope you have not damaged the fellow."

"Upon my word no, sir," Reynolds called back cheerfully.

45

"These sardine grubbers take more killing than a donkey. He'll be right as rain in an hour." He lifted his right foot and drove it with casual precision into the unconscious man's ribs. "You'd best soak his thick skull," he said to no one in particular and tossed the shit-stained spatula he still carried onto the deck before Dunn. "Wash that off and stow it."

Again, for a moment, rebellion glistened in Dunn's eyes like unshed tears. Then, as the radiant face onto which he looked down smiled with anticipation—the baby plump cheeks rosily brightening, and the small, sure hand closing on the butt of the Navy Colt—the light dimmed in Dunn's eyes. They became dull, almost vacant with a hate so profound that he did not seem to be contemplating Reynolds at all but to be looking beyond him to some revealed reckoning in which Reynolds was merely another factor, or an aid perhaps, like a crystal ball, to focus the seer's vision.

"Pick it up, Dunn," Reynolds said now, and there was hunger in his voice, a longing both mad and wistful, as he waited on what the other might do.

From where he leaned against the midshiphouse, the old Portuguese said, "Do orders, Senhor Dunn," in an urgent, careful voice, like a woman who sees a child in a situation where even the sound of her warning might tilt it into disaster.

Stiffly, as though forced by the pressure of a powerful hand on the back of his neck, Dunn bent and picked up the spatula. The black and emptied eyes he fixed on Reynold's face as he straightened were almost tired now, and there was an odd fatigue in his slow walk forward among the women and children beyond the midshiphouse to the pump on the foredeck. Two of the Portuguese followed, carrying by the ankles and shoulders the limply jack-knifed body of the man Reynolds had knocked senseless.

At the pump, Dunn bent again, grasped the brass nozzle of the coiled hose and dragged a short length of the canvas tube across the deck to the bulwarks. He thrust the spatula through a mesh hole in the netting, turned his head and nodded briefly to the two men by the pump. They began to work the double handle of the pump with light economical movements, and as the first jet of sea-water gushed from the nozzle, Dunn pushed it through the netting and directed the intermittent spurts onto the fouled wood.

When the spatula was clean, he drew it and the nozzle in through the netting, turned and went back to the pump. He looked down at the unconscious Portuguese and then up at the other two. They nodded agreement and, as they began to work the handle again, Dunn sluiced the still face on the deck until the stunned man wriggled, gasped and sat up spluttering.

He looked about him vacantly as he sat up, like a man waking from a drunken sleep and not remembering where he fell into bed. Then, as the two men came from the pump and grasping his arms heaved him to his feet, understanding and memory began to quicken his glazed eyes. He lurched forward from between the two men, looked about him once more with that drink-bemused air, staggered to the bulkhead of the forecastle and rested his forehead and crossed forearms against it. The water from his dripping hair and soaked shirt ran down white-painted wood as slowly, with the anxious care of a man trying to lift a cracked egg from a box, he felt below his ear and along the place on his neck, just behind the hinge of his jaw. Then he turned sluggishly, pivoting on one shoulder, and looked back with a bewildered and melancholy resignation at Dunn's expressionless face and the troubled sympathy of his two countrymen.

From the moment of Reynolds' leap over the poop rail, through his blurred terrible attack and the brief time when Dunn had balanced on the edge of certain death, to the washing of the spatula and the revival of the unconscious man, no more than three minutes had passed. Yet to those who had watched the concentrated and purposeful ferocity, as to those who had suffered it directly, it seemed that time itself must have been tricked, frozen by violence as by the uttering of some malignant spell. So that when Hogarth called impatiently from the poop, *Mr Reynolds! Mr Bullen! If we do not set to, we will be stowing the blacks again until midnight,* his harsh voice was greeted with a sort of relief, by the sailors and the slaves alike, releasing them from the painful rigidity of positions held in a century's sleep. Three of the older slave children began to cry, loudly and ecstatically.

47

CHAPTER FIVE

While the ranks of male slaves were being hosed down, one of the pairs tried to heave itself over the bulwarks. The two men had waited until the sailor trailing the hose had played the bright gushes of water over the section of six or seven pairs in which they stood and had passed on, leaving the linked figures who had hopped, gasped and huddled under the stinging jets to uncluster slowly and settle on the deck again.

It was then that one of the pairs in the rear rank had leaned the hollows of their backs against the bulwarks and under the astonished gaze of the Portuguese who stood three paces from them suddenly, wordlessly, flung up their heels, swivelling where the rail caught their arched spines, their shoulders and shaven skulls pushing the net out where they had, somehow, undone the water-soaked, swollen knots of the lashing.

They seemed to hang, balanced in time across space, for a moment that was not so much unprobably stretched but without beginning or end, their black, upraised hands like claws pulling from the bright air the weight that would topple them into the sea. Then they were gone: the soles of the four feet making pale streaks as the stiffened bodies toppled out of balance. And halted. Hung head down as the free left foot and ankle of the one on the left tangled in the netting. A wild, incredulous shriek rose from where his head hung out of sight as his shackled right leg was wrenched out and sideways and then down, grotesquely twisted at knee and hip by the suddenly arrested weight of his partner. He shrieked once more before the hands of the Portuguese, who had watched them begin their wordless and astonishing bid, closed round his enmeshed ankle, as his shackle-mate hanging below him lunged and flailed to pull him loose: a scream that seemed to rise beyond anguish into some reverent and nearly soundless question.

48

Then Price, trundling heavily, but moving very fast as though mounted on uneven wheels, Calder, the old Portuguese and one of the others had reached the bulwarks and were beginning to hoist back to the deck what the netting held. From beyond the midshiphouse where the women had been washing themselves and the children, dipping ladles of sea-water from two big tubs, there came a long sigh, a groan of held breath slowly exhaled. In the ranks of the men as they stood waiting to be hosed or sat with the sheen of water drying into dull patches on their skins, there was a stir that seemed to begin in the section from which the pairs had flung themselves and to travel accumulating force in each group, until it was one massed and murmurous tremor, random yet menacing, like branches in a wood whipping in a sudden gust. Reynolds stood at the centre of the deck between the two front ranks, his gaze shifting steadily and rapidly from side to side, poised again on his toes, his hand closed round the butt of his revolver, crooning.

All right now . . . All right, my dear black friends . . . There is no cause for concern, I assure you . . . Reynolds is here. Reynolds your friend . . . Stand back, lads. Don't fright 'em . . . Now, now. Easy. Easy . . . Price, take those two out of sight . . . That's right, you sons of Ham, you children of darkness, howl if it makes you feel better . . .

Until under the assurance of the soothing and incomprehensible patter the ranks became quiet and the frightened eyes turned to him held a sorrowful yet trusting bewilderment.

On the poop, Hogarth slowly thrust the revolver he had drawn back into his belt. He said in a heavy, furious, voice, "Mister Bullen, how did the blacks do it, eh? How did they untie the lashing without us seeing 'em at it?"

"The knots were cut, sir," Bullen called back. "Cut clean." Anxiously he raised the loosened section of the net from which the three severed lengths of rope dangled. "I can't imagine how they could have done it."

"With a sharp instrument, Mister Bullen." Hogarth's voice was almost weary now, as if disgust had replaced the leaden anger. "You and Mister Reynolds see that you find it before we stow them again. Or find out what they have done with it."

But Reynolds was already hurrying back from where Price,

Calder and the two Portuguese had laid the pair on the deck, forward of the midshiphouse under the starboard rail. Densely resilient, brisk as a ball of rubber, he bounced aft calling, "You'd never believe it, sir. The cunning dog had it in his mouth. Lodged snug as you please between his gums and his lip." He waved at Hogarth, a dark sliver held between the thumb and forefinger of his right hand.

"What is it, Mister Reynolds?"

Lightly skipping up the companionway between quarterdeck and poop, Reynolds dropped into Hoggarth's extended palm the sliver he carried.

"Ah, yes," Hogarth said, and then with a return of that flat, reined-in fury, "Where would he have got this, Mister Reynolds?" His hand closed with careful tightness around the little triangle of snapped-off dagger-point which Reynolds had passed to him.

'Not aboard, sir, I'll warrant," Reynolds said. "Back in the barracoons I should think." He looked forward along the decks to where the pair were laid. "They're Angolans. From the lot we took on at Benguela. You'll remember the numbers of tame blacks there. And that metal was not forged in Europe. Somebody passed this to him in Benguela, sir." He shook his head and added with a sort of cordial admiration. "They prepared for this with care. Feel the edge they put on it. They must have been honing it on their shackles ever since we left Africa. The obstinate rogues."

"Which one had it concealed?"

"The fellow who tangled himself in the net, sir." Reynolds now shook his head with glum exasperation. "We have suffered a loss, I fear. He will not walk again if I am any judge."

"The other?"

"Oh, he will heal. The shackle skinned him badly while he was hanging, but with attention we should have him fit for sale at Pernambuco."

"Still we have lost one," Hogarth said, "and but for a fortunate accident we would have lost two. This is a bad business, Mister Reynolds. I do not blame you. Your handling of the situation was admirable. But we shall have to exercise special care for a while. The blacks have been seriously affected.

We may have uncomfortable echoes of this before they settle down again."

From behind them a woman's voice said, "Captain Hogarth?" on a note of distant question, and they turned to where Hogarth's wife stood before the doorway of the poop cabin. In the shadow of the bonnet she wore tied under the chin, her face was still, remote, as if she were glancing, in an unoccupied moment, at the vulgarly drawn pictures illustrating a banal story.

"My respects, ma'am," Reynolds said and inclined his head and stepped back a pace from Hogarth, glancing with interested and sardonic relish from the face in the shadow of the bonnet's wings to the expression of sudden, wary deference under the wide brim of the straw hat.

"My dear," Hogarth said and stepped forward stiffly, "do you wish something?"

"You have had trouble, Captain Hogarth? I heard a man scream, and then there was shouting?" She stood, straight, plump and composed in her chill and bitter distance, her hands clasped at the stomach of her pale blue cotton dress.

"An incident, my dear," Hogarth said carefully, as though each word was a weight he laid carefully on one end or the other of a balance. "We had an unfortunate accident. Two of the blacks tried to drown themselves. I trust you were not alarmed. We have the situation in hand."

She nodded once, acknowledged the information, not so much ignoring the dutiful concern as letting it pass her by, deflected. Turning, she re-entered the little cabin.

Hogarth came back slowly to where Reynolds waited. He said, without emphasis, tiredly, "Very well, Mister Reynolds. That will be all. See the blacks are fed now."

"Yes, sir." The downy eyebrows lifted again in question. "And the crippled one?"

"You and Alex see to it when they are battened down. We cannot afford to have them excited again. Can you keep them quiet until then?"

"Yes, sir. He is hardly conscious now. If he comes to and looks like disturbing the others, I'll have Alex dose him with laudanum."

51

"Yes," Hogarth said as he turned away to his stand beside the wheel, "that would be best. It would not take much to fret them again." And then with a return of tautly controlled anger, "I'll tell you this has been an ill business, Mister Reynolds. Our first loss. It must not occur again."

Part Two

THE MIDSHIPHOUSE

CHAPTER SIX

As Louis Delfosse used to say, *Two of us could take and hold that country, Alex, if you were only a white man,* and he'd look across the Rio Grande hungering for what was on the other side. The cities and the women and the gold and the silver, not just the pukey scrawny Mex cattle we was lifting and the *cantina* whores you could get the sickness from by just looking at them, let alone dipping into what they had between their legs.

I can't do it alone, he'd say, *and there isn't another man except you can see it as I see it, and they'd kill you before we could even get started because you're a nigger. Kill us both.* And he'd laugh a little dry laugh back in his throat. *That's history, Alex. The man is nothing without the time. And this isn't our time. We're kings without a crown because of your black skin. They'd hate you so much for that they'd forget they really want to be ruled, need to be ruled, just as much as we want to rule them.*

He knew plenty, that Louis. A whole heap of plenty. Everything else in him had spoiled except what he'd learned from those fancy high-talking teachers old Jean-Paul Delfosse used to bring over from France and Germany and England. The books and the words were the only things in him that hadn't spoiled rotten by the time he come to his manhood. He was a bad mean boy too. The worst I ever saw—except for me. But that weren't anything to what he became when we was men riding across the river. But he knew things, and I kept with him because of that. And because of what we'd done together when we was boys on the Delta.

Well, he didn't know enough not to try after that girl-child. For all I warned him. Not even wanting her, really, but wanting to hurt an old man who would have taken any hurt but that.

I told him, *Don't do it, Louis! Sometimes you got to know*

53

*which corners a man won't back into unless you stuff him there
dead, If you got to have the girl, you better kill the old man
first. I don't know how I know this, Louis, but I feel it so sure.*
And he laughed then, the same dry small laugh sounding in the
back of his throat, that never seemed to come out to you but
just remained there inside him, alone. It was only the sort of
hurt a man couldn't take, even if he had to die trying not to
take it, that Louis Delfosse could get any pleasure from. The
other kind of hurting you have to give out, so's to get where
you're going, he liked that too, but only the way a man likes
to have his boots fit comfortable. And that day when I went
across the river to pick him up there was more blood over the
floor and walls of that little adobe hut than it seemed rightly
could've come from one man. The old man dead beside him,
too, but he hadn't bled much. A little thick squeezed-out trickle
from under his heart was all. But Louis's blood had covered
everything—as if all the badness and evil he had inside had
come bursting out at the last. And I wonder sometimes if maybe
he hadn't hoped for that too, and hadn't kept looking to hurt
somebody bad enough for it to happen as I'd told him it would.
He must've died hard, he was maybe really dead before he
ever got to his gun, but what he had on his face was the nearest
thing to true smiling I'd seen there since he was a little piece
of a chap. But then maybe I never did much real smiling myself
after him and me got to be twelve or around that and started
into doing the things that would've ended it all for both of us
then if enough men with two ropes had ever caught us one
night far enough outside Delfosse territory. As they could've
too, even inside it, if old Jean-Paul hadn't finally allowed to
himself what he had kept trying to pretend wasn't so and
shipped us out. *You're worse than he is*, he told Louis, and
pointing to me on the floor where he'd knocked me down,
*because you're a white man and a bad white man will always
be worse than the worst nigger. A rogue nigger is only a dog
turned wolf but a bad white man is a fallen angel. I should let
them shoot you now, and then burn you, the white and the
black together, but there are others who will kill you for me
where you're going. I hope they do it quickly. That's the only*

54

blessing I give you: that they'll kill you quickly when the time comes.

So this evening after we'd fed and stowed the niggers, I told Reynolds about that time. I don't know why—except it's this dead calm pressing us down so nothing seems real, not even liquor. As if we was all dead already and serving out our sentence.

Reynolds, he laughed, like I knew he would. Not laughing at me, but as if it was all a travelling raree-show put on for him special and he was applauding me and Louis and old Jean-Paul for the quality of the entertainment.

"You dog," he said, and laughed again. "I have never imagined you to be just a simple sea-cook, Alex. You may have deceived all the world and his wife but I can always smell the beast, even before I see him there hidden in the undergrowth peering out and hungry, oh so hungry. Always hungry for the fat snoring prey that believes itself secure. What happened then?"

"When?" I asked him.

"After the old fellow sent you packing? When he was forced to repudiate his only son and his pet Negro." Reynolds shook this time, silent, as if he didn't want to waste any of the sweet laughter inside him by letting it out too soon.

"We lit out for the border," I told him. "Where the hell else could we go? The South ain't no place for a nigger who don't have someone like Mister Delfosse to run back to. Especially if it ain't no place for a free nigger. There's always men waitin' for a chance to use you real cruel just for bein' free. An' what would we have been goin' North for? Ridin' an' fightin' was all me an' Lous was good for. Oh Louis, he could have taught school, I reckon. Or found himself a place writin' an' figurin' in some bank. He'd had a heap of learnin'. Maybe he would have found some gal with a rich daddy. An' I'd have driven his carriage like my old man did for Jean-Paul. But all that would have killed us both sure as the rope or the guns they had waitin' for us if we ever showed our faces back in the Delta."

God he knows why I needed to tell Reynolds all this. Maybe it's because he got something in him that Louis used to have. Beside a man's got to talk with somebody and him and Hogarth are the only men on this stinking tub who ain't plain trash,

When I'm obliged to kill him I'll be real regretful it's got to be that way. But a man like him you don't leave to your good luck to take care of for you.

"That fellow, now," Reynolds said when I'd finished telling him how me and Louis had lit out, "the one you and I have just disposed of over the side. What were your sentiments concerning him?"

"About what you felt," I told him. "Weren't anythin' much to feel. He weren't any good to me, all broke up like he was. Weren't much good to himself, come to that. He went easy, not knowin' a thing from all that laudanum we give him. So he can't complain he didn't get somethin' out of it. I've seen men go out a lot slower and a lot worse than he did. Men who'd have kissed your hand and called you Jesus Christ if that was what you wanted, just for you doin' them the favour of drawin' a knife quick and merciful across their throats."

Reynolds wasn't laughing now, but looking at me steady from those eyes of his bluer than anything I ever seen in a man's head. Only one woman I ever saw got eyes that the colour could turn to black in some lights, like the grapes old Jean-Paul used to have him sent special from France. I know all the blues of the white man's eyes—from where they're clear and light and blind like they was made of glass, to something not grey and not green but like two bits of ice broke from the edge of a pond in winter where the dirt and the water mix. Or maybe like the shine on a bullet spun off a rock. Ain't a nigger looked straight into more white men's eyes and's alive to remember it than me. Sometimes I used to push it pretty close though. If it'd been the South and not the border I'd have been dead for sure. Even with Louis to back any play I made. And I ought to remember that. I don't have to—but I ought to, for remembrance. He backed me three times when it wasn't easy for a white man. He rode out of four maybe five places where it'd been good makings for him but not for me. And stopped lead twice he wouldn't have needed to stop but for me. And him knowing I'd have left him anytime and anywhere to die if I didn't need him. Jesus Christ. *Louis Delfosse!* You and me with what I got waiting to be taken now! We could be kings. Like you always wanted us to be.

So now Reynolds said, "I mean, did you feel no sense of kinship? A twinge of guilt, shall we say? Or if nothing so strong as guilt, knowing you as I think I do, Alex, was there no feeling that you were perhaps treating a brother in blood with less than the loving kindness a brother might have expected?"

The way he says things you'd believe Reynolds wouldn't bother to lower the glass from his lips if you was to come to him and tell him his mammy was lying dead in a whorehouse. And you'd never make a bigger mistake than that. He's a joker, all right. When they laid Christ on the cross, he was the one laughing as the nails went in. But he's serious. He don't do or say anything he don't know what it's for.

"What sort of damn fool question you asking me, Reynolds?" I said. "He weren't any kin to me. An' him and me never entered into no agreement, neither. Except I contracted to feed him between Africa an' Brazil. Maybe that's why he tried to drown himself. Maybe the son of a bitch didn't like my cookin'."

Reynolds laughed again, throwing his head back into the shadow and then leaning forward over the table with his face all bright and merry and red and the yellow hair pale and shiny under the lamp hanging above us.

"Alex," he cried, "oh, Alex. Your austere certitudes are an inspiration. You speak as one having authority, not like those scribes and Pharisees who have congested the libraries of the world with elaborate justifications of their fatuous premises. My father has ten thousand books, and has read seven thousand of them. At least that was his inane boast the last time we conversed. The only discernible effect of such a labour is that a bovine but once useful squire has become an overburdened ass. His commentary on Plato, in three volumes, is distinguished only by being duller than the tedious prig who inspired it; and of course it completely fails to note the significance of the one interesting contribution Plato made to thought: that in this world there are those made of gold, those made of silver, and those made of brass; and that the whole business of life lies in maintaining these distinctions. But then I don't have to tell you that, Alex. You know it without ever having wasted your attention on that dreary Greek usher. I envy you, my dear fellow. Upon my word I do."

"I've heard of Plato", I told him, "an' a few of the others. I ain't sayin' as I read 'em, you understand. Exceptin' once in a while I'd take a little peek to see how they looked down there on a page. But there weren't much need for me to bother. Louis Delfosse used to do the readin' for us both. Anything I wanted to know, he'd tell me."

"An admirable division of duties, Alex," Reynolds said then, "and one that I would have expected only of you. The true kings of history, the men of great and decisive action, have always kept clerks to perform the debilitating labour of reading for them. And what do these clerks read? From what do they weave their insipid and attenuated speculations? Why, the very actions for which their menial service has freed the kings."

"Now you're takin' a line of territory I never been in, Reynolds," I said. "Maybe I better have a little more of this brandy, see if I can't at least ride in your tracks even if I can't keep up with you. What the hell is an old black man without a dollar in his purse or a country he can go back to doin' in the company of those kings you mention?"

"What indeed?" Reynolds said, and helped himself to four maybe five fingers of the Spanish brandy I'd laid aboard for myself at Vigo before we made the run down to Setubal to take on the Portuguese hands and pay off the white men—the English and the squareheads—Hogarth had gotten to work us out of Bristol and across the Bay. He paid 'em all off except for that old man Calder, who knows a ship the way a field-hand knows one hundred acres of cotton or a mule knows a trail in the mountains. Him and that mean trash, Dunn—and Reynolds should have killed *him this afternoon and saved me the trouble of having to do it for myself later. He's trash but I wouldn't leave him at my back anymore than I would spread one blanket over me and a rattlesnake, or stand close behind a mustang that ain't been broke yet. And that little Boyo. I hope it don't have to go as far as killing him. No time I ever held with killing, except it had to be done to get where you're going, or to get out of where somebody else figured he ought to go and you in his way.

And all the time while Reynolds and me was drinking, I was watching him, and not feeling too easy about that last reckoning of his. The one about the kings. Nothing I ever said to him could have led him so close . . . But with a man like Reynolds, you have to keep remembering he opens his eyes one morning and smells the air and knows a lot of things he doesn't know how he knows them—like a catamount or a lobo wolf. I should've kept my mouth shut or at least just talked my way around things the way we've done ever since he took to stopping by after the niggers are battened down for the night. Maybe it's this damn calm making me foolish and loose at the mouth. It ain't being alone or waiting it out or nothing like that. I'm used to all that, God he knows. I seen plenty of times when there was only me and a few bastards you'd never know was there until they jumped you for what you might be carrying, or just jumped you because they'd got nothing else to do. I seen a lot of days alone in wild lonesome country, and I come through all right . . . Maybe I'm getting old, like I told Reynolds. Can't take it the way I used to.

But thinking that, or even feeling it, and you're a fair way to losing everything. Losing before you've even shuffled the pack and dealt. I learned that much, a long time ago, along with everything else I had to learn.

So now I stopped thinking it and said to Reynolds, "You looking worried, man, an' that ain't like you. I seen you a lot of things but bein' fretted ain't in your line."

"It is on my mind," he said, "that you and I may well have the same office to perform, many times, as we now just did. There will be more for the deep, Alex, if this calm continues. Those two this afternoon: they were a portent. We are running to the end of our allowance."

"I can keep feedin' 'em," I told him. "There's enough left to bring 'em in to the market—unless there ain't goin' to be no wind blow across the sea ever again. They won't dress out as much if we *don't* get a breeze soon, but they'll fatten up pretty quick once we drop anchor an' lay fresh grub aboard. Cap'n Hogarth ain't goin' to start sellin' until they're sleeked up a bit. Sure we're goin to lose a few more, but how many traders you ever hear of got this far without loss? An' we hadn't lost a one until those crazy Angolans decided they would rather do without the pleasure of our company. Hogarth an' you, an' me, we've herded 'em an' fed 'em an' doctored 'em like nobody ever has before. When we get movin' again an' they get a little healthful breeze freshenin' the blood, they'll perk up right smart. Anyways, we could lose up to a hundred, hundred an' fifty, an' still be paid off with more than you'd get from ten years on any lawful run you know of."

"You misunderstand," he said. He was hunched over then, sort of drawn together thoughtful; and when he looked up from staring down into his glass, he wasn't really looking at me but at something out there only he could see, and I knew that the calm was getting to him too and that he needed somebody to lean his mind against for a spell, same as me. "My concern is for their spiritual resources rather than our ability to keep them in fair health. Past a certain point melancholia can become a disease as infectious and as lethal as the cholera. Heaven knows, our fortunes below have little to be sanguine about in the most favourable conditions. In this unnatural stillness, I forsee despair breeding, becoming epidemic. Those two this afternoon were the first victims, Alex. We would be poor physicians if we did not recognize the symptoms."

"They'll do", I told him. "They'll droop an' spook a little maybe, if we don't soothe 'em, but they'll make it. They want to live same as anybody else."

"Now that is precisely where we may have miscalculated," he said. "Do they? May they not decide, unanimously, to exchange the burdens of a tangible servitude for the problematic freedom of death? I have heard of these tacit agreements."

"You may have heard of 'em", I told him, "but you sure as hell never seen one. They want to live, the most of 'em. Most folks want to live, pretty deep, most of the time. That's why you got slaves. There ain't a chain forged or a guard sharp an' quick enough to stop any man findin' freedom if he wants it bad enough."

"Alex," he said, and he seemed to shake himself light and loose again, the way he generally is, as if he could bound clear from the deck up to the top mainyard if that was his manner of recreation; his eyes not dark and steady now but dancing like little fish turning so quick you never see them move but just see them somewhere they wasn't while you watched. "Alex, my

60

shipmate and fellow criminal, you are as generous with your wisdom as you are with your brandy. I shall wrest two fortunes from this voyage yet. The share, the very generous share, I shall receive from our good captain, and the education you have afforded me so prodigally. I shall invest both my dear fellow, to the fullest advantage. You will be proud of your pupil, I promise you."

"You Reynolds," I said then, "I admire talkin' to you but you sure get some fanciful notions. You're an entertainment."

But he ain't nobody's fool, that little hard white man. And he has the right of it about what could happen to the niggers if that goddam breeze that's out there somewhere don't find us soon. I seen it happen with cattle. All that beef that just lay down and died on us in the Sonora desert. Not just because they was dried out and half-crazy with no water, but something went out of them, or maybe come into them, and they didn't want to live anymore. You could feel it the night it happened, plain as the wind in your face, and the next day they was all dead across less than two miles, just dropping one after another as we drove them.

CHAPTER SEVEN

1

The stars were crowded so thickly that the sky was only the black lining to a mesh of hot and busy gold.

And even to the boy Joshua, as he mounted the companion-way to the poop, that field of light seemed to demand a moment's attention. It was nothing so much as awe, or even exaltation. He had no more experience of these than he had of trust or pity. To his small, efficient and quite deadly mind such feelings would have seemed cumbersome and endangering—had he been able to comprehend that they existed. But for a little while, standing by the rail, looking out and up, he sensed obscurely a pleasurable fullness that was different from, more pervasive than, a crammed stomach in a warm bed. He longed for something to touch; and he felt strangely, consolingly, freed of his skin, as if he were a lump of sugar slowly dissolving in the clearest water.

The image formed in his mind before he realized it, and frightened him. He stepped back from the rail quickly, alert and suspicious, ready for flight or combat. The great sky, the sweetly painful longing to touch and to be absorbed, had been forgotten by the time he had crossed the yard of deck to the captain's cabin.

The Hogarths had finished their dinner. On the small table, the two cleaned plates, the three emptied dishes, spoke of steady, dutiful appetites. The captain sat in the one easy chair the cabin contained. Like the settee to which Eliza Hogarth had retired, it was slip-covered with a patterned chintz from which the colours of the red roses and the yellow had long since faded to dark brown and dull lemon.

The silence in the cabin was stale and old, like the trapped

62

heat. That was how he had found them, always, ever since the voyage began and, for the second time this evening, a fanciful and vivid concept formed itself in Joshua's mind: the captain and his lady, it seemed to him, were sitting at opposite sides of a room so large that you could scarcely see the walls, but only two small figures half swallowed below the edges of their respective horizons.

The image did not frighten him: he toyed with it a moment for its novelty's sake and then abandoned it. Hogarth and his wife beyonged to a world as nearly far from his comprehension as the constellations outside. In his brief life, he had begged from this world; stolen from it; been abused by it and hidden from it; come, by a cunning he was yet to realize he possessed, nearly into manhood despite it.

But until the evening, four months before, when he first carried dinner to the couple in the poop cabin, he had never been physically closer to any inhabitant of that world than his hand in the gentleman's pockets or—once—when he had lifted a gold-bordered cameo from the throat of a lady who had been ill-advised enough to pause and brood above the heart-stopping, blue-veined pallor of his angel's face. Fifty words of the English tongue would have been more than sufficient to carry the burden of such intimacies as he had established between Captain Hogarth's class and his. And in all his life before he found himself aboard his ship, he had never used more than twenty-five consecutive words of that fifty for anything but lies, whining appeal and fraudulent conversion of the emotions. For him, as he entered the cabin, the palpable silence was only what was customary between a gentleman and his lady. He was not yet capable of imagining any human exchanges other than those based on immediate hunger, lust and ruthless preservation of the self.

He said shyly, holding a round Benares tray to his chest as Mr Alex had taught him. "May I clear, ma'am?" and skirted, as widely as the space allowed, the chair in which Hogarth sat, before approaching the table. He was confident now of the woman's kindness but still cautious about that remote and potent figure in the chair. It seemed impossible that one having so much authority would not one day, in sudden wrath or in a fit of absent-mindedness, destroy whoever came first under his eye.

"Yes, Joshua," Eliza Hogarth said, "you may clear. We have finished, thank you."

The hanging lamp above the table had been turned low because of the heat. In the soft radiance, the woman's smile suddenly restored her youth and placid comeliness; and in the shadow-dappled light the two harsh, vertical creases between her eyebrows were camouflaged and the faded hair glimmered.

"You are well, Joshua?" Hogarth said suddenly. He sat in darker shadow than his wife and the dry, deep voice issuing from the pale blur of his face was almost disembodied. "You have not been affected by this still heat? I observed you this afternoon. You appeared to be in good health. A little less colour in your cheeks, perhaps, than a boy of your years should have but that is only to be expected in the tropics. The blood runs thin. However, you are a sturdy fellow and a little thinning of the blood is beneficial. See to it that you perform your duties industriously. Occupation is a sovereign remedy against the ills of the flesh, Joshua. Remember that."

"Yes, sir . . . Thank you, sir," Joshua stammered. The oracular interrogation from the shadows behind him had been quite unexpected. In the four months that he had served the cabin, the captain had nodded to him perhaps three or four times— with a wide and distant benevolence to which he attached no more personal significance than that he enjoyed it when it happened. Occasionally he had conveyed small messages to one of the officers or to Mr Alex in the midshiphouse. Now he was being asked to respond adequately to a question which was more like a statement and he felt that a satisfactory answer was beyond his powers. For a small space of time, his confusion gave way to something like mutinous resentment. As though he were being searched for goods everyone knew he had not stolen. He was being unfairly put upon.

"Yes, sir," he repeated sullenly, and continued to stack the dishes, plates, glasses and cutlery on his tray, as quickly as he could without clatter. "I keeps well, sir. An' I does my work, sir. Willin' an' careful. Mister Alex'll bear witness to that, sir. Anytime."

64

"You have proved worthy of your hire, Joshua," the woman said. "Have no fear on that score."

She leaned forward into the lamp's glow, and again the years were lightened and the sad, angry mask dissolved by her smile. Then the small grey eyes lost their moment's glow, became once more dull as they turned briefly to the shadowed figure in the chair across the cabin. "But you must remember that it is not only among the idle or the lazy that Satan may find his home. A man may build a palace, Joshua, but without the fear of God it is a hovel of corruption. That is why I teach you your letters. So that you may be able to remind yourself daily from God's own book of God's love and swift justice."

"Yes'm," Joshua said contentedly.

This was familiar if testing ground.

He had assumed when he was first taken aboard—after four days or so of astonishment, suspicion almost, about having three full meals to eat every twenty-four hours and a box to sleep in with three blankets to cover him if he wanted—that such luxuries would have to be paid for. Paid for with something more than the pleasant work in the warmth and the food smells of the galley: work that he found a mildly exhilarating sort of play, really, once he was sure that the big, fierce-looking black man intended him no hurt, even when he made a mistake or was careless, and seemed prepared to treat him with an absently amused, proprietorial kindness. But he had known that there would have to be more of a return on his part for the extraordinary good fortune into which he had stumbled and, when the payment was demanded, he was again suspicious, almost worried, by its pleasant, unexacting nature.

A week after sailing, with the barque shaken down and running steadily if heavily across the turbulent Bay, the lady had sent for him one evening after he had served the two officers in their cabin under the captain's, and he had entered to find her seated at the little table on which he was learning to lay the bewildering profusion of cutlery and plates. A Bible, a slate framed in pale, wooden slats and a pencil were laid on the table before her and she was alone, her face sad and still in the lamplight. Before she released him, over an hour later, he had learned to form a shaky capital A—the squeaking of the new,

still sharp point on the new surface had been strange but bear-
able—and he had heard the story of the Creation and the Fall.

He had quite understood the inevitability of the latter event.
Stealing was a matter of simple exchange, always punished if
you were caught. It was necessary to steal : but being punished
was the other side of it if you were slow or clumsy or unlucky.
That was natural. He could not quite understand why God had
left the apple tree unguarded if He did not want the fruit stolen,
but he did not question His right to deal with the thieves as
He saw fit. Adam and Eve had got away quite lightly, in fact.
Not prison or even a beating, but only dismissal from a gentleman's service for lifting a trifle off his property.

Joshua's world had been full of such tempted, discovered and
cast-out servants : a maid who had put a deliberately forgotten
sixpence into her apron pocket; a footman caught drinking
from the pail of beer with which he was swabbing a parquet
floor to deepen the lustre; a pantryboy who had tried to smuggle
out a scrag-end of mutton under his jacket.

The letters came to him quickly after that night. He was a
bright child, and his fingers had been schooled to make swift,
delicate purchase of small objects. The pencil was no problem.
By the time they reached the Bight of Biafra he was signing his
name, transforming the synonymous, open copperplate with a
remarkably personal touch : crowded, angular, parsimonious.

His progress through the Bible—or rather through the Bible
which Eliza Hogarth selected for him—confirmed such assess-
ments of life as he had come to make. Having to sit listening
attentively, answering short verbal tests on what she had read,
memorizing words and then recognizing them in another context—all of this when he would rather have been playing his
privileged pet's role in the forecastle among the Portuguese—
was sometimes tiresome. But patient and concentrated attendance on adult whim had been habit with him for so long that
it was nearly an instinct. And in the stories she paraphrased
with a sombre yet vivid relish—tales unfolding on transgression
and terrible penalty, arbitrary cruelty and suffering or abject
despair, despotic power and anxious submission—Joshua found
something both stimulating and profound. This was more or less

what life was about. She had told him that God ordered life. The two propositions made a logic that was consoling.

Only one thing had begun to trouble him. As with bitter, glistening eyes and a face lively, sometimes nearly flushed, with the heat of her conviction, she taught him about sin, described for him how it waited—insidious and cunningly painted in a thousand attractive designs—to seize on all but the few who had earned a measure of God's strictly apportioned mercy, he realized that there was one sin so great, so hideous in shape, so detestable in God's eyes that all other sins except blasphemy were like misdemanours compared with it.

He had an intimate knowledge of this sin which her oblique and elaborate hints made far more horrendous than any explicit description. He had lain next to it as a baby, been frightened by its scuffling and agonized wails in the dark as a small child, spied on it with a choking excitement a little later and committed it many times during the past three years with a succession of ignorant or frightened little girls. And now, over four months away from his last, thin spurt into the body of the waif who had demanded a penny of him and foiled his intention of snatching it away afterwards by placing it in her mouth before lifting her skirt, he was committing the sin again—two, sometimes three times a week—in his dreams: in the unbidden but overwhelming urges of desire that were part memory and part invention.

But these dreams and imaginings, he now knew, were as bad as that last, quick, stand-up coupling in the dark under the canal bridge.

If anything, the punishment for them would be even more painful for they were the actions of one who had been shown the light but who still chose to wander in the darkness from which he had been rescued.

And sometimes he would come awake slowly, as though swimming up to darkness through warm, thick currents full of bright visions like undulating fish, and his mouth would dry, his stomach clench with guilt, as he gradually realized that it was the captain's lady against whose naked body dreaming Joshua had pressed himself.

Even now as he lifted the corner of the worn linen tablecloth

67

(in which the scent of lilac bushes still lingered), sliding the tray onto the space he had uncovered, she appeared, fully formed, bright-skinned, gliding towards him as she had last night; her face gravely kind and eager; her private parts tantalizingly shrouded in a mist through which one could not quite see.

His flesh began to stipple with panic as he felt the stirring and swelling begin inside his trousers. Hurriedly he lifted the tablecloth clear and holding it by two corners let it hang before him, folding it slowly with fussy care, lengthways again, then draping it over his forearm so that it still concealed his front, all the while running through his mind images of himself scrubbing the floor of the galley, scouring pans, emptying slops, tying the various and intricate knots the old Portuguese had taught him.

By the time he could no longer spin out the business of folding the cloth, the bulge at the front of his trousers had subsided.

"Will there be anything else, ma'am?" he muttered, his eyes turned down to the tray with its load of thick, blue-patterned bone china and the heavy silver that always, it seemed to him, looked so large and crowded on the little table.

"That will be all, Joshua. Have you had your supper?"

"No'm. Mister Alex allus likes to eat after we're done servin' yourself an' cap'n an' seen to the officers."

"Well go and eat then, child, but don't dawdle. We have the Lord's work to do and the Lord's word to learn. I shall expect you in half an hour."

"Yes'm," he said with resignation and, lifting the tray, he turned to leave.

"Tell Alex I wish to see him then," Hogarth said, the voice from the shadows distant and heavy, as though it were falling slowly from a great height above mists. "I shall be on the poop. by the taffrail. He knows where to find me."

"Yes, sir. I'll tell him, sir. Is there anythin' else, sir?"

"No. Run along now, Joshua."

"Thank you, sir."

Almost, as he scuttled thankfully from the cabin, Joshua could have wished himself back among the easily comprehended cross-currents, the brutal but predictable exchanges, of the life from which he had been salvaged casually on the grey, iron-cold February afternoon four months ago when Price had selected him from the cluster of boys at the dock gates: picking him out with the same detached appraisal that a man might use in choosing the likeliest from a litter of mongrel puppies.

2

"You took your time," Alex said when the boy stepped into the galley. "I figured maybe the cap'n an' his lady had invited you to sit down an' dine with 'em, an' I was just fixin' to eat your supper myself."

"Oh, Mister Alex, sir, it wasn't my fault. They kept me talkin'."

"Talkin' was it! My, my! Now that's somethin'. Any fool can share a dinner if he's invited to it, but to talk with a man you got to be able to bring somethin' to the feast. I hope you kept your end up. Didn't go lettin' me down mumblin' an' shucksin' like some field nigger who ain't never been nearer to a gentleman's table than his mule."

Joshua crossed the galley to the shelf beside the small stove on which they prepared food for the officers and crew. He placed the tray on the shelf and began to take the plates, dishes, cups and saucers, glasses and cutlery off it, stacking them in the tin bucket, half-full of sea-water, that was keeping warm on the residual heat of the damped stove.

Now you can handle all this truck careful, boy, Alex had said to him that February afternoon—after he had made his mark on a long sheet of paper, scratching two wavering crossed lines to the right of the calloused forefinger, thick and solid as the peg for a circus tent, that Price had stabbed onto the long paper—*this here is quality stuff a' just gettin' to wash it an' dry it nice an' put it away trim an' shiny is better'n you deserve. An' this silver now, boy. I don't want to see you leavin' that about all wet, to drain off. You dry that too, an' once a week you clean it with this powder, an' then you polish it till you can see your face in it clear as if it was a mirror, an' none of the powder left in these little bumps an' whirly bits on the handles neither. There is a whole heap of empty water between here*

and when we're goin' an' a boy that don't do his duties to my
likin' wouldn't make more than a little splash in any of it.

Then he had smiled. At least Joshua who had been watching
the hollowed-out black face above him with a fascination beyond fear, almost beyond his habitually alerted suspicion, saw
something at one corner where the wide lips with their thickly
curled back edges joined what might have been the memory
of a smile. It had not lit the impenetrably expressionless eyes,
nor moved the broad, flat planes, the low escarpments and the
shallow depressions of the wide face, but had simply touched
one corner of the blackness like a flake of light instantly swallowed: as if the man was not really amused in himself, nor
even aware of the object of his raillery, but was acknowledging
some distant and gigantic laughter that encompassed them both
in the same inexplicable joke.

Then the man had said, *Well now, I suppose you're figurin'*
that bein' a member of this crew all of two or three hours makes
you entitled to a share of the rations. All right, then sit down
an' let's see you eat. That way, at least I'll know somethin'
about you for sure and had jerked his chin at the small table
in the middle of the midshiphouse where he had been seated
when Price brought Joshua to him. *Here's your boy,* Price had
said, *I've seen better and I've seen worse* and the man had
looked up from the penny notebook to which he was transfer-
ring figures read from a sheaf of papers by his left hand and
nodded, going back to his figures after a glance so brief that it
had seemed to the boy he was already watching the point of
the pen trace another figure on the completion of the nod. *You*
sit there, boy, he had said, not lifting his head and waving his
left hand to a corner of the midshiphouse where there was a
small stool. Outside, the dank tendrils of cold wound closer
about the afternoon, pushing up the Avon before a wet west
wind under a sky of low, dirty clouds that frayed to tatters on
their eastern edges. But the midshiphouse was warm with the
radiance from the small stove. The boy could see hard, nearly
opaque waves of heat dacing from the plump curve of its black-
leaded body; and he had sat at his place in the far corner for
two, perhaps three hours after he had eaten more meat and
bread than he had ever seen in a day of food. All the while the

black face under the lamp was bent over the notebook, or was in rhythmic deliberation between the papers and the notebook, and the big black hand (a lean, almost, thin hand, but big) gripped the pen, not clumsily but with taut purpose, as though it were the hilt of a sabre or the handle of a revolver and copied words and figures from the pile, each paper lifted methodically from the pile and turned face down as it was finished with. Until stupefied by the luxury of more heat than he needed the boy fell asleep, wedged in the angle made by the two bulkheads.

And woke to see the the fine-drawn body (on which the black broadcloth shore clothes hung closely, with a hard elegance, like the uniform of some austere and legendary corps of battle) lengthened above him by the perspective of his position so that the face seemed to lose itself in the shadows under the ceiling.

He had scrambled to his feet then, tense and poised for bolt-ing, one side or the other past the possible reach of the long black arms and big black hands, because to put himself beyond the grasp of any adult male until the situation was clearly defined was always the sensible and the economical thing to do; and the man had said, *Now you ain't got any cause to alarm, boy. You ain't wore out my stool any more sleepin' on it than you would have settin' upright. An' there sure as hell weren't no advantage to me in your keepin' awake unless you can read a bill of lading.* Quietly, without gentleness, but with a level and dispassionate observation of fact as if he were reading to the boy from a contract of his simple privileges and simpler uses in the scheme of things.

It was the same tone the boy was to hear him use, in the days after they had sailed, to any man on board: a measured and impersonal address that was not so much arrogant as effortlessly assumptive of an authority and position beyond challenge, that conceded to the officers—even to the captain—no more than the politeness due between equals and that put the crew at a precisely defined, intractable distance.

How precisely measured and how intractable, the boy was to see demonstrated one afternoon as they were beating south by east round Finisterre. One of the English hands (from among those signed on for the run to Setubal) had put his head in at the opened galley door and said in a cheerful, bantering

71

grumble, *Come on, darky. Stir stumps, then. Here it is past
six bells an' the starboard watch off an' still perishin' for their
supper.*

And Alex reached him before he could turn from the galley's
entrance, not seeming to hurry but simply closing the distance
between them with a steady, almost contemplative air of purpose, gathering in his left hand a fold of the man's jersey, still
holding in his right the big, curve-edged knife with the sharp,
indented back of blade, which was unlike any other sailor's
knife aboard although always worn like any other a little behind
on the right hip. It was a tool which might at any moment have
a use: an article of clothing, almost, without which any man
on board would have felt not quite dressed. *You*, Alex had said
without anger, without any particular emphasis, his left arm
bending slowly and evenly like a rope shortening around a
capstan, not so much dragging as warping the man in close to
him, and again in that level, musing voice: *You man! Listen!
You can call me Alex, 'cause that's what they named me. Or
you can call me cook, 'cause that's what I am. But I don't
answer to anythin' else, you understand. Leastways, I don't
answer as how you might like.*

Now, as Joshua finished what he had brought from the captain's cabin, Alex said, "Bring us our supper, boy. Unless you're
figuring that starving us both to death might be a good idea,"
and poured what remained of the bottle before him into the
short tumbler almost concealed in his right hand.

"Cap'n wants to see you, Mister Alex," Joshua said as he
opened the twin doors in the belly of the stove. "He says he
wants to see you as soon as you're finished."

"Yes," Alex said, "I guess he does at that."

CHAPTER EIGHT

At the taffrail, Hogarth stares through the star-drenched night to the horizon over which he has beaten so painfully with his cargo of invested ambitions. All the journeys of his life, the criss-crossings of the globe, the residue of profitable command converge on this random circle that could be a grave. He turns as a soft thud on the deck tells of someone approaching. His face passing through the glow of the sternlight riding above the rail seems not so much harshly matured as to have been suddenly bereft of youth before it had time to acquire youth's signatures.

"Alex?" he says to the figure coming towards him past the cabin, blurred in the obscurity under the awning.

"It's me, cap'n."

"Good."

Hogarth turns his back on the ship again and looks out once more to the last horizon. Alex joins him at the rail, leans the hollow of his back against it and with arms across his chest, face turned to Hogarth's, waits silently.

"I did not expect so orderly a conclusion to this afternoon's business, Alex. At first there, I thought we would be half the night settling them. But they went below quietly enough."

"It could have been trouble, cap'n. If those two had finished what they set out to do. They might have stampeded on you then. But those two fallin' down on the job like they did took the heart out of it. An' then you got a good-officer in Reynolds. He gentled 'em down right pretty."

"Yes. We are fortunate in having obtained Mister Reynolds' services. Without him we would have suffered loss before this ... You also, Alex. Your contribution to the success of this venture will be greater than your return. I fear. You understand.

We made an agreement. I will add to your share. Equitably. But it will not be what you deserve. It will be my token, my substantial token, of appreciation."

"I understand, cap'n, an' I thank you for the thought as I thank you for the promised token. Like you said, we made an agreement an' I knew what I was signin' on for. I ain't got no call to hold dissatisfaction over what I'll get out of this."

Hogarth turns abruptly and paces forward to the break of the poop deck. For a minute he stands there, the wide, square shoulders humped behind the thrust-forward head as he looks along the length of the barque past the glimmer of heavily drooping jib and the motionless tip of the bowsprit to where the wide fall of stars plunges below the curve of the earth. Alex remains as Hogarth left him: arms crossed across his chest, unmoving, studying the hunched, rudimentary blur twenty feet away against the luminous night. Hogarth returns. His heels strike the deck as if trying to crush anxiety into the unyielding teak. In the pool of light from the lamp riding on the taffrail, he turns his face to the black man who keeps his eyes fixed on the place from which Hogarth has come.

"I must have a wind, Alex," Hogarth says, in a harsh, astounded whisper. "If I do not raise a wind I am ruined."

"You got five days, cap'n," Alex says, without looking at him. "Maybe seven if you stretch it. The food ain't all that worry. I know what to do with it an' half-rations won't kill nobody. But we don't get some rain down and an' we goin' to start needin' water in five to seven days. About that. Then you start buyin' time. Thirty, thirty-five niggers over the side each day will buy you a day more."

"I do not wish that. It must not come to that."

"It come to it this afternoon when Reynolds an' me put that broke-up one over the side. Wishin' an' willin' is one thing, cap'n, an' what you got to do sometimes is another. We better start thinkin' now of what we'll have to do."

"Murder," Hogarth says. His voice still holds the tone of bitter astonishment. "Murder. After all my care, my scruple, to come to murder." Then he shakes himself and says, with flat anger, "No. You're right, Alex. We must not try to escape our

74

consequences. I would give much to avoid what we may yet have to do, but I will not console myself with regrets if it becomes necessary."

"Yes, cap'n,' Alex says, "that's about how it always is when you're goin' any place."

Part Three

OFFICERS' MESS

CHAPTER NINE

1

Three days from Africa, Reynolds had stopped one of the women as the slaves were filing below for the night. In those first days on the open water, the slaves' terror and desolation had not yet become dulled by habit. A reverberation of hope, of flaring panic, would run along the ranks, seeming to accumulate strength and intensity the further it travelled from the original protest or spark of fright. Tense and sweating—cursing softly and growling reassurances—the sailors would close in then on both sides of the iron-linked, multi-limbed file of black flesh, as if trying to shut the air from the flame at the end of a rapidly shortening fuse.

It was in those moments that Reynolds had first shown his true value; over and above, that is, his learned competence as an officer of the marine. Skimming like a dragonfly between the clamorous hold and the untidy toss of dark bodies on the deck, ceaselessly and loudly prattling, he would pat a shoulder vigorously or rub his hand affectionately over a shaven scalp, shoving back into line a dangerously excited pair who might have influenced those behind them. Occasionally linking arms with the slave nearest him and executing a few blithe, fantastic steps of his own invention, to the accompaniment of an old and lively song he would gradually contain the surge of feeble outrage and despair that had begun to gather force by replication, feeding on itself as it spilled out of the black entrance to the hold into the wide, bright possibilities of sky and sea.

He would never, himself, strike any man, but sometimes in his darting, antic progress, he would stop and point and say urgently, with absolute finality, *Him! Hit him!* and be three yards along the rank of bonded flesh before the nine tails of knotted leather curled around the shoulders of the one he had pointed to or before the stock of the whip rang on the head or before the butt of a Springfield was driven between ribs and diaphragm. And always where he would say *Him! Hit him!* was the place where protest might have become revolt and the reflex gestures of despair have grown into a final challenge.

On the third afternoon out from the low, black coast where they had lain for one week waiting for the final consignment that would fill the last unprofitable spaces in the hold, Reynolds had stood at the edge of the hatchway as the last pair of males had stumbled and clanked down to where Mr Bullen, Price, Dunn, Calder, the old Portuguese and four of his younger countrymen were performing the tedious but delicate duty of seeing the cargo laid out on the tiered planks and shackled to the one-inch chains that were run the length of the hold along each plank. Behind Reynolds, the women and the children waited, unfettered, in loose coagulation between the mainmast and his back.

"All secured, sir," Price had called from the hold, his level, heavy voice made flatter, more leaden, by the thick air through which it rose.

Reynolds had turned then and nodded to the three Portuguese who leaned against the bulwarks beside the huddle of women and children. The three men crossed the deck and began to herd their charges aft to the open hold, nodding and smiling encouragement, their hands laid almost shlyly on the smooth shoulders and backs, their voices low, pleading, nearly deferential.

And as the first woman began her descent, Reynolds had reached into the thick of the slowly moving cluster, closed his hand round a wrist and pulled a girl out, drawing her to his side and then behind him, his seal-sleek little body braced against her first startled lunge and subsequent flung-back weight, without a word, looking up at her with that derisive and conspiratorial smile.

Then he had seemed to forget her. Or at least to make no more count of her existence than if she had been a stick planted in the deck behind him against the moment when he would pick it up again. When Bullen came scrambling in untidy

78

agitation from the hold, Reynolds still stood at the edge of the hatchway, bland and comely, smiling faintly with that affable derisiveness, his hands clasped behind his back.

"Mister Reynolds," Bullen had begun, "my tally makes one woman less than—" and his gaze went past Reynolds to where the girl stood in rigid and bewildered terror, her eyes frantic as they looked into the hold, at Reynolds, around the deck, back to the hold, at Reynolds again—"Oh," said Bullen, "but are you? I mean?"

"My apologies, Mister Bullen. My heartfelt apologies. I would have advised you had I anticipated my intention. But I did not, my dear fellow. Upon my oath, I did not. It occurred to me on the moment. A *coup de coeur*, as it were. Insofar as we can distinguish one of the creatures from t'other, you will agree that I have chosen well . . . Look at her, Mister Bullen," Reynolds said, not turning to look at the girl behind him. "Is she not a splendid specimen of her kind? Rest assured. She will not disturb the harmony of our mess. I will keep her in my stateroom. A release—or should I say a recreation?—from the exhausting demands of our vocation."

"But . . .but . . ." Bullen had stuttered again "Mister Reynolds, sir . . . I mean . . ." His words floundered in the space between them as if stunned by the bright, mad derision of that blue gaze; then stiffly—"Very well, you know your own mind best, I suppose."

He had turned and disappeared into the hold again then, in a tangled, flourish of legs and arms that seemed certain to pitch him head first into the darkness, and Reynolds had waited, smiling gently, almost dreamily now, rocking a little, heel to toe, with the dip and rise of the deck, breathing deeply and steadily as if drawing from some exclusive source of his own supply of sweet air.

When Bullen and his party began to emerge from the hold he had nodded genially and said, "Well that's it then, Mister Bullen. Another day nearer our journey's end," and had waited until the hatch cover had been lifted on and fastened, the men sent forward, and Bullen had gone aft to the officers' quarters under the poop.

Then he had looked up, for the first time, at Hogarth on the

79

poop deck, his eyes still bright and dreaming, but darkened a little now by the ironic question they posed. Hogarth had descended from the poop and crossed the deck to where he stood. Not looking at Reynolds, nor at the girl, but at some point through the space between them far out over the swift, steep green of the sea, Hogarth had asked, "Is this absolutely necessary, Mister Reynolds?"

"I fear it is, sir. I am of an ardent nature; I freely confess it. It is a cross I do not always bear with the stoic fortitude, that discipline of self, on which a man may rise to the heights. But then I have never aspired to those heights. I freely confess *that*. Besides, you will concede, sir, she *is* a handsome wench. I trust you do not object to my choice."

"Object, Mister Reynolds? No. I understand that choosing as you have has always been one of the prerogatives of your rank in this trade. I had hoped, however, that my officers would feel as I do about such a sordid tradition. But, then, you owe me only your efficient and faithful service; your private conduct is your own affair. So long as it does not affect the discipline of my ship. You will keep the woman out of the way except when we air and feed the cargo. I will not have her roaming the deck, setting the men at each other's throats. You understand?"

"You may depend on me, sir, to do nothing that will fall short of the highest standards you expect of your officers." The clear, lilting voice was grave, its light burden of private and sardonic laughter sourceless and trembling in the air like the music of a stream over pebbles.

"See to it then, Mister Reynolds," Hogarth had said tiredly. "See to it."

2

I told that fool Bullen that my decision to take her was made for me. A moment's irresistible and unresisted madness. He assumed that I was teasing him and I will admit he has evidence enough to justify such an assumption. But when he came from the hold—ludicrous and vulgar as his disapproval was, obligatory as it became for me to augment it—I spoke no less than the truth. The desire churning in my bowels at that moment was so close to pain that I was weak from the effort of containing it. I owe Bullen a debt of gratitude for thrusting his ridiculous face before me when he did: it is a face that would transmute the carnality of Priapus himself into laughter.

All the same, I could feel her at my back, this ignorant black savage, even as I wasted irony on Bullen. Feel the profound and terrible force she carried that had reached out and seized me before ever I hauled her from among the women. It was more than the urgent lust that has nourished me (and which I have happily cultivated) since my seed first swam out on a dream. It was an ecstasy like—like vertigo. I had to clasp my hands behind me so that Hogarth on the poop and the men would not see how they trembled.

Bad. Very bad. Dangerous. One who intends to get as much as I do from this world must be above wanting anything too much. He must take when he is ready and the time appropriate; never fall to from mere greed. I do not like to think that there may be anything outside me that can move me to an action I do not calculate.

Strange ... strange ... For two months along that infernal coast, I had seen enough of them naked to rouse Origen's statue if nakedness was all that was needed. And yet they were no more to me there than shaven apes. Handsome enough some of them, to be sure, but not for my use. That Portuguese factor at Benguela who inquired with such a heartfelt solicitude as to whether I would not prefer a clean sambo boy after I had refused his offer of the slut who had served his execrable dinner. He was a decent little dago and I shall always remember with warm appreciation the tolerant scope of his hospitality, his genuine distress that perhaps all was not as it should be with my virile member when I declined the boy also. His food would have poisoned any creature other than a goat or a sailor but he meant well. He had a kind heart. In the fortnight we lay off Benguela, I swear he never had more than five of his niggers flogged and, of those, three were only warmed gently; for his amusement, as it were. Their skins were hardly broken; and they did not let enough blood between them to fill a thimble. I do believe the good, generous fellow even had one of them— that big, coffee-coloured girl who looked as though she might have been sired by an Arab—strung up and tickled in my presence in the hope that the spectacle would have a medicinal effect on what he considered the premature degeneration of my manhood. What a disappointment it must have been for him when I failed to arouse. And for her too, perhaps. Who knows but the bitch had agreed to conspire with him in a joint stock venture: an investment designed to wring a dividend of hapless lust out of cold English Reynolds?

But that never was my way. That was never Reynolds' way. Proffered goods are insipid and of little value in the long run. To take, to seize, to hold. And to dispose of what has been taken when one grows weary of it or sees a greater prize.

Sometimes the cloying hypocrisies of the world—the sentimental falsehoods I learned so early to swallow with such apparent trust and to regurgitate with such cunning whenever it served my purpose—sometimes they no longer amuse. They lie beneath my heart, indigestible as stones. And around them I can feel the accretion of something beyond anger, beyond simple rage.

It is an abhorrence so profound, a hate so consuming, that I am disembodied, made ethereal by my regard for the truth. Holy. *Yes, Holy!* In another age, I would have been sanctified for the unsleeping zeal with which I smelled out and hunted down the pretenders and heretics: those who tried to conceal their corruption beneath ritual observance and fraudulent utterances of piety. My path to Heaven would have been lit by the blaze of a thousand fires. I would have ascended on the incense of a thousand burning bodies, to the music of screams more truly repentant than prayer.

Perhaps that is why I chose the sea. We cannot distort it into lying shapes as we do the land. No parks, no palaces, no fine cities fashioned from the miserable stunted flesh of the many so that the few may write each other encomiums on their achievements. How many slow deaths to build and keep a gentleman's manor! How much blood and children's bones stirred into the feed for a gentleman's horse to quicken the brute's fastidious appetite?

But the sea will not be moulded into our excremental falsehoods. It will not record the shape of any keel. Christ could walk it to the end of time and leave no more mark of his passage than will this floating barracoon we choose to call a ship. When I come into my small fortune at the end of this, when I begin to make that fortune work for me, the world shall learn the purifying terror of the sea's indifference . . . *The world shall learn.*

3

She had come to understand what he was; although she could never hope to *know* him. He was *Elegwa*: evil without purpose, accidentally embodied; a spirit without a role in the complex exchanges of good and bad; a thing outside the decent order of worship and propitiation. You closed your eyes and threw oil-soaked bread before it and the dogs ate the offerings. No more than that. A random element. A fact, not a necessity. Beyond explanation, and therefore worth no more than a few expiatory gestures. But for his extraordinary body, he would not even have been interesting once you understood what he was; recognized that he was outside knowledge; inexplicable except to *Obba Oloroun*, to God. And perhaps even God was not concerned with explaining him.

So—as a virtuous woman aware of the traditions she had been taught, must observe and pass on—she had tried to put him in his proper place. That first evening he had covered her— no, not covered her like a man but plunged himself into her— his body plump yet surprisingly firm, like that of a large rat in a disturbing dream, strangely weightless though oppressive; his clenched face swinging above hers like the moon of her first flux (now immeasurably distant, now close enough to touch); and with what he thrust between her spread and passive legs somehow not connected to the squirming dream-creature she scarcely felt on her body, but simply hard and long and severed —yes, severed—planted in the moist darkness where its new roots might grow and find purchase. After that evening when she had had to respond with all her pieties if she was not to become a ghost forever without home or purpose, she had withdrawn herself. She was safe now, she was fairly sure; although it had been a near thing. For a little while on that evening, she had felt herself close to being consumed. She was a virgin and, at the moment of passage into womanhood in a transition so different from what she had been trained to expect and undergo, the unhallowed experience could have overwhelmed her; devout and proper observances could have been forgotten. She could have vanished forever into the kingdom of his ghosts that took the form of dogs gulping bits of oil-soaked bread ... And, without her spirit to serve as a crossing between the spirits of those who had formed her and the spirits of those who would be formed because of her, there would be only confused wandering and homelessness. They would not have, even, the place conceded to the dogs that ate the oil-soaked *eyori* around *Elegwa*.

Yes. It had been a near thing. Very near ... Such is the fragility of the flesh into which the self is born and must be carried, as a duty, for a little ... But she had remembered, and committed herself to *Obba Oloroun*; and to the *orisa*; and to the *obbi* she had shared with the boy who was to be her *onrokore* —her husband—how many *oddou* ago?—and whose mother had brought her gifts for many further *oddou*; until one day when everything had been destroyed by the man with guns and fire who came down the great creek from the north. Strange men, with cloth wrapped around their heads and nearly concealing their faces, who had taken her with them, leaving her without ceremony, like a slave, among others as strange; who, in turn, had passed her onto strangers, until she had come to live in this ship, shut in the dark with a lot of people, many of whom were not only strange but disgusting. Most of whom did not know God's name but who called strange sounds that might have been their words for the dogs eating the oil-soaked bread. Perhaps they did worship the ravenous dogs. Anything was possible among people who had no sense of order and ceremony.

It was possible, even, that she had died when the men who appeared on the great creek had begun to fire their guns and the houses began to dance in the flames. Or perhaps she had died on the way to the shore of the great lake where the air smelt thin and sharp. She could not remember very much of that journey except that many from her town had died. She had seen them left on the ground, impiously, without ceremony, so that they would become ghosts without consolation, unable to communicate with the living or with each other. Each doomed to circle the place of death, in silence, forever.

She had said as much to Tadene (who was her uncle's second wife) in the first few nights when they were lying in the darkness of that dreadful and improper place below. She had whispered it across the body of the woman who had been placed between them on the wooden sleeping place that was not big enough for a single child. The woman had been brought to the house on the shore of the great lake—along with others, men and women, who looked ugly like her and spoke her ugly tongue. She had not been brought by the sort of men who had driven Tadene and herself on the long journey she could scarcely remember. The men who brought the ugly women and her people were so yellow they were almost green; she had never seen men of that colour. They were dressed like the white men who came into the house by the great lake later. She had heard that men could be white and live. And when the white men came into the house where so many strange, ugly people were shut with her and Tadene, she did not think they were white but red. They were wearing masks of skin painted red. And then, two days later, they had returned with more ugly people speaking ugly voices she could not understand. The green men came back with them and the men in red masks walked up to her and Tadene and looked at her and she was satisfied that she had not been told the truth. Nobody could be white and live. One of them said something in angry tone to one of the green men and took the cloth from his shoulders and she had felt her stomach tighten with astonishment. For he was white. Shoulders, chest and stomach were white, and the red mask fitted closely to his neck.

There was so much to understand, so much to be forgotten—so much disorder—that she began to feel she might indeed have died in the burning town or on the journey or in the house on the shore of the great lake. For there would have been none left to bury with pious and proper ceremony and everybody knew that those buried without due observances by the living became ghosts with no memory and no place.

But Tadene had said she was alive. That they were all alive. And she had accepted this because nobody knew more about the ceremonies of passage between the living and the spirits than Tadene. She was a disagreeable woman, but so proper and devout that her uncle had always dutifully visited her house, four nights in each month, even though all her children had died a week after they were born. Once when the married women were attending to Tadene after her fifth child had died at the empty breast, she had heard them say that God had intended Tadene to be a man but had changed his feelings when it was too late so that although Tadene had all the appearances of a woman outside, she did not have the things in her belly and her breasts to form and nourish a child. She had been shocked, for she knew *Obba Oloroun* could not change his feelings. His feelings *were Obba Oloroun* and the world. If they were changed then impossible things would happen—like the spirits leaving their proper place and taking flesh again, leaving no room for the living. Or *Elegwa*, even, evil without purpose, might be greater than *Obba Oloroun* and the dogs would have the world in their care. She had hoped when she had heard the women speaking such an impiety in Tadene's house that Tadene was still too weak to understand what they said, for so devout a woman would have had to protest and she had nearly died in the delivery of the small, feeble creature who had hardly looked like a baby at all.

She was glad that Tadene had not died then, because it was Tadene who had kept her alive on that long, terrible journey when the men with cloth round their heads beat them and left people dead on the track without decent ceremony of burial.

As it had been Tadene who had forced her to eat the strange, horrible food when they went up into the sunlight each day. Even when she vomited it, Tadene had made her eat again from the stinking mess in the great copper pot which everybody shared. Perhaps that was when the white rat who belonged to *Elegwa* had first noticed her and wanted her. For he had been very angry when she had vomited the strange food and had come up to where she was crouched with all the strange, unblessed food in a pool on the wood as it had gone into her stomach.

The white rat had frowned and said something to her in a voice so soft yet terrible that she had even forgot her shame at having vomited before so many strange people; forgotten even the memory of the taste of the food that made her want to vomit again although there was nothing left in her stomach to vomit.

The white rat had said something to one of the white men who were perhaps from a different people because they did not eat with the white rat and did everything he told them, and this white man had gone back to the little house with the low roof behind the great pole on which was fastened the great pieces of cloth that swelled with the wind.

The white man had returned walking behind the tall black man who wore clothing like the white rat and who sometimes walked between the women and the chained men, looking at people as though he knew them but never saying anything; never frowning, never smiling; just looking at them as a man might study the surface of a river before casting a net.

The black man was carrying the instrument made of iron which they had seen him push into the mouth of one of the men who had refused the food. The instrument made of iron opened into two pieces and the man's jaws had opened with it and the black man had put a hollow tube of iron narrow at one end, wide at the other, into the mouth of the man who had refused food and ladled the strange, unblessed food from the pot the men shared and poured it down the man's throat while two of the white men had held the man's arms behind his back.

The man had vomited, the food welling out of his mouth and running down the sides of his face which the black man in white man's clothes had forced back. But the black man kept ladling more of the food down the tube even after they were all sure that the man must choke to death. Until the man ceased to vomit back the food, ceased to writhe in the hands gripping him, and they could see his throat moving as he swallowed.

Then for the only time since they had seen him, and the last the black man smiled and patted the stomach of the man he had stuffed and rubbed it like a woman trying to gentle wind out of her child. He had taken the man's tin bowl and filled it with water at the big drum fastened to the little house and brought it back and watched while the man filled his mouth and spat out the filth through the net that the white men had tied too high for them to jump over. Then the black man had filled the bowl from the men's copper pot and the man he had forced to swallow had eaten all of it while the black man watched. The white man who was always standing on the platform when they came into the sun, looking down on them, had said something in the language she was beginning to learn from the white rat and the black man had nodded without looking up, keeping his eyes on the eating man.

So when the black man had approached her on the day that she had vomited she had begun to cry. She knew that she could no longer eat the disgusting and unholy food. She must starve, but she could eat no longer. Yet she knew also that the black man would put the iron instrument in her mouth and open it and then pour the food through the funnel until she drowned.

And then Tadene had done what nobody had ever seen Tadene do. She had knelt before the white rat and held his legs behind his knees and begged him to be patient in the language of the people and called him in his own language what these people called themselves. *Massa*, Tadene had said, *Massa*, *Massa*, *Massa*, and turned to her and fed her, a little at a time, from what was left in her bowl, scooping up pinches of the disgusting stuff and putting it gently into her mouth, speaking the words a mother speaks when her baby is being weaned. The white rat had laughed and slapped his thigh and said something to the black man who did not even nod, as he had that time when the white man on the platform had spoken to him, simply looking steadily not at her but at Tadene. Then, still without looking at or answering the white rat, he had turned and gone back to his little house.

For three days after that Tadene had fed her in the way a mother feeds a weaning baby until she was able to force herself to eat enough of the unblessed food to please the white rat and the black man and all the other *Massas*.

Tadene had told her that they were both slaves. But that was impossible. Even Tadene was mistaken there. She did not know why the *Massas* were taking them on this horrible journey across this huge lake of salt. They must have some dreadful purpose. But she and Tadene could not be slaves. She had seen the slaves in her father's houses. Slaves were strangers who you sometimes bought to help if there was too much land for the people to till.

She and Tadene were not strangers. They were the *people*.

4

I think it must be her magnificent, her invulnerable, insipidity. She is a pretty little piece to be sure, and if you dressed her in the fashion she'd have half the rosy creamy misses in the Park wishing that God had made them a pair of tits like hers and a back so fine to sprout above a crinoline. They'd sneer at her black hide, of course, but there ain't one of them wouldn't accept a drop or two of her blood if it didn't show and gave 'em what she has to rouse a bulge in the front of a young gentleman's trousers. She'll be off the auction block and into some Brazilian dom's bed before you can say knife. And if she has the good sense to fetch him a son or two, she'll end up free and comfortable. The Brazilians treat their niggers well. So they ought. Most of 'em, including the Emperor, are half nigger themselves. She ain't breeding for me yet. Pity. It would be capital fun if she presented one of those yellow Brazilian swells with a blue-eyed mulatto boy seven or eight months from now. The little dago would be so proud of himself. I never met one yet who didn't drone on interminably about his Visigothic forebears.

But it ain't her figure and her soft little hole why I keep her. If it were only that I'd have sent her back to the hold long ago. These cabins ain't made for accommodating two powder monkeys, let alone an officer of my standing and his lady. Good thing I can put the bitch to squat in a corner when I ain't coupling her. And to tell the truth I like to see her tucked away there all naked and wide-eyed and waiting when I come off watch. If I didn't know she must, I'd swear she never sleeps. She's always awake and waiting no matter what the hour. Stark terrified yet, although I ain't laid a hand on her in any fashion save lust, and I ain't one of those who get their pleasure from using women cruel when I feel to mount.

No, it ain't her figure why I keep her here closer than a Turk keeps his harem. It is her beautiful insipidity. Almost inspired.

89

Close to genius. The properest, most genteel, nicest little miss.
She makes my silly bitch of a sister look like a whore and God
knows I never thought I'd live to find any one could beat
Georgiana and her mincing prissy ways and her ostentatious
self-sacrifice and her three times to church of a Sunday and her
eyes rolled to Heaven so she don't have to look at what happens
in the farmyard at her feet. I'd like to have her aboard for a
day, just to see some of the bucks when we bring 'em up.
Especially the young fellows who get erections after they've
aired a bit and we've hosed 'em down and fed 'em. There's one
of them, one of the Balubas we got in Angola. *Christ*, he can
show you a clear foot and a half when Eros seizes him and he
couldn't be a day over fifteen. I should like to have Georgiana
have that bobbing up and down like a clipper bowsprit before
her. Only thing is she'd probably hope for more, the hypo-
critical bitch. The *lucky* bitch, since the richest part of her
satisfaction would come after, when she was whispering the
sad tale of her embarrassment to the drop-jawed cows at tea in
the vicarage drawing-room and every one of them wetter between their legs with excitement than the Empress Theodora
astride the knob of her bedpost. She always had the best of it,
Georgiana. The bitch. The bitch. First born and no title so Papa
can leave everything to her as he intended from the moment he
laid his damned eyes on me. Georgiana will get everything, and
a duke's second son if she don't grow too long in the tooth. I
hope he gives her the pox before she has broken his back with
her dutiful writhings. I saw her in the folly on the island in the
middle of the lake, with her skirts bunched up around her waist
like surf on a lee shore, as she poked and poked away into her
cunt with her forefinger and held that book in the other hand,
her mouth open, her eyes like a blind woman's and the rash of
fury on her pale face like German measles. I found the book
later. The bitch, the cunning bitch, had hidden it underneath
that pile of sanitary cloths in the little cedar chest where nobody but she and her maid would go since in our house we
don't admit that such things are part of a lady's wardrobe. And
it was in French and I was six years old and Georgiana spoke
perfect French because my father had brought over Mam'selle
Carnot to governess Georgiana before she was two. She was

supposed to do for me too when I came along but she never had much time, and if I speak French as well as I do English it's little thanks to her. She and Georgiana would never stop to tell me what they were saying when I was three and they were speaking rapidly. They would talk and laugh or talk and sigh (because Mam'selle Carnot was another of those pious, randy bitches who would like to see a great Baluba cock at full erection with its single eye searching for what she has between her legs) and never stop to tell me what they were saying.

I never saw the book again. The next day it was gone. And most of it didn't mean much to a boy of six. Georgiana spoke and read French better than most French girls in their best convents. I heard Mam'selle Carnot tell my father that. When I was five. And he, the old fool, grinning and twisting and patting Georgiana on the top of her mousy hair and jabbering compliments at old hairy-cunt Carnot, because I saw her once in the bathing house on the lake's shore that we used in the summer. I did not know she was in there and walked in and she was hairy. All I could see was a great coarse black mat spread half across her stomach and Georgiana in her shift. Georgiana screamed and came outside and boxed my ears until I fell on my knees and vomited onto the grass. She told me that I was a wicked boy and God would punish me, and that the only restitution I could make which God would accept for my having caught Mam'selle Carnot without her stays or pantalettes would be for me to lick my vomit from the grass. I could scarcely hear her, my ears were singing so. And when I would not do this dreadful thing, Georgiana bent forward, in her shift, with her tits nearly falling out and pressed on the back of my neck until she could rub my face in my vomit. Then she went back into the bathing house with the sunlight making a confusing transparency of her fine cotton shift where it hung below her buttocks at the fork of her legs.

I washed my face in the lake, plunging my entire head in and wishing that I was not so afraid of the pain that would come if I kept my head there and breathed deeply until I could breathe no more.

Then I walked back across the long quarter-mile of fine grass to the great house which Charles the Second gave my father's ancestor as his reward for changing sides at the last minute and went to my room and cried.

I cried for two days. Not at meals or before the servants, of course. But in between. Only Deidre—the coarse, freckled Irish slut my father had picked up on his last visit to County Clare when he went to look about my dead mother's estate—took notice that I was crying.

Damp pillow, she said on the second day when she was changing my bed linen—it must have been on a Saturday for we changed bed linen and still do for all I know, on Tuesdays and Saturdays in our house. *Damp pillow,* Deidre said, as she felt the case. *Dry eyes now. You're entertaining the Divvel, Masther George. The Divvel shares your bed.*

And who knows that she was not right. But I had no need of her ignorant slut's commentary on top of Georgiana's violent sermon.

Still, I must not be ungrateful to those dedicated tutors of my childhood: Georgiana, my father, Mam'selle Carnot, animals like Deidre. They taught me well. To believe in myself, to believe in my future, to take my pleasure whenever and however the opportunity offers itself. Faith, hope and lust, as it were. And the greatest of these is lust.

5

"Bitch," said Reynolds. "You are a *bitch.* Come on my little black beauty, my heathen bunkmate, I'll have you speaking English prettier than the Queen before we get to Brazil. *Bitch.* You are a *bitch.* Say it slowly after me, *I—am—a—bitch.* Come now, you ain't stupid, that's for certain, for all that you're so pi."

Half an hour before, he had leaned over the edge of his bunk and shaken the girl by her shoulder as she lay curled up and asleep on the mat. He had felt the stiffening tremor under his hand as she came awake instantly. Quickly, yet moving as though she still slept, she had scrambled into his bunk and begun to do the things he had taught her. All of the things she could do without feeling that it was she who performed them but some ghost who had borrowed her body. All of the things except one.

This one thing was so unnatural, so unbelievable, that she had not yet been able to tell Tadene of it. When she was doing this thing, she could not pretend she was another. She had to suppose that it was the custom of the *Massa* women, since not even this white rat, this *Elegwa*, could have conceived of such a purpose for a woman's mouth or have imagined that a woman should uselessly swallow his seed and eat his children. Such a practice had to be the custom of the women among his people. More than anything else that might happen to her among the white rat's people, the thought of being among women who initiated such intercourse filled her with a special terror. Cruelty and death, even slavery, she could understand; but not this.

Squatting cross-legged and naked at the foot of the bunk, Reynolds grinned at her. His yellow curls were dark and flattened with the sweat of making love in the heat of the little cabin. In the feeble radiance, more shadow than light, of the low-turned hanging lamp, his eyes were almost black. The glow of the moonlight coming through the opened porthole fell on the damp, pale skin of his shoulders and chest, giving it a bluish tinge.

"Come now," he repeated. "Here's old Reynolds taking time out to improve your education and all you do is crouch there looking as if I were going to eat you. Where's your manners, my girl. I'm sure your mamma taught you better than that . . . *I— am—a—bitch* . . . Try it slow if it don't come easy to your heathen tongue. One word at a time."

He nodded encouragingly to her she crouched at the other end of the bunk, pressed hard against the bulkhead, her gaze wide, unwinking and fascinated.

"I—" Reynolds said and nodded again and pointed.

I—

"Excellent . . . Oh, bravely done," Reynolds told her . . . "*Am—*"

Am—

"Better and better. A man could not wish for an apter pupil . . . *A—*"

A—

"*Bitch*"

Bitch

"Splendid. Now altogether after me . . . *I—am—a—bitch.*"

I am—she hesitated, frowning with concentration—*a bitch.*

"Bravo!" The small firm body opposite her rocked with pleasure as Reynolds clapped his hands. "Once more! Repetition is the half of learning . . . *I am—*"

I am a bitch, she said before he could finish.

"You shall have a reward for this," Reynolds said. "Upon my word you shall. Now rememeber, *you*," he pointed at her, "*bitch.*"

I am a bitch. I am a bitch.

Her gaze was less wide now. Less blankly fascinated. But she became very still as Reynolds leaned forward and put his hand between her legs. The small animation of the previous second vanished from her face.

"No," Reynolds told her, "not that. Twice in half an hour, in this heat, is enough for Reynolds. No, I am merely continuing our lesson . . . This, *cunt.*"

He ran his finger lightly in her furrow. "Now don't disappoint me. You have made such splendid progress into our noble tongue . . . *Cunt.* Say it. *Cunt.*"

She looked down at his head and said *Cunt* in a sullen whisper.

"And these," said Reynolds tapping her under her breasts so they bobbed. "*Tits. Tits.*"

Tits

"By God, you'll be reading Shakespeare next," Reynolds leaned back and pushed the middle finger of his right hand up and down up and down into the hole made by the thumb and forefinger of his lightly clenched left hand. "This," he told her, "what we do . . . *Fuck . . . Fuckity fuck.*"

There was suspicion in her face now, almost a timid anger; her lips tightened and she turned her head away.

"What is this," Reynolds said, "does my prize pupil sulk? Does miss tire of her lesson so easily? Oh this will never do. This will not do at all." Again he made the gesture, leaning forward and thrusting his hands before her averted face. "*Fuck,*" he repeated. "*Fuckity fuck.*"

In the same sullen monotone she said *Fuckity fuck*

Reynolds, his face bunched and bright with pleasure, patted her on her shoulder.

"Splendid," he said. "Absolutely splendid. And yet there are the bigots among my race who maintain that your kind is ineducable. I'd like to see some of them master the essentials of your language as quickly as you have ours ... By God, it's a pity we're selling you in Brazil. It would be pretty to think of you adventuring your English among those dainty simpering misses in Virginia or the Carolinas."

He swung his feet abruptly over the edge of the bunk and stood, stretching his plump, shapley little body taut with pads and ropes of concealed muscle. From the easy chair in the further corner of the little cabin, he took his clothes: drawers, nankeen trousers, shirt and blue jacket. He dressed quickly.

"Eight bells soon, my dear," he said cheerfully to her uncomprehending face. "I relieve that fool Bullen at eight bells but I always like to get to him early to see if the opportunity for a little diversion presents itself. I sometimes feel that the idiot understands less of what I say than you do."

He stopped smiling suddenly and pointed to the mat on the deck beside the bunk. He watched her as she slid over the side of the bunk and lay down on the mat. He continued to watch her with a still face and eyes remote and speculative until she turned her own eyes away.

Then he nodded, smiled absently, turned and left the little cabin.

For several minutes after he had left, she could hear the rapid thudding of her heart. Yet she was content in one small thing. *Elegwa* had begun to teach her the language of his people. This was the first time since he had taken her from among the women that he had talked to her. Up to now he had talked happily to himself, or perhaps to ghosts only he could reach. Now she knew what his people called woman ... *Bitch*. And when a woman went to a man's house—as she would have gone to her betrothed if the people with cloth around their heads and the guns had not come down the creek—it was called *fuckity fuck*. That was the white people's word for marriage.

It was not much to have learned but she knew how quickly

you could acquire a strange language once you began to grasp a few important words.

Perhaps the next time he lay with her, he could tell her his people's word for *man*.

And perhaps when she came to live among the women of his people, she would be able to persuade them that their custom of eating children was wrong.

Rather, it would be better if Tadene told them. The younger ones would listen to Tadene although she was childless and often so angry for no reason that everyone was afraid of her.

But Tadene was wise, and she would know how to speak gently and convincingly to young women who practised dreadful and unholy acts in their ignorance.

Part Four

THE FORECASTLE

CHAPTER TEN

1

"The truth av it, Ned," said Dolan, "is that you're afraid av that black gintleman. An' the knowledge av it ain't any easier to digest than the grub he serves. Not that he don't do better than most in his place could, mark you. Considerin' what he has to start with, I'd say he's—"

Dunn's hand—narrow as a woman's for all its big bones— came down on Dolan's shoulder, curved and rigid as a clamp of pale metal.

"You," Dunn said, his voice thin and hard, as though forcing itself up through a windpipe as rigid as the hand which crushed Dolan's shoulder. "You, Dolan! You've got no call to be saying I fear any man walks a deck, or land for that matter. There's officers, Boyo, an' a couple of 'em cap'ns maybe, at this minute, still bears the marks of how much Ned Dunn fears 'em. Caught 'em, didn't I, as they was coming back to the ships. In streets where they couldn't call on other men to tie me to the gratings an' flog the strength out of me. Just them an' Ned Dunn face to face. Man to man. An' I never fouled 'em in fight any worse than they could have fouled me, had they the mind. I ain't afeard of no man, Boyo. No officer nor his bos'un on the sea. No high an' mighty gentleman ashore. I chooses my time, that's all. When they can't call on no bastards like you to aid 'em in holding down a man . . . An' in particular, Boyo, I ain't afeard of no nigger who walks the deck as if it weren't good enough for him. As if he were the rightful cap'n of a clipper fallen among scum an' just waitin' for his letter of appointment that's on the way to be delivered."

Old Calder's hand closed around Dunn's wrist, in a grip light but vibrant with warning. Nobody aboard knew Calder's full strength; as no one could guess his age.

"Leave him be, Ned," he said, in that even almost ruminative tone through which he seemed to sift each experience impartially. "You're a strong man, an' I would not like to see you do Boyo here a mischief in your anger because he speaks the truth. You'll do well to have a bit of fear for Alex, Ned, an' I've seen a deal of killin' gentlemen in my time. When I was a boy younger'n Joshua there was officers you couldn't have marked on any street—no matter how foul or fair you fought. I seen what they'd do to each other, Ned, in their duels, an' come back laughin' an' toastin' each other wi' no more thought than if it was a dog they'd shot or run through 'stead of a Christian an' a fellow officer like themselves. An' for nothin', Ned. For a bit of a word or a fallin' out as you an' I wouldn't hardly raise a fist for. You wouldn't have been puttin' any marks on one of them, Ned, I tell 'ee straight. Why Cap'n Colinton or any o' that breed would a' put a sword through your navel an' carried 'ee back to the snug o' their inn an' roasted 'ee in the embers wi' no more worry that if you was a chestnut. So leave Boyo be, 'cause you can be cruel strong when you is roused an' he's a slight man. Handy as any I've ever sailed with, but not filled out like you an' me . . . An' he had the right o' it concernin' you an' Alex. Wi' no shame to you, either. There ben't a man aboard wi' any sense hasn't taken the measure of *his* quality. Not even Reynolds—an' Reynolds would fight a shark for its meat if the fancy took 'im. Even them poor ignorant blackies we got below, you see how they hol' breath an' watch 'im until he passes when he's inspectin' 'em to see they're gettin' their vict'ls down."

Calder's hand had slowly tightened around Dunn's wrist to the rhythm of the measured, placid voice, so that it was almost with astonishment that the younger man noticed his suddenly numbed and darkly congested fingers. He gave a brief, embarrassed laugh as he looked down into the heavy old face from which the years seemed to have eroded everything but an uncompromising and benign purpose. He lifted his hand from Dolan's shoulder and began to rub the wrist which Calder had instantly released.

98

"So it's niggers as gentlemen an' officers now, is it?" he said and laughed again, the same uncertain embarrassed snort. "You and Boyo will be suggestin' to him as how he an' Hogarth ought to change places next. Hogarth in the galley cookin' the swill, an' Alex on the poop givin' the orders an' couplin' Hogarth's lady in between times . . ."

"I never said no such thing, Ned, an' you know it," Calder protested in gentle distress, almost apology. "Did I now, Boyo? Did you ever 'ear me say as how niggers should be gentlemen an' officers an' that Alex were such?"

Boyo, who had been tenderly kneading the trapezius muscle near the neck which had taken the most of Dunn's furious grip, grinned and shook his head in delighted appreciation and then he laughed as Calder's face and Dunn's creased in uncomprehending frowns.

"Christ an' all his saints," Dolan said. "You two! If I was to sail the length an' breadth av this world until the conversion av the Jews, I'll never find a pair like you again. You've spoiled me for the future . . . No, John, you never said anythin' about niggers as officers an' gentlemen. As for you, Ned . . . if you don't understand what John an' me was in agreement on, then I don't have the ejjication to enlighten you . . ." He grimaced as he rubbed his palm on his neck and shoulder. "Jaysus, Ned! If they're ever in need av a strangler instead av a hangman in Dublin Castle your fortune's made. You'll have me personal recommendation writ in me finest copperplate."

"Ah!" Dunn said sullenly, as if afraid of what might next be said, "I'm sorry if I hurt you, Boyo. It was just your sayin' what you did 'bout me an' that nigger cook. You caught me with sails set wrong like. I didn't mean you no harm."

Dolan stopped rubbing his shoulder, his hand still on it as he looked into Dunn's angrily pleading face.

"No," Dolan said drily, "you didn't mean no harm, Ned. There's no harm meant in you . . . It's only what you have is so like it only the Holy Father himself could explain the difference."

It was forenoon on the seventeenth day of the calm.

For thirty-six hours—from seven bells of the middle watch two days previous—Hogarth had not left the poop beside the

99

helmsman, except to take his meals, to pace the deck when stillness became intolerable, or to go to the little canvas booth
erected against the taffrail that served as the privy for him, his
wife, the officers, and Alex. All others of the crew used a similar
little booth in the bows, save that they might piss over the
bulwarks during the night watches, when they were sure the
captain's lady was asleep and not likely to come from her cabin
and see them. The slaves urinated and defecated where they lay
below; although sometimes, after feeding, one of the chained
men would haplessly empty his bowels where he sat: before he
had time to rise, obliging his partner to rise with him, as he
stuck his arse over the rail to shit through a space in the netting.
The sailors would hose him down afterwards, washing his waste
off the deck and into the scuppers, with no more sense of strange
duty than if they were grooms cleaning a stable. The women
being unchained were seldom caught short like the men: they
would squat to piss into the scuppers, or push their buttocks
into the yielding net. After the third day out from Africa, the
other women had taken to forming a screen around any of them
who had to void. They would stand, shoulder to shoulder, in a
semi-circle around her facing outwards, until she emerged.

By this, the seventeenth day of the calm, the slaves were
evacuating their bowels and their bladders less frequently and
with fewer occasions of urgency. The gradual lessening of their
water ration which Hogarth had ordered from the twelfth day
was beginning to have its effect. Only the pregnant women and
the children were given their full measure of two quarts per
day. More if they wanted it; but it had to be drunk under super-
vision so that they would not try to pass any of it to the others.
The air was so unnaturally dry that only the most rigorous
exertion could make the skin shine with moisture; otherwise
sweat dried as it started. The sailors now had taken to licking
at little pinches of salt cupped in their left hands while drinking
their rations. Faint, nearly imperceptible creaks and groanings
sounded throughout the whole ship in the first hour after dark
as heat escaped into the retreating sky and wood began to
shrink, as if the ocean itself were tightening around the hull.

On the sixteenth night, Reynolds had ordered the jolly boat
lowered, and he and the nigger cook Alex had sat in the stern-

sheets (Reynolds leaning forward like a coxswain, Alex seeming to recline in an armchair) with Dunn, Calder and two of the Portuguese at the sweeps, pulling clear of the ever-widening, dully-shimmering band of waste, under a moon as huge and bright as a guinea taken from a giant's pocket. They had pulled across a sea like black, tearing satin for nearly a mile until Reynolds said, *Hold, lads*—in the way that he always gave an order, as though he were telling you a fact already gone like the time. And even out a mile on the clean deep from the black, ribbed silhouette of the barque, they could taste in the far back of their throats, the stench of what crawled to them across the water.

Christ! Reynolds had said softly, almost awed. *Christ, Alex, they'll smell us clear to the Admiralty. We'll have every scut of a midshipman boarding us to claim seizure if we don't get a wind to blow us out of our stink.*

All right, Dunn, you take us back now, Alex had said and Dunn, who was manning the bow sweep, had dug the blade into the moon-smeared water to turn the head of the boat round before he had realized that he was obeying, and by then it was too late because Calder and the Portuguese were already pulling to the rhythm of his stroke.

When they had hoisted the jolly boat, Alex had said to Reynolds: *We'd best inspect stores now. No sense cookin' ourselves down in that hold after sun-up. Dunn, you an' Calder get the lanterns.* Not even looking at Dunn, he turned and went forward with that long, light, toe-and-heel step that looked like a contemplative amble until you measured the distance he had covered while you were looking at him. Even bouncing Reynolds had to put out to match pace with him.

They had descended the narrow, iron companion ladder into the forward hold, the darkness seeming to curl back softly from the pale twin radiance of the lanterns. The air was locked in contending scents: sharp cheese, cloying brown sugar and the harsh tang of highly salted beef. Covering all the smells, like a warm, damp blanket, was the heavy, almost suffocating weight of cornmeal and brown Patna rice. The residual, trapped heat of the day had the substance of raw silk curtains as they moved into the belly of the ship.

101

You know your judgin', Alex had said to Reynolds, *but I reckon you'll need to have a couple of ton of that meal, an' another ton of rice shifted centre of the hold, first thing. Come we get a piece of a wind south-east tomorrow an' this tub'll lay over on her port side like a sow on her farrow if you don't shift that weight. It's been three pounds of vict'ls I been feedin' each nigger for a fortnight now an' that plays hell with the distribution of your ballast . . .*

I'll see to it, Reynolds had said, *in the morning . . . Calder,* he had added as he moved further into the recesses of the hold to where the lashed-down ranks of great water casks were stowed. Alex had followed Calder with his held-aloft lantern and Reynolds, and they had returned to Dunn and the two Portuguese through a glow parting the darkness.

. . . a day's ration, Alex, Reynolds had been saying, as his voice and face emerged from the gloom into visibility, *a full day's ration spilling—like blood from a severed artery. A whale could sound in the water we've leaked in forty-eight hours. Those damned staves are warping like rope.*

His light, urgent voice had ricocheted around the bulkheads and the covers of the hold: urgent yet detached—like the tenor in an opera commenting in recitative on the tragic turn in the story. *Iron tanks,* he had said then. *Iron containers, Alex, every vessel on Her Majesty's service uses 'em now. Why didn't you purchase iron casks, Alex? And every merchant man beyond a coasting trade. Sound iron against heat and warp? We could come to the end of our venture because of your damned wooden casks.*

And Alex, his baked black mask of a face shimmering into definition above and just behind Reynolds' shoulder, had answered: *You go buyin' enough iron casks to water the cargo we're carryin' an' you might as soon send a letter to the Admiral of the West Indies Station, Mister Reynolds. They'd have reckoned we was carryin' slaves sure'n if we had showed 'em a bill of lading. You get that old man, Jerome, doin' some cooperage tomorrow, an' squeezin' them barrels a little tighter, an' we'll be all right . . . We've got enough left to keep us ridin' straight in the saddle for a spell yet.*

He had come from behind Reynolds then, and taken the

lantern from Dunn's hand—as if Dunn had offered it him in bowed mute servility—and they had heard him ascending the iron companion ladder to the wooden companionhead set almost flush with the deck, and his curious, long and dismissive stride taking him away from them.

So that now, just past six bells in the forenoon watch, they were coopering the last of the great casks that had warped enough to justify winching them with slow care from the hold, risking a sudden widened gap in the staves through which too much bright water would come gushing. Each full cask after it cleared the hold had been eased above a sound and empty one and tilted until it too had been emptied. Then it had been scrubbed inside with stiff brushes and large bunches of mingled witch-hazel, garlic and mint. Then the old Portuguese, Jerome, had supervised them as they had put the great tourniquet of hemp around the cask and tightened it until the staves creaked and bent and he could with an astonishing, almost dainty calculation prise the iron hoop free with chisel and hammer and carry it across to the large brazier and pincer it into the white-red surface of burning charcoal.

Here on the deck, forward of the forward hold, enclosed by the awning and by the canvas breaks stretched between deck and the awning edge in case a cat's paw, stroking unexpectedly across the flat water, should lift a spark onto the baked, dry paint or varnish or timber of the ship, they had laboured since change of watch in a still heat that had entered them like a drug. They were dazed, almost elated by it as they waited until Jerome finished his precise hammering at the anvil before placing the altered hoop into the charcoal and bringing it back, fading red in the pincers, to drop it around the cask and ladle sea-water over it, producing another heady incense of scorched wood and steam. Always, it seemed improbable that the loose belt of metal surrounded by a penumbra of viscous heat waves could shrink enough to close the edges of the staves on each other. But always, as the first extrusions of the fresh caulking of pitch and hemp fibres which they had worked between warps oozed out, the old Portuguese would nod and say, *Loose rope, now,* and when five minutes later the iron was cooler than the

103

wood of the deck, a man could hardly have put the point of a knife into the space between the two staves.

Then it was winching up the cask with the water for the healed cask again, and winching down into the hold, and stowing, and lashing so that, unless the barque turned turtle and sailed keel-up, not a drop of water would seep or a stave start loose from its neighbour.

They were brilliant with the instantly evaporating sweat being sucked out of them.

Old Jerome above his brazier, with his metronome hammer going against the cherry-glowing hoops of iron on his anvil, seemed to be diminishing by the minute like a flawed, streaming, candle.

From below them in the hold—as half the watch waited to stow and lash each freshly coopered cask—they could hear the light yet troubling music of Reynolds' profane exhortations.

Alex would appear at intervals, as each repaired cask was being refilled, with a small chamois bag from which he would scoop a handful of finely shredded fibre with a curious, bitter, clinging scent and sprinkle it onto the surface of the water in the half-filled cask.

It's bhang, Ned, Calder told Dunn. *I knows of it. They swear by it in India. You can smoke it or eat it in little cakes or boil it and drink it or just let it soak, like what Alex is doin'. Some of our lads would mix it wi' a pipe when I was in Trincomalee, an' say as how it kept 'em contented an' healthy like. They kept healthy as any hands I ever seen, I'll grant that, an' they certain sure were good-natured messmates, but I never tried on't, myself. Maybe it's right for niggers an' that's why Alex mixes it with the water . . . I heard enough about this trade when I were a boy, Ned, from those who had known it afore the Act, an' it was some bad times they could remember, wi' the poor blackies takin' fright an' raisin' mutiny or dyin' as if they was spiteful . . . But our lot keep so peaceful, an' we ain't had no sickness worth a mention, so maybe it's what Alex put into their water. They's deep, I tell you, real deep is niggers. They knews things. I seen 'em know things what I wished I could have knowed.*

They were waiting, with the three Portuguese who made up their half of the watch, for Jerome to finish his work with the claw, chisel and hammer on the last hoop. Sweat from the old man's skull ran through his wet, dangling hair, from his chin and dropped sizzling on the iron. For over three hours he had been the only man of the crew who had not been able to pause for more than it took to drink a ladle of water, yet there was a liveliness, a purposeful, happy animation in his movements and a still concentration in his face, which the others did not have. After seventeen days, he was the only soul on board, except for the cook and the boy Joshua, whose skills were being fully employed. All the others felt unused, uneasy—a little wearied and guilty, even—as all the constant, busy habits by which they were accustomed to survive became increasingly irrelevant to the small, soundless, indifferent world on which they were trapped within the confines of their own excrement.

"You all are figurin' on turnin' salt water into wine, I reckon. Or else into what Moses struck from the rock," Alex said from two feet behind and a foot above where Dunn lounged against the cask. "'Cause I tell you, Dunn, you put water back into this barrel an' stow it, an' in three days you won't have no need for a doctor. Any priest can get to you in time is about all you'll have use for . . . Jesus Christ, Calder, you know better'n this. You call this cask cleaned out? Why you didn't just shit in it while you an' Dunn an' Boyo was engaged in all that leisured conversation I was observin' a minute gone?" He leaned over Dunn and rubbed his palm briskly up and down the inside of the cask. "Look at that now," he said, straightening and showing them the faint brown stain on the salmon-pink flesh. "I've seen privies cleaner than that in hospital durin' the cholera."

He leaned over the crouching Dunn again and breathed deeply from the empty cask.

"They smelled a right smart better, too, than what you was aimin' to put our water back into. You think I'm goin' to waste my good herb in a cess-pit? Calder, you an' Boyo better get the dagoes scrubbin' an' rinsin' before Jerome finishes or else you might as well empty the water over the side."

He straightened again and looked down on Dunn who had straightened with him.

"You ain't no officer yet," Dunn said. "An' we ain't any cook's
105

mates, neither, to taste your sauce for you. You speak to us civil like, you hear?"

He spoke in the carefully apaced monotone of a man who has been running hard and who has breath enough for only word between inhalations. The face he turned up to Alex had assumed an awful simplicity, like the faces of the insane, moved only by their single, interior purpose.

From his height Alex looked down on Dunn with a detached, almost distant amusement.

"My, my," he said, "you do get your dander up easy, don't you? Now if you was thinkin' of saying what's on your mind to say, I'd advise you against it. But if you *must*, I'd be right happy to oblige you."

"Oh come on, Ned," Dolan said, his voice rising and falling anxiously. "Watch'll be over an' we'll not have finished an' Reynolds ud like nothin' better than the pleasure av broilin' us here like chickens for anoder coupla hours."

He pushed his little body between the two big men and they stepped back out of their circle of accumulating violence. Alex laughed softly and nodded with indulgent admiration at Dolan as he began trying to heave the great cask onto its side.

"Give us a hand—for God's sake—will ya, Ned," Dolan grunted as he pulled and swung, histrionically, at the lip of the great cask. "An' you, Calder. Will ya stop pickin' Cap'n Hogarth's pocket an' do some av the work for which he's payin' you like a lord ... Or maybe you're just standin' there takin' a private wager wid yourself as to when I'll rupture beyond redemption ... Christ, the company a fella has to keep at sea ... The disgrace av it."

In carved, watchful stillness Alex watched as Calder and the Portuguese hurried up and the cask was pulled onto its side. In still-dreaming hate Dunn regarded Alex for a moment before he turned to join the others scouring the cask. At his anvil, old Jerome finally looked down and cursed as his hammer struck unyielding metal that had cooled while he had waited for what he knew must come eventually between Dunn and Alex.

"Alex," said Reynolds, and Alex turned to see Reynolds' pert, boiled moon of a face framed between the low cowling of the companionhead and the deck on which he was resting his elbows. "Alex! A word in your ear, my dear fellow."

Alex crossed the deck to where that bright, pink face was set into the dark of the hold behind.

"How long you been there, Reynolds?" Alex asked; a smile no thicker than a thread was laid briefly across his face.

"Long enough," Reynolds said, "to see that interfering little Irishman save Dunn's life. You intended to kill him, I take it, had he gone for you?"

"I was sorely tempted," Alex said, "an' I'm not denyin' I might have yielded to temptation but I was only fixin' to ruin him a little. Just enough to take the wildness out of him. But if I do any more'n that, I'll lose the other two, Calder an' Dolan. They'd fret an' go all sulky on us, an' we need 'em workin' happy a sight more than the way we need the satisfaction of puttin' Dunn over the side dead. He's a natural-born heap of trouble, an' he will be all his life, but once we fetch to Brazil an' pay off I just might find the occasion to make a reckoning with him."

"If we ever do pay off in Brazil," Reynolds said mournfully. "If we don't get a capful of breeze tomorrow, Alex, we'll limp up that coast with half the cargo jettisoned and half the rest not worth unloading for the lack of water to keep them on their feet."

"Now you don't go fallin' all flat on me, Reynolds," Alex said. "You've been down that hold a might too long. You come by the midshiphouse in the second dog watch an' smoke a little herb with some of my brandy an' eat a few raisins to put a little sugar back into your spirits, and you'll be all right. I've got a game soup too in a tin, and recommended by Mr Soyer himself to the nobility an' gentry, that will make a heap of difference."

"Game soup, by God." Reynolds' restless eyes stilled, widened with a child's unpretending greed and anticipation. "You do yourself well, Alex. I'll wager you're provisioned fancier against the monotonies of a voyage than any admiral."

Alex chuckled: a small, soft exhalation that was laughter only because it could not be anything else. From a distance greater than his height he looked down with a speculative, absent appreciation on Reynolds' upturned face.

"Well, now," he said, "maybe I wouldn't be seein' an' raisin' no admiral with what I've got in my hand; but there's a few things laid by that would admire for a gentleman's palate to taste 'em. Those Portuguese chandlers in Setabul an' São Tomé were right grateful for the sort of trade I steered their way when we was provisionin' against the bellies I'd got to keep separated from the backbone between Africa an' Brazil. I always did hold by a man eatin' as high as he can, whenever he can. It carries you when you're eatin' rough or nothin'."

They both looked then as Jerome supervised the winching up of the scund cask in which water was kept during cooperage; and as Dunn, Calder, Dolan and the three Portuguese of the half-watch tilted it against the rim of the emptied and repaired one.

"There's enough casks below in need of attention," Reynolds said, "to take us until well into the second dog watch. That old dago can do it. He has the constitution. But I can't, Alex. And God knows what Bullen will pass as satisfactory when his watch relieves me. You will have to see to it. Call me if you feel my eye is needed."

"You put your head down, Reynolds. I need that water as much as anybody an' a sight more'n most. I ain't aimin' to see it wasted, but I'll call you if I figure you ought to be there."

2

She would come home of an evenin' so wore down with the work an' the hungry walk in the cold, you couldn't tell her from the old women: she was so hunched an' her face so grey. But she would put it off, God knows how, afore she stepped into the room. Always. She would come in as straight as the young woman she was, with a smile for us all, but with one particular for me I used to think. Maybe each o' the others—Grace an' Charlie an' David—were thinkin' the same too. Even to poor Arthur who could no more hold a thought in his head than he could hold the waste in his bowels. I would try to meet her at the end of the street, so as to see her straighten an' smile afore any o' the others, an' to hear her say, *There's my Ned. Come to walk his lady home.* But often the others was so fretful with hunger, an' if Arthur was into one of his howlin' spells, the time would pass on me and she would be at the door comin' in afore I knew it. Besides when the others was cryin' an' miserable, I could not risk them alone with father. 'Specially if Arthur was into howlin' like a sick dog without cease. Mostly father would sit or lie without more than a cough an' a curse all day; but he would come on sometimes, unexpected, and the young 'uns could not defend themselves. Father was why Arthur howled like a dog, I'm sure on't. From the time when he was a little piece of a chap an' half-mad with a gripe so mother told me afterwards an' father put his big hand on Arthur's face to stop his cryin', an' would ha' held it there until murder an' death had been done but for mother screamin' on his back an' me at his ankles. He shrugged mother off like you would shed a coat, desprit as she was, crazed as only a woman can be who sees her last-born bein' done to death afore her eyes, an' I held his legs fast even when he tried to kick me loose. But he had no boots, nor had worn any for two year since the last pair went for his drink. An' I brought him down at last, straight on his back, never lettin' go o' his ankles. An' when his head hit the floor an' I saw the first blood shinin' on the flagstone behind him, I thought I'd killed him. I hoped I had killed him, so's he'd leave mother an' me in peace to care for the young 'uns.

But he treated me careful after that. As if what I had done to his head had made him afeard I might do something worse one day when he weren't lookin'. An' he'd never laid hands on the others when I was there although he'd curse an' threaten for pride's sake. Him sitting there or lying in the bed an' wearin' the old dress our gran had left, 'cause there were nothin' else for him to wear as would keep him warm while he waited for mother to bring home what we ate with and what he drank with.

For there were nothin' else for him to do wi' his days. There had been no work for the men three years an' more. No work at all. Only for the women, an' only for those as were particular neat an' quick like mother. Even for children there weren't no work. There were no place for me along wi' mother until I were all o' eight year old, risin' nine. An' even then I suspect place was made for me 'cause mother was so quick an' neat an' they knew she'd work better if she didn't have to feed me.

He died sudden. Not even coughin' like he always had but

109

goin' quiet before our eyes, over three days, lookin' back without a word or a curse at the young 'uns as they looked at him. All except Arthur, who never let up on the howlin' until we gave him a cup o' brown sugar an' gin, special-bought, an' he didn't stir for two days save to foul himself where he lay in the corner.

We had to bury him in gran's dress for there were no clothes left for layin' him out. An' had it not been for free-given help we would not have had enough. Mother was near dead, herself, for the shame of that.

For a while after, it were the only time she did not smile an' straighten when she come through the door. The only time I seen her weep as if she was afraid for us all, sitting over the few bits of coal as could hardly warm the stone on which they burned.

He were such a fine figure of a man, Ned, she would say to me repeated, night after night when the young 'uns had been got to sleep. *When I was carryin' you nine year ago, an' there were work, he were so upright. Why did they have to waste a man like that, Ned? Waste him wi' no more thought than a drunkard would have for the value of a bright guinea?*

3

"Ned?" said Boyo Dolan.

"Aye?"

"Will you forgive me now . . . for the foolishness an' libel I was imputin' this mornin' concernin' your courage?"

"Nothing to forgive, Boyo. 'Twas forgotten as soon as heard."

"Sure an' I thank you for your kind lie, Ned. There's as fine a gintleman walks in you as ever druv in a carriage up to the Viceroy's reception. But I had no grant or permit to speak as I did, 'cept out av resentment, like you, at the lordliness av that black bastard's visitations to inspect the progress av our labour. You stood up to him, Ned, an' if I thrust between you after it was only to save you from yourself. You've a fine high temper, an' if it had found let it might have been a hangin' matter for you at the end av it. You understand, Ned?"

"Aye, Boyo."

"Then say somethin', for God's sake, 'stead av lying there as if you was only waitin' for John an' me to sew you into your hammock, wid a shot at your feet, preparatory to consignment over the side an' a prayer for your soul."

"Tis nothin' you said, Boyo. Nothin', I swear."

"So how's about a bit av revolution, then, to liven the occasion. Most evenin's you've cleared Peterloo, an' them Tolpuddle Chartist fellas, sweeter than a Galway blazer over a gate an' is poundin' down straight on a loose, breakneck rein for the starvation av Ireland an' the brotherhood av the workin' man. Be the holy, Ned, it's an enlightenment to hear you when you get goin' . . ."

"Boyo," old Calder said suddenly, with dispassionate finality. Put a cable round your tongue, an' a sea anchor at the end o' *that*, an' let her ride into the swell."

"What? I was only tryin'—"

"Heave to, Boyo. Heave to or else I'll sink you," Calder said without threat, with generous and determined promise. "Leave Ned be for the bye."

They had been called back on deck at five bells of the afternoon watch, stupefied with the first sleep of recovery. They had come out to Reynolds' delicately balanced, infinitely dangerous urgency, and old Jerome working with the blind assurance of a somnambulist walking a parapet. Alex appeared from time to time in the first part of the afternoon, as each newly coopered cask was half full, to sprinkle a heaped palmful of *bhang* into the water. But as the sun went down, he seemed to be everywhere, like Reynolds, and it was difficult, in their tiredness, to distinguish whose orders they obeyed with more gratitude.

On the main deck, as the afternoon lengthened, as the heat became heavier and as men collapsed and were hosed down into a new usefulness, Price and Bullen had seen to the clearing, feeding and exercise of the slaves: and to the terrible descent into the holds below with hoses, tubs of vinegar, red-hot one-pound shot to drop into the vinegar and little coal pots on which to burn the dry coffee berries to sweeten the air that had trapped the smells of the night's discharges from five hundred sick and abused bodies. One of the Portuguese (not really a sailor at all but an elegant, pale ladies' hairdresser working his

111

way to the promise of a provincial empire) had fainted below and would have drowned face down in a shallow pool of piss, liquid shit and vomit, if Price had not found him and brought him up on his shoulder and flung him face-down on the deck, so hard that the unconscious man had expelled a gout of the broth he had inhaled and had begun to breathe raggedly but deep.

The slaves—shuffling and clumsily jumping as the sailors urged and shouted and pleaded and heaved them into one of their measures of sustained activity—had scarcely looked at the prone figure in the space between their feet. Their eyes had kept turning to where Jerome and the half-watch at the water casks moved behind the screen of shimmering air spreading from the forge.

Once, Captain Hogarth came from around the mast and into the small inferno of the foredeck and Alex had immediately brought him water in a ladle from the cask they had just winched up. Hogarth had drunk it all, nodded as he handed the ladle back to Alex, and said to Reynolds, *You have done well, Mister Reynolds. But we must do better than this if we are not to lose more than we can afford before morning. I trust you are stowing well to starboard. I have no wish to take a fresh south-easterly with a loose ballast.* And at that moment, seeing Hogarth's face through the blur of exhaustion, Dunn had felt a confidence and security as close, as natural, as his own skin. With Hogarth in command, you could sail into any chance or danger and he would bring you out of it again.

Now they lay in their hammocks in the little territory nearest the entrance to the forecastle which they had claimed and established. Calder and three of the Portuguese had lifted Jerome into his hammock. The huge old man had been on his feet between brazier and anvil since eight bells of the first watch. As the last cask was lowered back into the hold, they had to prise his fingers from the handle of his hammer.

The last glare from the vanished sun had polished the water with a curious sheen of no recognizable colour. The caught ship seemed to fester into the gathering shadows of an immense loneliness.

"John?" Dunn said.

112

"Aye, Ned?"

"I wonder whatever happened t'others—Grace an' Charlie an' David an' Arthur. I was three years on my first voyage, an' when I come back there weren't a soul knew where they might ha' gone."

"They'd have to go somewheres, Ned. Where there was work like. But England's a big place, an' three year's a long time. They'd have gone somewhere for sure."

"But Arthur, John . . . He'd not ha' been good for any kind o' work. I wonder what would happen to him?"

"They'd have taken him, Ned. He'd have gone along with 'em."

"I looked for 'em, you know. I looked as hard as a man could look afore I had to ship out again. But it was as if they'd drowned . . . How's about you, John? Did you ever go lookin' for yours when you come back?"

"Me?" said old Calder comfortably. "Nobody as I ever *could* have looked for, Ned. There was nobody to remember after they put me out."

Part Five

THE MIDSHIPHOUSE

CHAPTER ELEVEN

When he was drawing on the stick I'd rolled him, holding the smoke a spell in his lungs and breathing fresh air onto it just like I taught him, I was watching his eyes. It's the only way you can tell when Mary Jane starts cosying up in a man. The eyes go all steady and sort of peaceful. Not foolish, but as if he's looking at something inside him he ain't ever seen before. Or as if what he's seeing outside him is new as Christmas morning to a little child.

I knew I was pushing luck giving Reynolds a smoke of the herb, 'cause a man can get a sudden understanding of what the trail signs mean when Mary Jane starts whispering in his ear. And God knows he's right smart even without it. But I need him yet awhile. Ain't any way I can get five hundred niggers out of this goddam calm and safe to Brazil without him riding point. And I surely didn't like the way he was looking this afternoon. As if he couldn't call on any more wickedness to perk him up. So I gave him another stick after his eyes became steady and looking inside him as well as out and when he got real hungry, as I knew he would, I put game soup and raisins and biscuits into him along with the claret and the brandy and sent him back to his cabin to do his ploughing. When he left he was going to her as straight and happy as a baby to the breast. Soon as I told him I'd take his middle watch you couldn't hold him any more than you'd hold a spring stallion. I'll give him this, though, he was all set to pace the deck and walk off his heat until I persuaded him that it was no chore for me to take his watch. Come morning and he'll be all spirited up again. All the sadness pumped out of him into that gal.

"Alex," he asked me as I was heating him up another tin of the game soup. He was stuffing Bath Olivers into his mouth as

115

if he had never known there was such a thing as biscuits and speaking around the crumbs and swallowing wine like a Mex priest after communion. "Alex, I ask your confidence. How d'you come to be aboard this enterprise? How did our captain discover you? He could hardly have put it about among the agents that he was in need of a cook able to fulfil the requirements of a slaver."

"There's agents in Bristol, Reynolds," I told him, "an' there's other agents who don't have offices or a brass plate to the door but do a powerful heap of business. Wouldn't be no niggers bein' slipped steady through the patrols to Cuba an' Brazil an' into every goddam sounding in the Sea Islands that can float a hull if it wasn't for them. You know that. There's some fine and dandy gentlemen's houses in Orchard Street an' Everton Hill, with matched pairs haulin' the carriages, because some fine gentlemen know how to keep the trade furnished."

"Indeed, yes," Reynolds said. "Your observation on the great English talent for masquerade is as trenchant as it is accurate. I sometimes indulge myself in the speculation that hypocrisy, a monumental and enduring hypocrisy, will be what my race bequeaths to the future. That the spreading of hypocrisy is our purpose—as the Romans bequeathed us that concept of well-ordered brutality they called law. But we will build even better than the Romans, Alex. We shall convert more heathens, perhaps, than the Catholic Church. For we have transformed hypocrisy into a religion with all the rituals, vestments and hierarchy of a truly inspired faith. We shall light the dark integrities of a thousand tribes with the revelation of our sanctimonious self-deceit."

I was watching him from where I stood over the stove, letting the soup come to a nice lazy simmer like a cat stretching itself awake. The words were feeding on Mary Jane and the claret and he was feeding on the words and it was doing him a power of good. I could see the face he liked to wear growing on him as if he was a woman prettying for a dance. And I was glad I'd taken the long odds and given him the second stick. With that and the soup and the wine and his running off his mouth on a long canter, I was reckoning he'd be ready for the gal and the sort of sleep you only get when you lie between Mary Jane

116

and a woman. I brought him the soup I had been heating up in the iron saucepan I never let any of my boys scour but wipe out soft myself and which never cooks for anybody 'cept me and a few like Hogarth and Reynolds.

"You get that inside you", I told him, "an' talk afterwards."

"But you," he said, taking soup and biscuits and wine and talking all at the same time. Letting the words run as if he had never drawn rein for a piece of a second. "You were never recruited from a dockside tavern as you drank yourself numb between berths. You present a question to me Alex; and I must confess that for me unanswered questions don't sit as comfortable on my mind as your noble repast does on my stomach. How did you hear of Hogarth and this venture for which every canting tractarian manufacturer in England would send us to the gallows because slaves ain't able to purchase enough of his shoddy goods so his son may buy in as a gentleman?"

"I heard about the same as you, I reckon," I said and I put a mite of unwelcome in my voice. Not much, but just to turn his head from coming straight at where he aimed to go. "I ain't sayin' I heard from the same source of information but it was put to me—kind of delicate, if you get my meaning—as if the man putting it might have been talkin' about the weather or the flowerboat gals on the Pearl River . . . An' you, Reynolds? You weren't polishin' the chairs in the outer offices, neither, along with the other paid-off officers, and hopin' some ship would put in with the third mate sick or mebbe even already dead an' put over the side. You left one good berth, I know, with promise of a better. You was waitin' for this, an' you grabbed ahold of it as it went by."

For a moment he stared at me, his eyes widened a space, with thoughtfulness like a little, steady match flame behind them. As if he was considering how I'd put myself up there along with him as if we was equals. I've been seeing that look all my life and sometimes I've had to kill when they couldn't rest comfortable with the thought. A few times I've taken real pleasure in killing but mostly its been only there weren't anything else to do.

There's a heap of owing to be paid by white men some day. But what's *owing*, anyway, 'cept power some fool's lent you,

117

same as a mule or a horse or a jackass, and you ain't figuring on paying it back?

Reynolds shook his head one quick toss, as if he was tucking the thought down where he could take it out again.

"As usual you have gone to the centre," he said, "while the rest of us exercise our considerations on the periphery. You are right. It is not *we* who found Hogarth. He knew where to find us. As certainly as though we were marked on Admiralty charts. It would occasion me no surprise to learn that he knew our features, each man, before he clapped eyes on us. He plotted a course to several hungers, Alex, and raised each with no more trouble nor error than any good navigator need allow for."

"What *I* will allow", I told him, and poured him three fingers more of brandy because I wanted him to keep tacking on the stretch he had taken, "is that you have a way of fillin' my hand with some fancy cards I never drew. I never said about Hogarth findin' us, 'cept Dunn and Calder an' that little Boyo, an' the dagoes. But anybody could've found them—the same way Price found me the boy, Joshua. They're the leavin's an' scrapin's of the world. The only difference between them an' what we've got shackled in the hold is we don't have to feed 'em when they ain't workin'... You and me, now, we *heard* where there was somethin' worth a man's gettin' out of his bed for. Just as it's you an' me will get this ship to where it's bound before it turns into the biggest goddam coffin an' floatin' hazard ever drifted across the course of lawful traffic."

He laughed then. And when he flung himself back and stayed loose laughing, I knew he was into himself again and cautioned as I wanted him. His mind was going to what I said the way your feet go beneath a table when you're sitting close beside a woman with the band playing but you don't want to dance, neither of you, cause what you're both dancing sitting is the beginnings of what you're going upstairs to dance.

He was that pleasured with what I'd said about needing him to get us safe and profitable out of the calm. And God knows I was speaking as true as Jesus at the Last Supper when I said *that*.

I need him. I can't do it if he ain't himself.

"Alex," he said when he'd finished laughing (and I admired

118

the way he approached his brandy, letting it come to him a step at a time instead of him rushing it, frowning when I made to top up on what he had drunk and putting his hand over the glass), "I am a man restored. You have brought Reynolds to himself again. For I must confess that I have been a melancholy, useless dog these past three days . . . As though this damned ship were at the end of the world and those on it the last souls in all history. There! You know the extent of the vapours which I shall deny should you ever charge me with having entertained them. You are right, of course. As you are always right. It is you and I must see to it that Hogarth brings us safe into the first of our inheritance. Two voyages more and we shall have gained, if not the treasure itself, at least sufficient to purchase the key that unlocks the frowning portals of the treasury. What say you, eh, Alex? Can a man not anticipate a bright future on the profit from three cargoes such as we carry?'

"He can anticipate a rope round his neck," I told him, "or comin' grey out of prison if he's lucky. Mebbe you ought to think about *that*."

"Nonsense, my dear fellow. D'you think I'd let some interfering fool advance his career and exalt his smug heart by taking you? What is of even greater significance, d'you think I'd let them take *me*? No. I am set on my course and will not be turned from it by trifling risks. Men who allow themselves to be deterred by disagreeable possibilities must resign themselves to disagreeable certainties—such as an obscure old age without fortune or influence. And that I will not do, Alex. Upon my oath, but that is not Reynolds' way."

His voice was light and perky then, with the laughter coiled in back of it as smooth and ready and alone as a snake under a bush. Looking at him then I come to understand as if I hadn't rightly figured it before that he made twice of most of any man I ever met. Which means I got to be twice as careful when it comes to killing him.

"You," I said then, slow and thoughtful, as if I was asking his pardon for showing more fret than a man should. "You, Reynolds, I don't know what you ate when you was growin' but it didn't do you any harm. I ain't sayin' that I am particular took with the idea of runnin' another cargo like this one. An' another run after that is goin' to take a lot more out of me than a man pushin' my age can afford. But with you an' Hogarth to take care of things, I reckon I can live it out contented enough."

"Hogarth," he said sudden, as if he had only been listening to the sound of what I'd been saying until the word he'd been waiting for come up. "Now if you are enigma, Alex, what am I to make of Hogarth? Why do we find his like sharing a berth with the likes of us on such a venture?"

"For the same hopin' as any aboard, I reckon," I said. "Ain't no quicker pickings a man can make than in this trade, less'n he strikes a mother lode somewhere. An' this is sure 'cept you get took by the patrol. Most prospectors I ever run into couldn't find the price of what's in a spitoon even if it was sellin' at two cents a glass. Hogarth ain't no different. Like I told you, he's seen slavers climbin' into their carriages an' hats lifted as if they'd never smelled what come to us last night across the water or put a foundered body over the side."

"No," he said then, and shook his head determined. "You misunderstand me. Rather, I believe you choose to misunderstand me. I know what Hogarth expects to have for his use after three voyages in the trade . . . But *why*, Alex? That is what interests me. Why does such a man come to such a desperate wager in company such as ours?"

"Seems to me," I said, "that if Cap'n Hogarth measures high as where you mark him, there's nobody or nothin' could have brung him down to where we reach."

"Don't play the simple sailor with me," he said. "We know what we are and no damned pretence about it, thank God. But Hogarth, now, is a different article entirely . . . He's a gentleman spoiled."

"So's you," I told him, "if you think what you've engaged for isn't your callin'."

"I'm a spoiled gentleman," he said, not light and bouncing, not sad either, but steady like a banker at blackjack calling the cards. "Oh, I come down grand enough. There's been a Reynolds at Style two hundred years almost to the day, and money to go with it. In my father's house there are many mansions, although I shan't have the pleasure of inheriting the meanest of them. But I don't come down as grand as Hogarth. I wouldn't care to set about matching my forebears with his, even if mine could put up a guinea for every penny his could. He's old breeding, Alex, and he sets my philosopher's nose pointing and twitching as you do. I wish to know not what he may acquire—which is either great wealth or nothing according to vulgar chance—but his entelechy."

"His *what*?" I said. "Jesus Christ, Reynolds. You do try a man who ain't ever seen more of a schoolroom than what he could lookin' through a windowpane. What in hell is this entelchy Hogarth's got an' you can't wait to rustle?"

"You know", he said and smiled as far as the bottom of his nose. "You know. Unless you lied to me t'other night about what I suspect is your comfortable acquaintance with those Athenian pederasts who grope in our breeches across the centuries . . . It is Hogarth's soul I would like to run to earth, not the degenerating flesh of his actions . . . Why does he turn to this sordid trade? Why does he have as a wife a person no more suited to his station in life than Calder to a quarterdeck?"

He was drunk then. Not drunk with the game soup and the brandy and Mary Jane making him feel himself again. But drunk the same as any Pawnee or Dakota buck I ever seen riding alongside a buffalo until it went over the lip of a bluff and broke its neck below. He was clear, clean, crazy drunk with hunting down what he was smelling to be the truth.

"Mrs Hogarth?" I said. "Now what sort of a tack you comin' up on, Reynolds? I don't like women aboard any more than you do. An' I don't like captains' wives any at all. But Mrs Hogarth is a fine lady an'—"

"Gammon, Alex," he said, not looking at me for the first time, staring down into the drink he'd only wet his lips with. "She is not a captain's lady. She is a respectable woman enough, I grant you, but not a suitable wife for Hogarth . . . Come, my dear fellow, you know quality, and you know she ain't that. How would you have regarded her in the days when you lowered the carriage steps for real ladies? And I speak only of her condition. I do not refer, yet, to the plain distress between 'em."

And then, standing up—as a host has the right to do when the hour's late enough and enough liquor been drunk by the gentlemen—I sent him on his way up the deck to his cabin to what I wished him to have while he could still relish it and remember it.

Part Six

THE POOP

CHAPTER TWELVE

1

Her breathing was light and regular but he could not yet be sure that she slept. Lying on his back beside her, breathing lightly and evenly also, he held himself in anxious readiness, like a man in a jungle thicket waiting out the passage of some large, dangerous animal. The master's bunk was more commodious than any other but narrow enough if considered for two. Her curved spine beneath the cotton of her nightdress moved slightly against his arm with her breathing; yet they might have been lying on the opposite boundaries of a wide plain. There was no comfort where they touched. There was not even the consoling discomfort of joined warmth in the stale heat of the cabin. There was only a strange numb distress of the flesh and nerves: a heaviness through which no blood seemed to course. The foolish and exhausting habit of unhappiness hung between their touching bodies like a cable.

The moonlight filtering through the chintz curtains drawn across the opened port seemed to stain the darkness of the cabin with gradually diminishing strength, as if it were a clear, shallow tributary flowing into a deep lake of shadow. And to Hogarth, lying in quiet beside the woman he wished asleep with all his heart and hope, the first dimmed radiance immediately above his eyes was like the reflecting wall of a *camera obscura* across which the images of an untouchable expectation passed upside down.

"Eliza," he said, hardly above a rhetorical murmur, "are you asleep? This heat makes it difficult." He paused, and felt her breathing back swell against and fall away from his arm. "Even I find it trying." There was no catch or alteration in her breathing, but with the weary caution of the unforgiven he tested

123

again softly: too often had the silence and the dark of their shared bed seemed to engender remembered wrong as other beds might encourage mounting lust. "I shall take a turn on deck for a while," he said; and when he was satisfied that she really slept he rose.

He shucked his nightshirt and dressed in the dark with the swift, sure absent-mindedness of one who has learned early to come naked from the deep entombment of youthful sleep and fully clothed to the dangerous necessities of a plunging deck in less than half a minute. He put on only his shirt and trousers, and his slippers. As he stepped onto the deck beyond the cabin his deliverance from the tense moments of exploration in the bunk was like the tidal sweep of the first strong drink through a body just stepped in from a cold journey. At nights, the estranging darkness and his confidence in the usual soundness of her sleep ensured that his escape would be longer, more exhilarating. The cooler air from the sea, replacing the heat that still rose from the baked wood of the deck, was not so much a breeze as a touch, a presence, in the roots of his thick hair. For a moment, looking down the length of the barque, in the moonlight, he was humbly exalted—freed from any vulgar, selfish consideration—as he saw the intricate and beautiful wholeness of the world he commanded and as he enjoyed the knowledge of his proven competence to command it. For a moment he looked up at and across the packed, golden, silently fretting constellations which he could name by heart and by which he could steer to any landfall his mind envisaged.

For a moment, and only for a moment, in that night between the stars and the sea which he loved with a full, sufficient passion he would have denied, Hogarth was at peace for the last time in his life.

2

She could measure his passage along the port deck outside the cabin although he made no sound in his slippers . . . Break to taffrail . . . taffrail to break . . . with a pause each time, at the taffrail, as he breathed deeply and gazed across the wide-open fan of silvered black between the stern and the horizon.

She did not need to hear him or to see him to know where he was and what he did. She could have aimed a pistol or plunged a knife, with shut eyes, into the heart of the very spot where he was about to be on the instant before ball or point found its target.

She could measure him as exactly as she could measure the laconic and inexorable drum-tap of her heart.

Once her heart had moved to a very different beat; but she would no more remember it accurately now than a person can hear two measures at the same time but must listen to what is nearer and louder and must move to it, even though longing to move to what sounds faintly and unformed and far beyond.

Sometimes as she watched him, covertly, across the cabin—as she re-read another of the great voyages from which he could quote as easily as a country parson from the burial service or baptism or the churching of women in the prayer book—she could almost force herself to make the gesture and utter the words that might free them both if not into happiness at least into its possibility. Country bred, she knew that the male initiated nothing except that to which he had been invited. In the prosperous, multiplying farmyard of her upbringing, she had learned this long before she could form words around what she had learned.

But always between the starved, endlessly punished longing to touch and reconcile there rose the cannibal hunger for what could never be restored. A hunger as consuming and fruitless as the need of a duellist to restore lost honour. A hunger, although she could not know it, as imbecile and determined as that of a gun-shot hyena eating its own entrails in dreadful conspiracy with the hunter.

Constantly she had prayed for the grace of forgetting. Two small patches of murdered skin on the knees he had not been permitted to see or touch for ten years testified to the length and intensity of her prayers. And sometimes grace entered, like a bird flying into a room, beating in panic from wall to wall before hurling itself into the light held in the opened casement.

But always, after these visitations, the other, strict charge would seize her: to expunge, by righteous anger and true witness, the frailty through which all were entered and betrayed

125

. . . As she would expunge it in the boy Joshua before it grew
with him and before he had come to cherish it and hide it from
his witnessing self.

And always, as the great, burning joy of righteous witness
seized her, she would know that the wildly darting grace of
forgetting in her locked room of prayer was only that: a bird
sent by Satan to distract her from repentance. She would not be
as those foolish prophets that follow their own spirit, seeing
nothing. For the day of the Lord was at hand and only those
who lived already in repentance would be spared the destruc-
tion He had promised. Only the just could walk in His ways
above the fallen transgressors who had seen and followed vain
visions and lying divinations.

Open rebuke, in the unsleeping service one owed God, was
better than secret love.

In His mercy, God had punished her once for false, secret
love with brief, tearing agony from which, in her sin and ignorance, she had screamed for the deliverance of death.

But God in His mercy, had brought her through that pain
and terror which, she could understand now, were blessed lights
guiding her out of the lewdness and abomination that passed
as love and in which she had been mired until He brought her
to understanding, cleansed for His service.

Dry-eyed, unsleeping, heavy as any stone, she lay on her
back in the still, pressing heat of the little cabin, divining her
husband's regular passage between break and taffrail, grateful
to God for her deserved suffering and for the peace to come
that it promised.

3

Had my beloved parents lived, I would have accepted my grandfather's offer, nay *assurance*, of recommendation into the Navy.
But it would have dishonoured their memories had I permitted
myself to pocket so much as a guinea of his, let alone his influence. For it was bad conscience and fear of damnation and
loneliness that prompted him to have his man waiting my
return beside the graves only a few weeks filled . . . He who saw
his daughter decline into sanctified penury beside a man as

saintly as herself; when a word could have gained them pre-
ferment, or a gift forgotten the day after it was made could have
regularly put wine on their table and a dress becoming her
beauty on her back. It was only when I was closing the lid of
the chest on their clothing that I realized how small were her
shoes. I took them from the chest, then, and set them beside
mine. They were like the shoes of a child and my tears fell on
leather that no lady's maid would have tolerated beneath her
truckle. When I was a boy, even before my departure for that
second voyage, she seemed to fill the largest room with her
radiance, like flowers in a vase. I am glad I wept onto her shoes
for it left me dry with the strength to resist temptation when I
went to see my grandfather. And I am glad that they died so
hard upon each other, even though I was not there to see either
into their rest. For neither would have had enough heart to live
on alone. They had both given all their reserves to provision my
passage. If I can return to this world a tithe of the loving care
they heaped upon me then the world will owe a debt it can
never discharge.

My grandfather was very old and frightened in the library of
the London house of which I had heard my mother speak so
often. The Prince of Wales danced with my aunts in the great
room above the library, my mother used to tell me—as proudly
as though he had taken *her* onto the floor. I saw him once, when
he was king and visited the school, and I remember my childish
incapacity to discern in that swollen, crimson face and gross,
reeking carcass, the lineaments of the fine prince my mother
had described.

"We must see to your future now, William," my grandfather
said. "You have made a fine beginning, I am told, but without
a father to counsel a boy it must devolve upon me, eh? I must
stir myself about the interests of my dear daughter's only child."

It was a fair, sunny month's end in May when we spoke but
he had a fire laid that would have warmed the hall of a thane.
I had to move back a step from the heat.

"I am promised a position, sir," I told him, "on an East
Indiaman, after I have served my next voyage. There is much
advantage in that trade to be gained, sir, by a young officer
who applies himself."

"To be sure . . . To be sure," he said. "There are men of most respectable family in the Company's service. But we ain't talking of merchant traffic, William. Such a deck is no place for my grandson—or for a Hogarth," he added hastily. He must have read my face. "No! Percival Hogarth's son must have a seventy-four to command by the time he's thirty. And a squadron in line behind his flagship, eh, well before he's fifty. I shall wait on Conyngham at the Admiralty in the morning. And if Conyngham can't find'ee a berth, I'll ask audience with Billy himself . . . He may be king now but there's still three thousand pounds of debt due between him and me for which I've never asked settlement . . . No, William. You've left it late, you're all of fifteen—sixteen, is it?—but I'll see you flying your own colours yet in a gentleman's command. And there'll be something to sustain it more than your pay. I'll see to that."

"I am more than obliged, sir," I said, "for the concern you manifest, but I do not think I could match your ambition for me. I would come late to a place in the Navy, as you have observed, and I have made commitment to another service."

He continued to press me but I was adamant, as only a grieving boy of sixteen full of righteousness can be. And to tell the truth, it gave me a sense of luxurious power to disdain his offer so lightly.

"Your mother would have wished it," he said finally, when he saw he could not buy the ease of mind my acceptance would have given him. "You owe it to her memory to pursue a career more fitting to your rank than carrying goods for rich tradesmen."

"My mother, sir," I told him, "had set her heart on my entering the church. She would speak of my bishopric as though it were a fact already accomplished when I was but ten years old. Not the least of the many cherished memories I shall forever hold of her is her immediate and enthusiastic agreement on my choice of the sea. Her disappointment must have been a sad one, but she never revealed it to me."

"Your mother was right in trying to groom you for the church," he said then, with peevish anger. "You speak like a damned churchman."

128

And I will confess that my priggish tone was not wholly assumed.

When I was leaving, my grandfather tried to relieve his burdened soul by five hundred guineas, and the floor of his library tilted like a deck as I refused this unimaginable fortune.

"So you will take nothing of me, eh?" he said. "How you must hate me."

"I do not hate you, sir," I said. "You are my mother's father and it would be the gravest offence in the eyes of God and man to hate you. And, as an earnest of my respect, I *will* take something from you."

"What?" he said, sharp and eager, but puzzled also.

"Those!" I said, and pointed at the shelf where the great mariners and voyagers of history stood closely, back after touching back, behind brown, green and red Morocco and gold-leaf lettering. They were all there: Hakluyt, Magellan, Columbus, Hudson, Tasman, Bougainville, Drake, and Cook, the greatest of them all. My heart had found them, when I entered this strange room, before I was close enough to read the names. "I will take those, grandfather."

He stared at where my trembling finger pointed and then looked back at me, shrewd enough to apprehend instantly which books I wanted without any further words on my part.

'You have made a profitable exchange, William," he said and laughed a little dry chuckle. "Five hundred guineas refused in return for what you have selected represents a piece of trading even your future employers would admire."

But he knew that those volumes would never be sold or pawned. There was respect in his voice for all its dryness.

"It is the finest gift I have ever received," I told him, and it was all I could do to restrain myself from crossing to the shelf to touch the fortune that had come to me. "I will never forget your generosity, grandfather. I will send a carter this afternoon to convey them to my lodgings."

"No need, William," he said in the same dry, respectful tone, as though he were talking to a man. "No need of that. I have servants a plenty with little employment and great appetites. One of them will bring the books to you if you tell me where you are lodged."

129

The day on which I first saw him, he was riding Mr Llewellyn's sorrel mare down the combe towards the village. We know horses, and their riders, in our part of the world, and even though it was the Sabbath and our thoughts should have been on the service we all stopped to admire his seat and the pleasure the mare seemed to take in being put to a swift canter by one who knew how to get the best out of her.

"Surely that is Mr Llewellyn's mare," my mother said.

"It is Mr Llwellyn's mare right enough," my father replied, "but it is not Mr Llwellyn riding her—nor that lump Daniel, neither. They neither of them ever rested in a saddle so easy in their lives, for all that the one's a gentleman born and t'other a groom afore he could walk."

"Then who could it be?" my mother said, for the rider was still a distance up the dropping white road and the morning sun was in our eyes.

We were all surprised enough. Mr Llwellyn was jealous of his mare, a beautiful creature, and none but he and Daniel ever rode her; except that sometimes he would give her to one of the ladies who might be staying at the Hall—but always with Daniel to attend her.

"Perhaps it has been stolen, Mama," Peter, our youngest, said. "Mr Shewell told me last night there be gipsies camped in Long Wood and—"

"Hush, child," my mother said absently. "What gipsy would dare to steal a horse known to every coper in the country? Besides, can you not see by his clothes that he is a gentleman?"

"He must be staying at the Hall," my father said, "and he must be a close friend, or even a blood relative, for Llewellyn don't lend the mare for any ordinary man's use."

But it was only a pause in our progress to matins; country folk like to consider any departure from that which is fixed and familiar, even the most trivial circumstances merit careful examination. And who's to blame them since their health and livelihood depend on regular seasons and tried ways. We walked on towards the church bells until the rider caught up with us, and reined the mare in to a walk so that it would not raise dust on our dresses.

"Good morning, good people," he said. "Ma-am," and here he lifted his tall hat and bowed in the saddle to my mother. "I am relieved to see you so unhurried and to hear the bell still ringing. I had feared I was late for service, and that would never have done my first Sunday back in a Christian country."

With that he passed us; and we saw him put heels to the mare as he gathered her into a canter again; and the wide shoulders and the back as straight and limber as an ash plant.

"There!" my mother said. "Did you mark *that*, Peter? Did you observe how a true gentleman behaves? They're others of his sort who would have cantered past us without a word, with the dust rising behind the hooves in clouds . . ."

"He gave *you* a pretty bow, Mama," I said, with my eyes down; and she blushed and grinned and slipped her arm round my waist, squeezing it in mock chastisement.

"Eliza," she said, "you sinful girl. Such wicked thoughts on the Sabbath. Hold your tongue, miss."

My mother and I were close, although she loved the others deeply. And she was never more mother to me than in my need and shameful pain later on.

"A soldier, I'll be bound," said my father gazing to where the stranger was turning the bend that would take him out of our sight. "An officer of the cavalry returned from India, perhaps. You heard him say he was newly come from heathen places. And how brown his face is, though you can see it would be fresh-coloured in natural climates. What say you, Eliza?"

"You may well be correct, Papa," I said. "His face *was* very brown and he sits like one who must ride without fear of faltering ahead of one hundred troopers."

He nodded with a pleased affirmation on my reply, for it always gave him quiet comfort when I confirmed his most casual judgements. *I love and cherish them all equal*, I used to hear him say to one or other of his friends who held the larger farms of Mr Llewellyn, *but Eliza is the one with brains. Were she a boy I would make her a scholar—had I to borrow 'gainst harvest on't*. After I came home from Miss Arboyne's in Liverpool, he would seek my agreement a dozen times a day on matters about which he was as well or better informed than I; on circumstances or possibilities to which his man's experience gave him larger access. But it made him proud to hear me support what his natural wit had arrived at, in the speech that Miss Arboyne and Miss Findlay had taught me at the academy. Speech for which he had paid so handsomely.

But he would grow anxious, sometimes, at the number of my books when young men were like to call. (For I was much inspected, and once or twice asked for, after my return.)

A book's a fine thing, Eliza, he would say. A book of poetry in a young woman's hands and her reading from it with feeling, and rapid as if she knows every word afore she's had time to read all the letters in it, will rouse the admiration of any young man of respectable family. But so many books, girl, and so many of them so thick, and the print so close. That might give a young man pause, who don't know that you don't allow them to get atween you and the woman's duties you do as well, no better, than your dear mother, though I should not say that and you will pretend I did not. Follow my advice, Eliza, for I know the ways of the world and how easily put off his best interest a young man can be. Keep the thick books out of the parlour, and leave the poetry there for reading. A quick reading in a soft voice can do more to make a young man think serious than your best bonnet or a dress straight from your grandest Liverpool shop.

There were so many young men then. And some of them, like Jeremy Dodd whose father held Calcroft on the rich bottom where the combe widened, were fine-set, steady young men, already older than their looks because of the care they must exercise in the managing of their land and their command of those twice their age who laboured on it. My breath would quicken to the sound of the hooves when they came riding up to the farm in the evening. But only to the sound of the hooves. Not for them who made the hooves ring so smartly. *Not for them.*

It is a mistake to believe that young women are persuaded into love by what their eyes admire and what makes their breaths quicken when they are twenty-one and have time on their hands between dusk and going to bed. A woman falls in love where she thinks she ought to fall in love, and finds looks enough to convince love after.

When I next beheld him that morning, in church, I was pleased to see him because he was new and had been to strange places and was set as fine as any young man in the combe and beyond, although he was older. It was hard to tell the age of his brown, square face as I glanced across to where he sat at the front of the church in the Llewellyn pew, which was empty save for him. (After Lady Charlotte, Mr Llewellyn's mother, died, and the last Miss Llewellyn married away up to Scotland, the Llewellyn pew was often empty on a Sunday, even when Mr Llewellyn was home from London and Parliament.)

I thought his face looked drawn beneath the brown and the strong, big bones. Not sick, but as if it were but recently begun to quicken into full health. That would explain his good spirits on the road. There is nothing so exalts any creature as health returning to a healthy body struck down by chance. Everything you see or touch or smell then seems so new yet familiar.

His black coat was of a weave finer than any in the church; fine and somehow deep as if you could sink your hand into it as into close turf. It looked unworn: not newly bought, but fresh as though its wearer's shoulders did not often settle into it.

He sat straight without stiffness, face straight ahead and contented, so contented. Like the face of a man sitting before a fire after coming in from a cold journey.

After the service, when we were still gathered exchanging news and pleasantries under the lime trees for which our churchyard is famous, I saw him talking with great animation to our vicar, Mr Blagrove. Again I was struck by the contentment, nay gratification, on his face, as though Mr Blagrove was a man he had purposed a long journey to meet.

When the boy from the Rose and Crown led the mare up to the lych-gate, our rider shook Mr Blagrove's hand heartily and came stepping down the flags. He recognized us and his face lightened, and his dark glance, as he lifted his hat, was keen and kindly—as though we belonged to him and he was pleased to see us looking so well.

Before he was fairly round the bend in the road leading up to the head of the combe, he had the mare to a gallop. I do not

133

know why, but I had and still have the feeling that had we not all been there and observing him, he would have flung his hat into the air and caught it descending, like any farmer's son who has won the steeplechase at a fair.

I wished to know who he was and what had brought him among us ... but for no other reason, then, that he was not Jeremy Dodd, and had got his face browned in distant lands and had walked among throngs of little, smooth, brown women who wore scraps of cloth, without shame, instead of proper covering, and that he was the finest young gentleman I had seen ride in the combe since my return from Miss Arboyne's in Liverpool.

But I could wait upon my wish, since I knew my mother would discover all I wished to know as quickly and as sure as little Peter would lick the batter from the inside of a mixing bowl.

I knew that he was a famous captain of East Indiamen before we were one hundred yards on the way back to home, and that he was resting between voyages with Mr Llewellyn who had great interests with the Company, and that Mr Llewellyn had sent his own chaise all the way to Manchester to fetch him to the combe.

And that his name was William Hogarth.

5

With the taffrail at his back, Hogarth rests his elbows and watches Alex come from the shadow cast by the cabin's bulk and into the moonlight caught between the awning and the stern deck.

"Alex?" he says.

"You got close to five hundred men aboard like me, cap'n," says Alex, "an' if it wasn't Alex but one of the others, you might be askin' that question hangin' onto the rudder with your head stove in mebbe ..."

Hogarth smiles, with the appreciation of one in whom laughter is an appetite always ready for satisfaction although seldom satisfied.

"I don't think I make that sort of error, Alex. I would not be where I am had I made a habit of misjudging men."

"Well now," says Alex, "there's Bullen. You callin' him a right exercise of judgement?"

"Ah!" says Hogarth smiling. "Between wind and water, Alex. You've holed me squarely, you scoundrel. Yes . . . Bullen was an error. But not an extreme one. He performed creditably this afternoon, for instance, in exacting circumstances. He had a fine, healthy sweat on our cargo . . . After seventeen days such as we have endured, it takes an officer of some merit to encourage such a response. Allow me, Alex. I may have been less than astute in engaging Bullen, but he is dutiful—and tireless once you point his nose to the task. Besides, I more than compensated for my lapse with Mister Reynolds. Even one who sets so high a standard as yourself must concede that Mister Reynolds complements the deficiency of which you so unkindly reminded me."

"He'll do," Alex says, joining Hogarth at the rail. He leans forward, speaking into the star-backed, silvered night. "You signin' him on for the second run?"

"I would as soon do without you. He will come as first officer. I shall give Bullen the choice of accepting demotion or his full profit on this voyage. He could barely accept the former."

"He'll accept his profit," Alex says. "He don't want much. He don't really want the three voyages it takes to give a man enough to buy his place ashore. Enough to rent is all Bullen can see."

"Until he runs to the end of the rent, eh?" Hogarth says. "And discovers that he has been paying another for the privilege of being allowed to live . . . I will not accept that as the condition of my life, Alex. As you have determined to have command of your destiny, so have I . . . There is much to be done with a life, but the noblest aspiration is a cannibal feeding on the man who entertains it, without wealth and power."

Hogarth pushes himself from the rail and walks decisively half-way down the deck to the edge of shadow cast by the cabin. He turns and comes back to where Alex now leans back against the rail.

"I did not make this world, Alex," Hogarth says, as if he

had not broken speech, "and I have learned how it will unmake those who will not understand its manifest necessities. I did not purpose to do what I am doing. I am not here by choice. Had the world been different it would have found a different use for me, and I for it."

"Had the world been different, cap'n," Alex says, "you'd have been where you are now . . . like me . . . We'd have come up on it a different way is all."

"You believe *that*?" Hogarth asks, staring.

"I believe it," Alex says.

Part Seven

THE HOLD

CHAPTER THIRTEEN

1

The smells of the hold seem to have congealed into one substance denser than the air in which it is suspended: an exudation, foul, tepid and almost phantasmagorial, that clings to the face, hands and nostrils like mucus.

Something that does not rise from only the gross discharges of urine puddles, oozing shit, splashed vomit, the constant farts and belches, the sweat, mingled oils and furious heat of near five hundred living bodies packed on shelves as close as corpses from an epidemic heaped into a pit of quicklime. Something that exhausts the trapped air as effectively as the shallow breathing and sudden yells from nightmare. Some odour, perhaps, that emanates from stunned hope, outraged expectation and the helpless fear of the unknowable.

For three nights, Tadene has watched the man who is like no man she has ever seen before come into this dreadful place where she is determined not to die and leave her spirit trapped. There can be no good or proper place for her to die now. She knows that. Either here in the middle of an immensity of water across which a spirit could wander forever without finding a place to share with the living. Nor can she imagine that there will be any proper place to die, or any fitting passage into death, in the country to which she is being carried. For she supposes there must be a country. Even the white men who behave with such indecency, with so little discernible custom or observance that they might be mad, must need a land to share with their spirits. She has thought that the white men may not have spirits but has dismissed that as an impossibility. There could be no world without spirits; just as spirits could not exist without the world of men and women and children. But however strange

137

and unholy the land to which they are taking her, it will be better to die there, where her spirits will find some nourishment, than here, where her spirit must wander alone, starved, without the smallest consolation, forever.

To die here would be a great, destroying impiety.

She cannot understand the tall man whose skin is the colour natural to all real people—even to the strange people among whom she has been forced to lie naked, in whose presence she must perform the most intimate functions, with whom she must share food if she hopes to live.

The tall black man is quite plainly one held in the greatest respect by the white men who must wait on his judgement and permission before they can eat. He has his own place into which nobody but his white child can go, and from which the prepared food is issued. For three nights now he has come into the place where she lies chained from the place where food for all people is stored: a place which obviously only he can enter alone without the possibility of some random, hungry spirit entering at the same time and spoiling the food as it eats.

He has come, alone, for three nights, through a little door set low down in the wall, not more than a few paces from where she lies chained down in a darkness more dreadful and stupefying than anyone could ever have imagined, but which she must survive if the spirits of her ancestors and of her descendants are to know each other. They will never be able to do that if she allows herself to die in this foul, dangerous and unholy place.

She sleeps very little at night, in the darkness after they have been chained down, for she has a great deal to think about; and it is easier to think among the sounds of others sleeping— even under the weight of their stench and the noises of their distress.

The first night he came from the place of food beyond the wall, she had felt such fear that she had nearly voided and her breath had seized so that a swirling darkness different from the blackness in which they lay had passed across her eyes. She had not known there was a door in the wall between this place and the place of food, and when the light suddenly appeared she had been sure that some powerful and unpropitiated spirit had entered. For it was certain that many lost spirits must wander this endless water seeking a place to share with the living.

And then she had seen that the light was only one of those vessels with sides of white glass that contained a flame which had seemed so strange at first but simple enough when you thought about it. So when he straightened and held the light near his face, she was no longer cramped with the hapless dread you feel before a spirit whose needs you cannot know: she only waited, rigid with apprehension, for whatever new incomprehensible custom or ceremony the black leader of the white men was about to fulfil.

But he had only walked slowly down the narrow space between the wall and the shelves on which they lay chained, scarcely glancing at the bodies chained down, touching, from the floor into the darkness above the light he carried by his head. His progress was marked by the cautious scrape of iron on iron as those who were awake, or whom he had awakened, shifted to watch him. The shadow of his head and shoulders went before him, gliding over the shine of opened eyes and the closed faces that looked into troubled worlds of sleep.

She had known before he reached her that he would stop. How she had known this she could not say, but had felt only a certainty of search, a purpose in him of which she was the object. And feeling this, she had felt also the tense anticipation of the unpredictable leave her. He could not want her for the use that the little evil white man made of her sister's child, Mtishta. She was long past the time when any man but a husband would come to her for that.

So when he halted beside her, looking down, she had gazed back with curiosity, squinting against the light which he held above her head. His face above and behind the hard, white glare was flat, hazy, yet occasionally and incompletely vivid, forming from and dissolving back into the darkness, like a face in some very significant dream.

And then that flat, important, *messenger's* face had gone down into the darkness behind where she lay chained; down among the men, until she could see only a glow, no matter how hard she stretched against the chain and how far she turned her head on her lengthened, straining neck. She had heard his

139

voice, and another voice replying briefly on a rapid, breathy, humble pitch, but she had not been able to distinguish any word in anything that might be a language. In this place there were so many languages.

He had come back, the hard, white light in the glass held high, not glancing at her even as he passed; and she had watched the light lose its hardness and whiteness, diminish to a great, glowing eye as he bent and went through the little door into the place of food, leaving them in the darkness.

On his return, the second night, she had watched his light and waited for him, not only with interest but impatience. But he had passed her without turning his head, the light held high in his right hand seeming to cut his face in half so that the side away from it was swallowed in a small moving area of darkness deeper than the dark around it.

Again she had heard the murmur of his voice among the men, and the quick deferential voice replying, and then a rattle of iron. Then the glow far back in the darkness began to strengthen gradually, became the square of hard light, as he returned to where she lay. Behind him was one of the men and, though she could not understand why he had released him, she knew it was for some purpose of which she was to be a part and in which she would be happy to share.

As he lowered his light above her opened, questioning eyes, she had recognized the man behind him: the fat, young one, hardly more than a boy, with the woman's hips and the round face, whose eyes were always so quick when they came into the open in the mornings and who always finished the horrible food they must all eat if they were not to die before any of the other men. She did not know to which of the many strange people held in this place he belonged, but she knew him because she could not forget his deep-set, always-looking eyes and the eagerness with which he ate.

From behind the hard smear of white light, the black man in the white man's cloth had said something in the language she had heard used by many of the white men.

The man with the woman's hips, from a people she did not know, had come close, quickly and urgently, and said in the

140

language of her people, *Are you willing to do as this man asks?*

Yes, she had said.

The man had turned to the light and to the still, flattened face behind it and spoken another few words in the language of the white men, and was answered in the same sounds.

He says, the young, womanly, fat stranger had told her, *that he will kill you if you do not do exactly what he orders.*

Irritably she had said, *I will do what he orders. What does he want? And how do you talk in the language of my people?*

I speak many languages, he had told her proudly. *The two languages of the white men and the language of the Bakongo and the Luanda and many others and all the other slaves.*

You are a slave?

Yes. I have always been a slave. I was sold to this man who is like us but who is also like the white men. He says that this place belongs to him but that we must kill the white man to take it, when he releases us as he has released me, and that we must go to a country with him on this place after we have taken it.

Tell him, she had said, *that I will do as he orders and take this place but that I wish to go back to my own country.*

The fat, alert, woman-man had spoken back into the light then, in the language of the white men who were under the other white men in this place, and the face behind the light had opened briefly, with a curious sort of amused approval as the incomprehensible yet familiar sounds came from it.

He says you have no country anymore, the young man whose flesh glistened with woman's fat had said, *but that you must help him release all the people in this place when he tells you to do so and that he will take you where you will have your own country.*

What must I do? she had asked.

Wait, the young man had answered, *until I tell you how he will take this place from the white men and how he will release us all from this iron.*

Why? she had asked. *Why is he doing this? Why does he want us to take this place from the white men and to kill them? He belongs to the white men's people. He is a white man.*

The white men took his kingdom, the strange, womanish

141

man had said, *a long time ago, and now he will take it back.*

Even though he has no people here?

We will be his people if we come with him into his own country.

I will do what he says, she had told him, and the flat, still face behind the glare had dipped towards her before the man from the strange people had said, in the white man's language, what she had replied.

Then the tall black man had touched the shoulder of the fat one who could speak so many languages and they had gone back into the darkness where the males lay chained. She had heard the rasp of the lock as the fat young man was secured again. And then she had seen the glow of the lamp strengthening, and the tall black man had passed her without a glance, so that after he had gone she might have dreamed his coming and what had been said to her.

But it had been no dream, and now, in the congealed, nearly palpable heat and stench of the hold, Tadene lies chained against the girl from what she has learned are called the Bakongo people and who shivers all night in her trance-like sleep. Now she knows what she must do when she and the fat young man are released.

She does not fully understand how it will all be done, but she is quite content. Not even afraid that the white men may kill her when the tall black man moves to take back his kingdom from them. He will see to it that she is not killed, and she will be glad to live with him in his country and to be one of his people.

It is not where she would have chosen to die; but she knows that her life has only one meaningful choice left to it: to die in such a manner, even if the ceremonies are insufficient, that her spirit may yet be accessible to the living people.

And the tall black man in the white man's cloth is the only hope of such a choice. Between the hope of choice and no choice at all, she will gladly choose hope.

2

That dried-up old bitch is the luck I was waiting for. I knew there would have to be somebody to draw from in a cargo this size, but I couldn't have got better'n her if I had been dealing the hand myself. Nothing more comfortable to have at your back in the kind of business I've got in mind than a hard, hating woman. And she hates sure enough. I could see it in her eyes that time when I was going to have to pour food down the gal Reynolds took because she wouldn't eat. Right smart too. The way she carried on, all humble and scared, begging Reynolds and hugging him, and all the time it was there in her eyes that she'd have been at his throat if that was what would have served her purpose better. She'll ride herd on the niggers when I let 'em loose. No men I ever knowed won't fall in around a big, hard woman set on what she wants, same as bees round the queen. And with that Angola boy telling her and them what I want done, I can make it. So long as they don't go stamping and bucking around loose when I let 'em onto the deck. So long as they cluster like I tell 'em. If I could talk to her straight I'd feel a little more ease about everything. But she'll do. She'll do it the way I got set between me and the boy.

It's going to be that way, the way I've set it. Because it's been a damn long haul from the Delta to where I am now. And all I need now is a steady fresh of a breeze and a clear reach up to that goddam coast over there and I'll be into what I can take and hold and what I owe myself.

There ain't nothing owing to a man that he don't take when it offers, and I've taken what's been offered up to now; but there ain't no way I can take a breeze that ain't there and which is all I need to push me into what I aim to be. Into what I am.

Part Eight

THE POOP

CHAPTER FOURTEEN

1

Hogarth returned to the cabin at six bells in the middle watch. He was tired down to the bone with a weariness that owed very little to the time or to the measured back and forth pacing of the last two hours. With each passage from the break to the taffrail and back, memory had accumulated a new weight, become less controllable; until the past seemed to have become a formless and gluttonous monster with a life very much its own, devouring that sombre discipline by which he kept his nerve in balance and which he had come to substitute for peace of mind.

He entered the cabin with a care that was closer to stealth. To his overwhelmed, hurting imagination there was something dangerous, even malign, in every article and boundary of this austere territory he knew so well. He was horribly alone, wrapped in a sadness as strange and shapeless as his exhaustion—a sense of loss for something he could not name: because although it had been plain to him, it was inscribed in a language he could not read. He carefully lowered himself into the easy chair on the other side of the table from the settee. It yielded to his weight and shape like an accustomed lap.

As he carefully lodged his head into one corner of the angled back, he could see sleep as definite as mist rising from the level of his chest, obscuring his vision before he closed his eyes. And for a moment of longing so deep and so swift that it was like an assurance, he wished that he would never wake.

He did not wish for death; only that he would never have to wake into another bright morning.

She nearly called to him when he returned to the cabin. The words were there but in a language she could only understand, no longer feel. She knew the sleep he slept across the cabin in his chair and all that she could say and do to make his sleep a salvation in their bed; but there was no time for that anymore. The longest life was less than a breath and judgement was eternal. A chance had been offered her once to atone and it would not be offered again. The suffering that had gone before that moment when she had chosen the way was but the shadow to the terrible substance of the pain endured by those who turned aside even for an instant. For who could tell in what worldly instant we might be called to eternal judgement.

3

Why did Alex's words last night fill me with such dread and awe close to terror, almost close to superstition?

Had the world been different, cap'n, you'd have been where you are now ... like me ... We'd have come up on it a different way is all.

They sounded in my head like the strokes of a funeral bell. I felt utterly helpless; as if I had been carried bound to this time and this place to watch over the interment of all purpose and endeavour.

If he is correct, my life has been a waste. I will have lived with far less significance than a dog.

He knew what he was saying, fully understood the consequence of his terrible utterance. In all the time I have known him, from the days when he first approached me, I have never heard Alex use a word lightly. He considers, as he accepts the fruits of consideration, without anger or regret or remorse. Without pity—least of all for himself.

God in Heaven, perhaps he is the only free man on this ship. Perhaps he alone understands that he must act not because he chooses but because he is chosen for a purpose he may come to identify but cannot alter.

And if I recognize *that*, I must recognize that I am as much his creature as the blacks below are mine. I should have recognized that from the beginning when he proposed this venture. *His* venture. For I could only have been the missing need in a purpose we're both meant to fulfil ... My position, my little money, my skill—my very nature.

But how did he appraise me so readily? How could he have discerned that I was the one to bring us both to this place? And how could I have forgotten so quickly that it was I who surrendered to the temptation he offered. He has, in effect, invested me and all that pertains to me; and even if I get the captain's share, he will gain *his* for nothing. I laboured long and hard for what was put into this enterprise. I laboured for *him*: he has invested nothing save his appraisal of me.

And yet I feel no resentment; only a measure of astonishment at my obtuseness, nay, my superficiality.

For he must have perceived in me the instrument—no, let me call it by its true title, the slave—of the purpose we were both destined to fulfil, whether in this world or in another fashioned in a manner that I like to believe would have rewarded me with honour. He must have fathomed that self-pitying bitterness and maudlin corruption with which we so often delude ourselves as being righteous anger against injustices done to us.

Yes, Alex must have found me easy sounding that day he came aboard my ship as we lay in Havana. He must have read every shoal, hazard and shallow beneath the face I presented —with that confident knowledge closer to instinct which I have observed in the great pilots on so many of the world's treacherous deltas.

And yet what was he to me then? I an English captain, unencumbered owner of his own vessel—even if it were so modest a thing as the *Sure Salvation* when compared with the decks I had so recently commanded for owners who made no secret of their eager intention to recruit me into their ranks before I had added the profits of another half-a-dozen voyages to their ever-swelling coffers.

And *he*: a black. Albeit dressed as fine as any Cuban *hidalgo* in a suit of cream linen you could have drawn through a ring bolt without raising a wrinkle. And arrogant. No, I must not use that facile and inaccurate word which came to my mind as he strode aft to where I stood waiting for my mate and the customs officers to conclude their little exchange of bribery in the hold and ascend with the doctored manifest that would add a measure of illegal profit to the owner and captain of the *Sure Salvation*. God knows, I needed that extra and ignoble measure of profit.

No, arrogance was not the measure of the man who strode aft to me on that morning. And if, for a moment, I saw him in that light, it was because of his race and one did not take kindly to a black so unaffectedly at ease in a suit any Jermyn Street tailor would have been proud to see leave his shop on a gentleman's back. Nor did he bear himself with that deference and anxious hope of finding me in even temper which is habitual to any black, however dignified, when he approaches a white man in the slave countries. He walked the deck as though he had trod many better and thought little of what he now saw in the place to which business had perforce brought him. For he was no stranger to the sea and to ships. The quick and knowledgeable eye which he cast from the crosstrees to the capstan to the very set of the masts, and the shadow of disdain on his impassive face, filled me with shame. I should have felt anger at his unspoken impertinence, his damned nigger presumption, but instead I wished only to justify to him in what condition I had found the *Sure Salvation*; how much I had done to restore her to what she was even now—restoration accomplished on the profits of only two voyages from which I had taken scarce enough to feed Eliza and myself.

But the shame at the condition of my command—and the unseemly desire to share my censure of white men however deserving of it with a black—had gone by the time he reached me. Indeed, I felt angry with myself for having taken notice of him at all except as some agent perhaps, sent aboard by his master to seek my custom in chandling the *Sure Salvation*, or to negotiate favourable rates on some cargo up to Tampa which was to be my next port of call. The whites of Cuba and the slave states of America make great profit with little effort from

148

the industry and artifice of men manifestly their superiors in every respect save the curse of that race to which God has assigned them. I have seen one young mulatto carpenter in Savannah design and supervise the creation of houses as elegant as would grace a London square, while his fop of an owner, playing at being the architect, would have considered himself as doing an Adam or a Wren the greatest honour in offering them his hand as their equal.

So when Alex addressed himself to me, I made sure that my distaste for the gross and lazy system supported by the labour of him and his kind was plain in my manner.

But then it was very much an address he made, not a deferential approach—a polite address to be sure, but brisk and dry as between equals.

"Captain Hogarth?" he asked, although it was clear that his question was merely a rhetorical formality. "May I be permitted the honour of a word with you, sir?"

"Yes?" I said shortly. "What business do you represent? I am glad your master has the good sense to send a man who speaks English. I have but little Spanish."

For he spoke without any trace of the Spanish accent. Nor could I detect the sing-song flattening of our West India islands: a disagreeable speech in which vowels and consonants seem to be indolently assigned the same value.

He seemed quite unconcerned by my brusque reception. Indeed, in the shadow cast on that black, disconcertingly *interested* face by the brim of the wide-awake hat he wore—and which he had raised to me briefly in the precise and prescribed manner of one gentleman to another—I caught what might have been the twitch of an understanding smile. Worse, a smile of impersonal sympathy. In that instant, I resolved that were his master to offer me provisions at half the price of any other chandler in Havana, or cargo profitable enough to restore the *Sure Salvation* from her keel to the main royal, I would do no trade with him.

"Your business, man!" I repeated, very sharp. (But I did say "man", for I have never been able to bring myself to call a grown black, "boy": the loss of my dignity in so doing seems to me greater than his.) "You will observe that I am busy unloading.

149

If your master is in the chandling line, I am already provisioned. And I have no space in hold or on deck for so much as a box of cigars when I begin to take on cargo."

Again that knowing, that insufferable, flicker of a smile that might have been no more than a fleeting patch of sunlight entered under the shade of his hat brim.

"How much you payin' them, cap'n?" he asked, and gestured at the hold in which my mate and the two customs officers were coming to an understanding—in a language composed of halting English, primitive Spanish and fluent dishonesty—about the matter of undervaluing my cargo.

I told him. I swear I had begun to tell him to get off my ship before I had him thrown off, but what I heard myself saying was the price of the lowered duty on which we had tentatively agreed for the unloading of my cargo.

A full and fixed amusement came to his face then, but of a curious sort: not light-hearted but bleakly exhilarated, with a sudden, cold splinter in his eyes. I thought then—and I have often thought since—that I was seeing a black man's face for the first time. Not just the few singular features by which one distinguishes one animal in the same litter from another: but a face *whole* and one that belonged in company I would not care to cross or have look at me with less than regard.

"My, my, cap'n," he said. "If that's what they're askin' an' that's what you're payin', you might just as soon give them your goddam ship free an' clear, an' hope they'll get drunk enough to feel generous an' toss you enough to buy a corner in steerage on the next ship back to London . . . With your permission, sir, I would take a great fancy to have a word with those gentlemen below."

And with that—and certainly without my permission—he was down the ladder into the hold. Indeed, I heard him, speaking in Spanish, before I had properly realized that the authority with which he left me was as though I had conferred it on him rather than one which he had assumed as by right.

He returned to the deck fifteen minutes later, and I will always remember the respect and even pleasure with which the two customs officers looked on him, and the deference and embarrassment with which they treated me—as though they had not realized that they had been guilty of the gravest lapse in courtesy and punctilio in expecting me to descend to haggling with them when I had such a servant as Alex to conduct these necessary but vulgar transactions.

"You have guineas, cap'n?" Alex asked me.

"Why, yes." Had he asked me that amount of the pitiful savings I had lodged with Coutts at home, I believe I would have as freely confided it to him. "I always keep a few aboard. But why?"

"Give these thievin' sons of bitches fifty. An English guinea goes a long way among the smugglers on the Main now, an' it'll be less than what you'd have to lay out in Spanish dollars."

So I went to the cabin in which Eliza and I had shared our voyages ever since—ever since that day nearly five years ago, and in which it sometimes seemed we would share a thousand other voyages in sadness until the end of time—and unlocked the little iron-bound, steel-lined box of guineas bolted to the deck under the bunk. I counted out fifty and then, on an impulse, took an extra two. The fifty I wrapped in a sheet from an old newspaper—a copy of *The Times*, I remember, brought aboard three months before in Bridgetown; the two extra coins I put into my pocket.

I returned to where he stood beside the hold with the two customs officers and gave him the bundle of coins. He tossed it to one of them without appearing to observe the course of its flight. But it was caught expertly enough before it had scarce left his hand, and they left us saluting and smiling and as happy as any two jack tars with their gallantly earned prize money from some desperate engagement.

He called something to them as they reached the head of the gangplank and they laughed with a slightly hesitant but unmistakably obsequious appreciation before descending.

"What did you say to them?" I asked him, for my minimal, trading Spanish was quite inadequate against his rapid colloquial pleasantry.

"Nothing much, cap'n," he said. "Least nothin' as would be fittin' for a gentleman such as yourself to hear."

"Nevertheless, I would welcome a translation," I said. "I have been a sailor for over thirty years now and, although I will

151

not tolerate blasphemy, I appreciate the value of a little rib-aldry, now and then; and even an oath or two if it will relieve nerves under stress. What did you say to those two rogues to send them away in such high good humour."

He looked down at me, with his impassive (no, his consciously and habitually stilled) face opened now in a gentle, proprietorial amusement, as though he were assessing me.

"I told them", he said, "that with all that money you just give 'em, they could afford to stop their sisters workin' the streets and buy 'em both a couple of husbands—if the men was blind and with no bed to sleep on at nights except a bench in the park."

"Your humour is somewhat rough," I said. "Surely they must have resented such a brutal indelicacy?"

"Rough, Cap'n Hogarth? *Indelicate*? Sir, the things most folk have to learn to live with—just to keep on breathin'—any joke that's worse'n what they've got to live with is like prayer to a priest. But sort of said backwards, if you understand my meanin'. You joke 'em as to how things could be worse an' you put a little hope into them. So long as you don't touch on a man's mother, or go remindin' a woman she's a whore even if she is, there's a lot of rough jokes have given people the spirit for one more day of livin'."

The time had plainly come for me to assert myself, and the position my black invader had assumed with such casual assurance. His cavalier and economical handling of those two wretched, underpaid functionaries I could accept as I would have the service of any good dragoman or skilled artisan. But I was not in any mood to play the young Athenian pupil to his Aesop.

"You would appear to have the advantage of me, my man," I said. "You are acquainted with my name, although that you will have doubtless learned from the gazette. I do not know yours, (nor the nature of your master's business). Meanwhile, accept these as a token for what you have saved me."

He looked at the two bright English guineas I had dropped into his pink palm and then did a thing that set me tingling with indignation at an unthinkable impertinence—with a sense of outrageous impropriety that was far more upsetting than any anger. He stepped briskly to the bulwark and called to the little boys—of all colours from pure white through milked coffee to ebony—who dived from the wharves for coins thrown from the ships.

Olé, little ones! he shouted. *Here is English gold for the best man among you!*

I understood enough Spanish to translate what he said as the yellow discs glinted in the bright Cuban air towards the green water and a couple of dozen small, naked, male bodies cleft the green water almost simultaneously and threshed like a frenzy of sharks. Of the two boys who emerged, each with a guinea clamped between his teeth, one could have scarcely been above six years old: a quadroon the colour of pale honey from his long hair to his feet. The other was a black of perhaps twelve, with huge shoulders, a chest as deep as it was broad, and hands the size of a cutter's oar-blades.

The remarkable finale to this brief and violent drama was the silence that ensued when they had all regained the wharf against which we were berthed. They all sat in a circle around the lucky two; and the coins were passed from hand to hand; turned; examined; reverently fondled and returned with awe—as if to appointed priests—when each child had verified what had been thrown for them to compete for was indeed what had been promised. There was none of the usual chatter and discussion about the recovery of the small pieces for which they were accustomed to dive. Even when the two received their guineas back again, they sat for a long time, staring down at them, trying to imagine, perhaps the values of a substance beyond mere specie, or an achievement greater than their mere physical skill.

Had Alex proposed marriage, then, to the daughter I did not have—had he suggested that we claim descent from a common ancestor—he could not have done a greater violence to my sensibilities than his contemptuous disposal of my guineas.

I am not certain what words had begun to form in my affronted mind as we watched those common little wharf-rats below worship my money—but Alex spoke before I said what it might never have been possible to unsay.

"I have no master, Cap'n Hogarth," he said. "Leastways not

153

the kind of master you're thinkin' of. I come aboard to you because I hear you'll be needin' a cook, before you weigh out for Tampa, an' I'd be happy to serve the likes of you."

"You appear to show remarkable little concern for the rewards of service," I said. For the calculated insouciance with which he had flung away my tip affected me with a *physical* revulsion as inaccessible to what should have been a cool and even diverting analysis of his behaviour as indigestion or a toothache. My rank and class in this life will condone—or at least treat with a near-affectionate rough justice—minor offences such as theft, deceit, immorality, even murder, on the part of our inferiors. By such acts they assure us of our appointed rights and duties and obligations—even if we have to hang or flog or imprison them. But assumption of equality attempts to usurp our behaviour and earned attitudes, constitutes the challenge we must meet with implacable harshness: with cruelty if harshness proves insufficient a lesson. There is a frailer safeguard between the chaos of the mob and the order we maintain than there is between this cabin and the savage creatures below whose children may someday learn of the salvation which their parents can no more imagine than an ape can understand the sempiternal laws of our universe.

And yet even as I tried to dismiss Alex that day in Havana harbour—with all that chilling denial of recognition which is a more crippling and painful weapon of my class than the most direct abuse—I was aware that he was armoured against it, if indeed he was aware that I was employing it all.

"Hell, Cap'n Hogarth," he said, "if I'd guessed you was goin' to get so riled 'bout a couple of guineas flung to a few little chaps who don't see more than one dinner a week when they're lucky, I'd have suggested you do it yourself, sir, an' give yourself the pleasure. Look at 'em, sir. Ain't one of them won't dream tonight of the English captain who gave his nigger gold for them to show him how fine they could swim."

Thus he rebuked me for daring to treat him less than one of my rank, and thus I recruited him.

Or, rather, thus he recruited me.

For the next thing I found myself saying was, "What is this

about becoming my cook? I have a cook. He's ashore until two bells in the first dog watch, but . . ."

"You *had* a cook, cap'n." The interruption was so elegant it could have been the courtesy of one gentleman touching another on the arm to prevent him stubbing his toe into an unobserved fault on a sidewalk. "You had a cook. Leastways you had one of those bleached-out Caymanian sawneys looks as if they was fathered by their uncles or their own grandmothers. From what I seen of your crew—from the looks of *you*—that son of a bitch don't know much more than how to catch a fire an' boil water without burnin' it . . . Still he ain't goin' to be rottin' your innards, nor those of any other poor devil of a sailorman as never done him any harm for quite a spell. Mebbe never if the good Lord is merciful."

"What d'you mean? And how d'you know of him? Has the scoundrel jumped ship?"

"No, he ain't jumped ship, cap'n. Truth is, I doubt me he'll be doin' much jumpin' over anythin' again. He tried to take on a little high yaller gal down in that place they call Floridita, couple of hours ago, an' it seems as if she didn't want to be taken on an' there was this big stoker off that Spanish gunboat anchored down the stream—an' *he* didn't seem to want the high yaller lady taken on by your cook neither . . . So what with one thing an' another, cap'n, that Caymanian, who shouldn't be allowed to feed grass to a mule, is lyin' in the seaman's hospital with his leg broke an' his head a mite stove in an' a finger or two they're trying to sew on. I coulda told him not to go grabbin' for that knife the high yaller gal pulled from a place no respectable brought-up young lady would ever think of decoratin' with anything but a pretty little bow or some lace mebbe, but he never give me no time to offer him my advice, an' anyway I was afeard the high yaller gal an' that big stoker might take it into their fool heads I was a friend of his and send me to keep him company in the hospital just so as he wouldn't have to lie there all by himself bein' lonesome. Some of your other crew was in the Floridita too—which is how I came to hear about you and the cook. For they certain sure wasn't givin' him any assistance when the Spanish stoker and the yaller gal was makin' things all miserable for him . . . Fact

155

is, cap'n, when I left they was buyin' drinks for that gal and the stoker. If'n he gets himself too near to the boilers tomorrow he's like to burn like a Christmas puddin' from all the brandy they've poured into him.

I could not help myself. Against my every instinct and residual resentment of his insolence, I found myself grinning. Not smiling, but grinning like a schoolboy.

"You tell a good story, my friend," I said, "and most of it is sordid and customary enough to be true ... But d'you expect me to believe that real sailors, men who bend canvas, would buy drinks for a stoker. Come, man! That is an embroidery. You should have known better than to decorate your yarn with such an improbable touch."

"Cap'n Hogarth, sir." And here he too grinned—perhaps the only time I have ever seen his face so relaxed in the five years I have known him. "Cap'n, if these two eyes hadn't seen it, I'd feel just about what I truly understand you're feelin' now. Any man come to me without introduction—as I've just come to you—an' tell me he seen canvas-bendin' sailors buyin' drinks for a stoker an' I'd call that man a liar, an' prove it on his hide if'n he didn't allow as how he was tellin' a tall one ... But I seen it, sir. After they put the third glass into his hand, I *had* to believe it."

"It would appear that I signed on a bad cook," I said, cordially, but distant again, regretting my moment's lapse into egalitarian affability with this black freebooter who seemed determined to convey that he was choosing a captain rather than offering himself to a captain as a cook.

"If what I seen of your crew is the measure of how he's been feedin' 'em, cap'n, I surely don't know how you've got this far without mutiny, or how any man's had the strength to haul himself higher'n the crossjack."

"And you would like to offer your services?"

"I would."

"You have served at sea before?"

"You know I have, cap'n."

"On vessels of greater worth and founding than this, of course?"

"Of course."

"So why do you offer to me? If you are as good as you claim, there must be many captains who would be more than happy to sign you on. A good cook is rarer than a good mate or a bos'un."

"I'm between fortunes, cap'n. I need a berth. An' I admire what I can plainly see you mus' keep puttin' back into this barque. I like to serve with a man who cares scrupulous for what he commands."

"And when your fortunes turn?"

"Why I'll leave you for somethin' better. But you'll have had me for what'll help you make this into the ship you're aimin' at. I ain't only good, Cap'n Hogarth. I'm the best."

"You rate yourself highly."

"I rate myself as high as I am, an' I'm probably higher than even that. But a man ought to practise a little humility from time to time."

"I doubt that the wages I could offer would pay for your clothes," I said, "nor for your aristocratic disdain of vulgar guineas. There are men in England—white men, officers on half-pay—who would have brought home joyously what you flung to those children just now, and lived on it for a week."

"I wear good clothes, cap'n," he said "because they last longer an' cost cheaper no matter how long you have to wear 'em. An' they never look anythin' else but good no matter how old they get. Fact is the older they get the better they look, because folks feel you've had the right to wear 'em so long you just don't think about gettin' anything new. An' as for wages. If'n you an' me decide to sign articles, I don't want no coin passed across your table to me. You give me authority to spend what you aim on provisionin' your command for any voyage an' leave me to do the buyin'. I'll take my rightful fair commission off the top of what you want put into your stores."

"Ah!" I said, and a soothing, cynical relief, like the demonstration of a theorem which had hitherto been eluding me, brought me back to the reality of relationship between me and this black dodger who trespassed my deck so jauntily. "So that is your method is it? I understand why you are between fortunes as you put it. You purchase, with my money, at your discretion, and make your fortune with no accounting. No wonder

157

you need a berth. My only bewilderment is that you have lasted so long. I cannot imagine you could have met so many gulls and fools on the fine ships on which you claim to have served. How many captains have you beggared?"

To this day, I can summon up the—no, not the contempt—but the weariness, the *boredom* of disappointment, that animated his impassive face.

"I guess I made a mistake, cap'n," he said. "From what your crew told me about you, I figured as how I was goin' to be dealin' with a gentleman . . . How much was you figurin' on for feedin' this crew between here and Tampa?"

I told him.

"An' how much was you payin' that Cayman sawney for poisonin' your men?"

"Ten dollars a week."

"I'll provision you for half what that white mongrel could get from the best chandler in this stinkin' Spanish port, an' I'll take fifty dollars a week along with the personal extras the chandlers'll be happy to sweeten me with an' I'll have your crew fillin' out like gaming cocks two days after I start feedin' 'em—an' I'll bring you back change you'd never have seen if you or that Cayman booby tried to do the buyin' yourselves . . . But if you can't trust me for that, you ain't the cap'n I heard talked of."

And with these words he was about to turn on his heel, with a fine swing of the skirt of his linen coat, when I did what I had never done before, or even imagined doing. I shook a black man's hand.

"My hand on it," I said, and took his black paw with as true a feeling as though he had been a British officer sent to me with highest recommendation. "My hand on it, my dear fellow. And if you can cook half as well as you can talk, I am your debtor. How much will you need to provision us for Tampa?"

"Let those sons of bitches provision us," he said, "an' then I'll tell you what to give 'em. What they give *me*, for gettin' what you give them, is my business."

And it was then that the thought came to me, as I looked at my hand in his, and I asked him, with a sense of possible loss, of a possible loneliness: "You are not a runaway? You are no

158

Cuban slave, that's certain, but you are obviously from the Southern States and we shall be in a dozen ports there during the next three months. I could not afford claim laid on for illegal possession of another man's property."

"Like I told you," he said. "I don't have no master—except you since you shook my hand—an' you an' me can sail into any port from Tampa to New Orleans an' there ain't a man can touch me anymore than he can touch you."

And with that, he put his hand into the inside pocket of his coat and extracted a long wallet of pale, grainless leather fine and supple as silk. He observed my interest, and said, as he took a neatly folded, legal-looking document from it, "Belly-skin from a young Apache who figured that he or me was one too many for the whole goddam Mex border . . . Don't look like that, cap'n. He was dead when I cut it off him. He didn't even know what he was bein' deprived of. An' there ain't nothin' cures nicer than skin from a prime buck who's never been sick an' who's been shot clean dead just when he's feelin' real mean an' perky."

He was not playing me for effect; not boasting as he passed me the heavy-bonded document from the finely fashioned container. He was describing a simple ritual in which there was no room for hesitations and in which any subsequent compromise on the part of the victor would have dishonoured the defeated or failed to observe ancient rules that made the whole contest meaningful.

He was paying a compliment to my rank and understanding. Judicious flattery has always been the great seal between the true gentlemen of history.

Be it known, the document read, *that Alexander Delfosse is the free born Negro child of my freed and manummitted Negro, Polydore Delfosse, and his duly married wife, Eulalia. Born this day, February 4, 1819, in the territory of Louisiana, in the County of Orleans, and that said child, Alexander Delfosse, is my ward, charge and heir to freedom in perpetuity. In instance of which, I hereby assign property of $500 (Five Hundred Dollars) to said Alexander Delfosse, lodged in his name, and to be used at his discretion on his attaining maturity, in the*

Bank of Louisiana, as he sees fit. And that said Alexander Del-fosse, Negro, and born free by my manumission and will, is, in perpetuity, ward, charge and free man of all courts in the States, Territories and Occupancies of the United States of America, or in any Lands over which the United States of America, or its Officers, may Exercise control.

And that, in further witness of this document, I have hereby lodged copy of this declaration with the Supreme Court of the United States in the City of Washington, District of Columbia, the Supreme Court of the Territory of Louisiana, and with my bankers, Laporte and Royce, of Senlieu Street, in the City of Louisiana. So help me God as I now stand god-father to this free-born Negro child on this fourth Day of February, in the Year of our Lord, Eighteen Hundred and Nineteen.

> *Sgnd. Jean-Paul Delfosse*
> *& Witnessed by Marie Delfosse (his wife)*
> *Esmond Travalle (Attorney)*
> *Jacques Laine (Clerk to said Attorney)*
> *Polydore Delfosse &*
> *Eulalia Delfosse,*
> *their marks,*

Last witnesses being duly freed and manumitted Negroes by said Jean-Paul Delfosse before birth of their child, Alexander, whose Christian baptismal is duly attached as performed by an accredited priest in the chapel of my estate of L'Esprit in the Territory of Louisiana, United States of America, on the Seventh Day of February, 1819.

There was a smaller document, a gilt-edged card, with a border of illuminated, insipid flowers and a blue, gold and white figure of Christ on the Cross above the name of some church or chapel, the name of which I have forgotten, and Alexander Delfosse's name inscribed and notice of his baptism under the signature of one Père Joseph Bernard, and the date, *7 février, 1819;* and all in French.

I studied the paper legitimizing his freedom, and the one

authenticating his membership in our community of Christian souls, and returned them to him and watched as he stowed them with care in that handsome wallet.

"You would appear to be what you claim," I said. "If those are forgeries, they have been executed by a master hand."

Again that fleeting disc of a smile at the corner of his mouth.

"I'm what I claim to be, Cap'n Hogarth. You can be certain sure of that ... An' now, I'm goin' to see what you've got laid aboard 'fore I go into town among the chandlers. I don't doubt there's a whole heap of swill they'll take off my hands in 'change for decent vict'ls, knowin' they'll be able to sell 'em back again to some jobbernowl like that Caymanian who has pretty near reduced a fine man like you to somethin' looks like a nigger scarecrow in a cornpatch."

And he matched himself to his word. For in the three days between unloading my British goods from Barbados and Jamaica and loading tobaco and timber for Tampa, Alex provisioned the *Sure Salvation* in a fashion that would have had my crew working for half their wages were that the condition of their service.

A couple of large blacks, obviously very much in his fear or service, or perhaps both, brought his gear aboard that afternoon and the midshiphouse became his.

After that, I seldom saw him except in the early mornings when he departed; and in the late afternoons when waggons of food would be driven to the wharf and unloaded by blacks under his direction, and much of what I had laid aboard in Kingston was taken off and put into the same waggons.

Three times he requested me to meet him in the midshiphouse, where he spoke rapid, incomprehensible Spanish to pale Cubans, who appeared only too eager to stand well in his favour, and told me what money to give them.

It was astonishingly less than I had anticipated. He must have driven some ruthless bargains in return for the Kingston stores he had exchanged for theirs. Though I have little doubt they did not intend to suffer loss on the exchange.

One of them offered me a cedar chest of a thousand cigars and a dozen cases of their fine light rum, and Alex addressed

161

him with a furious scorn I would have hesitated to employ to a lascar wharfhand and ordered him from the ship . . .

But the cigars and the rum remained and were conveyed to captain's stores, under my seal.

"Hell, cap'n," he told me, "I know you don't drink none but a gentleman's ration of wine, an' a little brandy, an' that you don't like smokin'. But you pass a few of these cigars an' a couple bottles of this rum among the trash you'll be treatin' with in the Gulf ports an' they'll be totin' cargo for you on their own backs. Couldn't have them Cuban waggon traders, though, thinkin' that *my* cap'n was to be influenced in his buying by a few rolls of tobacco an' a couple hundred bottles of rum."

"But they're *yours*, Alex," I protested. "You are well aware that every favour extended to this ship these last three days is because of your enterprise. You must have the advantage of such goods when you begin trading in the Gulf ports."

"They're yours, cap'n," he said flatly, "an' I've put your seal on 'em; an' you can fling 'em overboard if you like once we clear into the Gulf. But they's yours to dispose of as you see fit . . . I've taken what I figure is rightly mine; an' that's how it's goin' to be between me an' you, Cap'n Hogarth, for as long as we sail together. I don't take more than I'm owed an' I've earned, sir. An' what I've took so far from what you've allowed me isn't a cent more nor a cent less than what's deservin' to me."

And it was then, in the twilight, that we saw across the harbour, the Yankee clipper heeled over under the north-easter swelling her full spread as she entered the channel under the Morro Castle; and even at that distance I knew her for what she was.

You could no more mistake one of the great slavers in those days than you could a racehorse for even the finest hunter; there was a *gait* to them, inspired by the desperate men who sailed them through the vigilance of the world's navies.

One hundred guineas a head for every soul landed to labour in the Cuban sugar fields or Brazil; and a man who eluded the blockade for three voyages could lay the foundation stone of a great and respected house in the New World. Still can, although the trade is all but done; and as steam improves it must end altogether.

"*The Raven*," Alex said beside me. "Cap'n Standish commandin'. He could take that ship in and out of a naval dockyard, at high noon afore the smartest crew could raise an anchor or sight a gun on him. He's pushin' his luck a mite, though, considerin' the number of hauls he's made from Africa to here an' to Brazil; but he's cleared close to a million dollars doin' it."

"You seem to know the gentleman."

"Me an' him is acquainted you might say. One time in Charleston he tried to claim me as one of his'n run off from his plantation—he's got a little dried-up piece of land in South Carolina, an' I fitted the description on the notice pretty close I got to admit. But when I presented those papers I just showed you, he ended up havin' to settle five hundred dollars on me for the damage an' pain an' disrepute he'd brought on a free citizen of the United States."

It was obvious that there was more to what had transpired in Charleston between Standish and Alex than what I was being told, but I did not press for a full explanation. The Southern States of America comprise a huge territory of complex, incestuous relationships which no stranger can hope to understand—least of all those strangers in the North with which it shares the continent. It is destined for a terrible suffering and humiliation not many years from now. I see the foreshadows of this plainer and plainer each time I touch upon it. But I sense in it, also, the beginnings of a great, tribal strength coming into being between its miserable blacks and its savage whites such as may one day astonish the world. They are creatures emerging from a wilderness who may yet stable their horses in our cathedrals and inherit our crowns.

"Captain Standish will bear you a grudge for that occasion in Charleston," I said to Alex then. "It might be advisable that you do not go ashore, where you might meet him or any of his men, until he has sold off his cargo. You are a free man, Alex, and signed to a British captain, but you are a black, and even I could not protect you if an honoured slaver or his servants decided to do you a damage in Havana ... Nor should you trust yourself if, meeting with him by chance, you were not seized with anger at the foul trade he still pursues among our people."

And here I must correct my previous statement about seeing Alex's face in open amusement only once in five years. For now he did not only grin, but laughed. A full, kindly and infinitely condescending acknowledgement by experience of my innocence.

"Standish don't ply no foul trade, cap'n," he said. "An' whatever trade he plies, it sure as hell ain't among *my* people. It's black men sells black men to Standish—exceptin' for a few Portuguese who don't hardly count as white. If it wasn't for all them black kings an' chiefs an' high an' mighties along the Africa coast, Standish wouldn't have no more than that little parcel of South Carolina scrub I told you of. An' if whoever sold my great-grandpappy or whoever to whoever it was looked like Standish or you is *my* people, then I want another people ... No, Standish is runnin' too damn close to where he's goin' to get himself caught and hanged. But that's because he's a greedy son of a bitch, or likes to risk a damn sight more'n than's healthy ... But he runs his trade brave and skilful, cap'n, an' I'd be a born liar if I didn't say as how I admire the fashion he's playin' it out way past where he should be pressin' his luck. Standish didn't make the trade he's bringin' in on the *Raven,* Cap'n Hogarth. The trade was there both sides of the water, jus' waitin' an beggin' for a Standish to do it. An' he's more man than the bastards who'll be biddin' on his deck tomorrow mornin' for the goods he's brought 'em 'gainst the chance of his own neck stretched 'cause he couldn't get enough wind to put his stern twenty miles ahead of some damn steam-patrol gunboat bustin' its boilers to even catch sight of his topgallants in a telescope.

"An' I goin' to say one more thing to you, Cap'n Hogarth, 'bout Standish and the trade. If there'd been one, only one, black man on every ship swore to kill one white sailor on every voyage made ever since the trade began way back—three, four hundred years ago—even though he knew he was goin' to get himself killed doin' it, there wouldn't have been no trade. If every piece of white trash who ever signed on to take charge of three, four hundred niggers across three months of ocean had never knowed whether he wasn't goin' to be the one endin' up with a chain wrapped tight round his neck or with his gut trailing in the scuppers, you'd never have had the trade ... If you don't promise a man a death solemn, cap'n, he'll take his chance on the hope you might forget about it. But you promise, an' keep your promise, an' you establish trust between him an' you."

And with these words he left and went to the midshiphouse he had so quickly made his new domain, as I watched the *Raven* come about as neat as a scull at Henley—flying, standing and inner jibs furled as by a sorcerer's hand, fore-topgallant, main royal, mizzen royal, jigger-topmast staysail and spanker-topsail clewed—and the beautiful ship turn to her rest on a breath into the jigger-topmast staysail as the spanker boom was swung across the plunge of her anchor below the surface of the harbour.

And I watched and thought of the value of her cargo, and of the principles that kept me from carrying the value of such a cargo ... For good as the man Standish might be, I knew I was better. As Alex had said about himself, I rated myself as high as I was—even better—but a man must practise a little humility from time to time.

And I looked, and thought of the other disdained, contemptuously uncomprehended principles because of which I had lost the chance of approved and authenticated fortune and found myself at over forty years of age, reduced to grubbing for cargoes from small men in ports of chance in such a vessel as the *Sure Salvation*.

Yes, principle, rectitude, a sense of honour—whichever of the fine titles we give to what we practise so ostentatiously as long as they do not inconvenience us unduly—had done me out of fortune and position more surely than the disreputable conduct, the breach of faith, into which I was so warmly urged and by which, I must confess, I was so nearly tempted.

For the Devil showed me an engaging—nay, ingratiating—face that November afternoon ten years ago in the great board-room of Llewellyn and Oates, and spoke persuasively, with a wordly wisdom, almost as though chiding me as an equal, to be conscious of my duty and social obligation. And who knows whether, but for those two whose example and love so brightened my childhood, I would not have allowed myself to be persuaded. It would not have been hard for one of my kind to justify betrayal as, at worst, an embarrassing necessity—and there would have been many to console me out of the embarrassment and even congratulate me on my sensible perception of duty's demand.

And I must concede that, at first, they treated my predicament with proper concern and my scruples with respect. They behaved with the most proper hypocrisy and regard until the hour began to grow late and they felt their dinners calling.

Nor did they have to—since they had summoned me to make as generous an offer as could have been expected of them ... Indeed more, since they were gifting me with a directorship on a new line for which I had, to be sure, begun to make a name in the East, because of my acumen and old acquaintance in those parts, but to which I could contribute little in the way of capital save the exiguous accumulation that had come to a captain who had plied those waters for well over twenty years and ventured his own pay on private arrangements which in no manner affected the profits he had sworn to seek for his owners.

Yes, I had served men like Harry Llewellyn well, ever since I had sensed that the East India Company with its political entanglements was no longer the best venture in which to invest for highest returns in that great ocean beyond Singapore where there are few rules and little interference from jacks-in-office scarce different from Whitehall clerks, too long established in their own systems and courts and procedures. There were profits to be made in that vast reach of water, on islands half as large as continents, by men with money and game enough to risk losing a plunger or seeing it come back to them ten-fold.

I had sensed this new area of venture for our race many years before the Mutiny was even dreamed of, and the dull, predictable career the John Company had become, with its fine salaries for its servants like me and its safe returns, regular as excise, for its directors. And I cannot fault Harry Llewellyn or Oswald Oates for the dash with which they put their horses

166

to the gate and were first in at the kill when I opened the East for them.

Nor could I ever fault them for the appreciation they were prepared to bestow on the man who had done nothing for them except venture their ships and their cargoes among people on his word alone, and who had established them, in five years, among the greatest merchant magnates in Europe.

It was more than material valuation of my worth to them, I think. There was *liking*. Especially in the case of Harry Llewellyn, who I had brought back to his faith. And Oswald Oates who was waiting on his promised title with the anticipation of a boy for his birthday present, and who was as determined to have me as his brother-in-law as was his gentle and obedient little sister fixed in her mind that William Hogarth was to be her husband once he was no longer merely her brother's chief captain but his fellow director.

And I am not unaware of the irony and irrationality of it all that my probity, my faithfulness to obligation, my subscription to the Christian usages which I imbibed as joyous habits from my mother and father, brought me no resolutions but only the final impatient dismissal by men who had looked on me as a friend who would enhance their fortunes, the refused flesh of a woman who had once offered herself to me as she would have turned her face to the sun, and now a cargo that I would have repudiated ten years ago had I been offered the opportunity to convey it from the uttermost darkness to the Gates of Paradise.

I will make amends. I will make amends. Perhaps that is what is contained in Alex's last words to me last night.

We are brought to wherever we are to make amends. And even with what I have come to, I shall seek to promote among the unfortunate of this world something of the loving sanctity of those two who made my childhood so joyous.

Those two whose nurture and example were responsible for my refusal to succumb to the persuasion of those voices in the boardroom in Old Lombard Square ten years ago, and my refusal of the understanding indulgence, the approbation, that would have glowed in those faces around the mahogany had I agreed to join them in a conspiracy which, to give them

167

their due, they did not see as a conspiracy at all but only as the necessary settlement of a small debt I had somewhat carelessly contracted . . .

Those voices!

I can hear them now, across ten years, clearer almost than I can Alex's last words to me a few hours ago. As I can see their faces duplicated in the shining wood. There was a warmth in that room—from the two great fires, from the deep carpets, from the furniture built as if for descendants who would be twice our size—but which was itself only a reflection, like the faces in the polished depths of the table-top of a more substantial warmth. One of the curtains had been imperfectly drawn, leaving a gap wide enough for me to see from where I sat the drift of a restless brown fog across the roofs beyond the window. It was a curious fog, now thick enough to all but obscure vision, now thin enough to half reveal buildings as through a veil of gauze. It kept presenting and hiding from me, the dome of St Paul's where it reared against the low, sullen sky, a quarter of a mile away . . .

"Now damme, William," Harry Llewellyn was saying to me that afternoon, and the genuineness of his exasperation was part of that warmth by which we were all so effectively insulated against the drifting, thickening and thinning fog and the raw air and low, blackening sky into which the dome of St Paul's was set. "Now, William, listen, damn your ears, and stop lookin' as if you ought to be taken straight from here and burnt at the stake or made to do unnatural penitence the rest of your natural life.

"Your sentiments do you credit, my dear old fellow. I say that upon my word of honour. And if there's a man around this table don't share my opinion on that then he's no gentleman. If you hadn't told us what you've just related, and hadn't suggested what you propose to do, I'd have lost a deal of the regard I've come to feel for the William Hogarth who's dragged me back to attendance at me own church, at the tail of me own horse, whenever he's been back in England an' a guest in my house . . . But what you propose is preposterous—although I would have expected no less of you. And I won't permit you to do it. I will not allow the finest captain in England and a gentle-

168

man who has become one of my most valued friends to ruin the great future I shall be honoured to share with him . . . Nor will Oswald Oates here, if I know my man. Eh, Oswald?"

Oates looked up from an abstracted contemplation of himself in the table-top and turned his face to me. He shared, in a masculine way, much of his sister's slight, nay, delicate, gentle, fair good looks, and Harry Llewellyn who had been at school with him once told me—when it was beginning to make sense that we were all close on our way to becoming partners—that he had been much teased and bullied there at first, for his girlish appearance . . . Until the day he had publicly slapped the face of one of his older tormentors and assured him that as soon as he, Oates, was of an age, and they both out of school, he would again slap him before a witness of gentlemen and leave it to him as to whether they both took the next packet to France to settle the matter with loaded pistols on the beach at Calais or Dunkerque.

"Oh, they toasted him for it, William," Llewellyn had told me. "They had to, y'know, for form's sake. They turned him before the common-hall fire like a little lamb on a spit, an' tossed him from a blanket so high I thought they'd send him clean through the ceiling . . . But there wasn't a bigger boy ever laid a hand on Oswald Oates after that night, and every one of them afterwards spoke him as respectful as if he was already one of them . . . For he meant it, y'know! Child though he was . . . And the dullest lout among 'em knew they'd witnessed a vow that could only be discharged by an encounter or an apology . . . Which apology he got, by the way, from the boy he had slapped —four years later when Oswald was seventeen and just down from the school. He got it in Ludd's gaming house, with a handshake from his old torturer, and much laughing and chaff and backslapping from the rest of us, and jolly talk of old schooldays and boys will be boys. But we were dead serious beneath the jokes and the pretence of tipsiness, because those of us who knew Oswald realized he had come there to claim his right to satisfaction on the body of a poor fool who was no more grown as a man save that he was a bigger fool than he had been as a boy."

And looking at Oswald Oates' face across the table that

November afternoon, I wondered how even rough, innocent boys could have made such a mistake about him, even when he was a child. For there was in his gentle, close to feminine, delicacy of feature, the pleasure of one who loves himself and loves his neighbour so near as himself, that he will live and plan for consummation once his desires for doing a favour or extracting a revenge are aroused.

"Harry's right, of course, William," he said to me then. "We cannot permit you the mistaken honour of this folly you purpose, if we have to put you in chains and ship you off to the Celebes or some other wild place until you come to your senses." And here an edge sharpened the genuine concern of his voice—a badinage and mockery not meant ill, but a knowing, sardonic banter that cut deeper than he could possibly have realized as he invited me to share his generous envy of, and sympathy with, my predicament.

"You sly dog, William. Hauling poor Harry off to church every Sunday these last five years whenever you've stayed with him, and reducing him to wearing a hairshirt when he rises to make one of his famous humanitarian speeches in Parliament; and all the while tumbling one of his prettiest tenants every chance she gave you Mondays to Saturdays . . . And I'll warrant she put plenty of chance your way, eh? Rain or shine, these country girls know where a gentleman in need will always find it snug to lodge."

"Oswald!" Harry Llewellyn protested, and I was satisfied, at least, that my influence on him over the last five years had roused that much Christian sensibility in a breast that would formerly have accepted Oates' callousness as the commonplace of exchange between our sort.

"Oswald! Eliza Manning is not a common farm-girl. She is the daughter of one of my most respectable, and respected, tenants. A man of substance. And she has been educated too. Dammit, Oswald, she is—she is a woman you'd be proud to strut with, her hand on your arm, down any street in England."

"And with a damn sight more than her hand on my arm," said Oates drily, "if what Hogarth's had from her by his telling . . . But tell me, Harry, is she a lady? Can William take her into the places where she'll have to be a wife among wives of

170

the men who're going to turn us into the enterprise that'll make John Company look like coastal trade in twenty years?"

"Well, no," Harry Llewellyn said reluctantly. "She's a fine, respectable young woman, and it's been my hope these last five years she'd marry young Dodd down at Calcroft. I'd like to see those two holdings merged under a good man and wife. But she ain't a lady, although she speaks as well as many you address at any reception and . . ."

"At *your* reception, Harry?" asked Oates, drier than stones rattling in a tub. "At *your* receptions in the Hall. You would wish to introduce her to the Duchess of Sherwood, perhaps, as the wife of William Hogarth, our partner who is going to help make this company the greatest financial influence in the land before the century is three-quarters through? Come now, Harry, I won't take your cant . . . William, I can understand. He's a Christian and more of a gentleman that you'll ever hope to be, and he's got a good woman with child and feels he must marry her . . . And I'm sorry, William, if I made light of your agony of conscience a moment ago . . . but it won't do, y'know, my dear boy. It won't do at all. We'll have to buy off this woman and her people, and buy them off damn generous. I'll stand surety to half of whatever you gentlemen decide. But Llewellyn and Oates can't go into what we're about to capture with a partner wed to a farm wench. If you were to be one of our captains only, William, it wouldn't matter to me if she was your landlady's daughter. But you're a sight more than that, and you know it. You're a Hogarth, and there's men you've never met who'll be claiming old acquaintance once its known that you're moving money around the world from this room. And you'll be worse than useless to us, and to yourself, if you insist on marrying a milkmaid . . . What d'you say, your Grace?" he added to our chairman, the Duke of Sherwood, who was our great catch: a lean, brutal, old stick whose hitherto worthless lands had suddenly begun to yield coal when he was reduced to living in one wing of a castle falling into ruin over his ugly head, and who now held the chairmanship of as many companies as could find somebody influential enough to introduce them to his new fortune and his ancient title.

"Heh! Heh!" said the Duke. It was one of his practices of

war that he pretended deafness, although he was no more deaf than the bats I have seen skimming between the rigging of any ship at anchor in port. "What's that you said, Oates? Hogarth wants to marry a farmer. How the devil can he do that? A man can't marry a man. That's sodomy. They'd have us all in gaol or hanged or something equally unpleasant. Why does Hogarth want to marry a farmer?"

"Not farmer, your Grace," Oates said. "A farmer's daughter. She is with child by him."

"Well, if it's a boy, we'll put him to sea an' hope he'll be half the captain his father is. An' if it's a girl, I'll help dower her into a good marriage with another farmer—but Llewellyn'll have to go most of it on the dowry if it's a girl. The woman is his people, after all, an' he should have kept a better eye on her . . . Hogarth can't marry the gel, of course. I believe me an' him are related if we go back far enough, an' my people were damn proud to get his into the family. Did y'know that, Hogarth?"

"No, your Grace," I said, and but for his age and the distance that separated us across the table, I believe I would have risen and boxed him across his pretended deaf ears.

"And, William," said Harry Llewellyn, "are you sure that pup is yours? I'll grant that Eliza Manning is no easy-open country lass such as would have entertained any great gentleman willing to drop his trousers as innocent and generous as if he'd asked for one of her fine apples . . . But she's a farmer's daughter, and you've been out of England nine months at a time these last five years. There's a dozen fresh young farmers around my parts could have put her in the family way while you were abroad an' only too happy to lay the seeding on you . . . I'm not blaming you, man. Had I your address and ardour, I'd have cuckolded you myself while you were abroad. I've seen her and lusted, and wished I had the presence you plainly have when you're not church-going and improving your soul or trying to save mine . . . But is the child yours?"

"It is mine," I said. "Eliza Manning has been as faithful to me these last five years as I have been to her."

And when Oswald Oates raised his girlish eyebrows, at my statement, I knew I lied . . . Because despite what had taken place between Eliza Manning and myself over five years, in the

172

bracken of the combe, in the long, green grass of the woods around Bourne, and in half-a-dozen rooms from Avon to Wapping, I knew that I had been faithless ... Not in the vulgar, physical way of faithlessness all too available to a captain with a full purse and a fine piece of Eastern jewellery bought for a song in some bazaar or purchased from some sailor for the price of a drink; but faithless in my heart.

The prospects which Llewellyn and Oates had opened before me—not only with the dry, cool calculation of mutual profit, but with the pleasure of men finding a new friend of their rank to share an adventure—and my ambition and God-knows-what unsuspected taint of false pride: all had combined to make me more faithless than the idlest young lecher with nothing more to do with his time than hunt the countryside for cunning foxes and simple, flattered girls. I was more faithless than that old brute Sherwood who'd shown no more concern when he'd heard that a fine woman was bearing my child unwed than he would had they told him I'd once broken my collarbone in a point-to-point. Both mishaps were likely to happen to a gentleman of spirit; and, indeed, the latter could be the more serious: a broken collarbone will mend but not a broken neck.

Yes, *faithless*: to Eliza Manning and to the memory of those two who had sacrificed everything to teach me the joy of Christian love and duty. Above all, I had been faithless to myself. For I had concealed from myself my plain intention to marry my rising, deserved fortunes to one of those—like Oswald Oates' sister, Caroline—whose cards were, increasingly, empty of other men's names for the next dance whenever I requested the pleasure in the sort of house to which Harry, Oswald and Sherwood saw to it that I was invited whenever I returned home.

I had concealed from myself my intention to become part of this vulgar trading venture practised so assiduously by the rank to which I belonged by blood, and to which I was returning through my talent, my ambition and my great capacity to make rich men so much richer that they would have to freight me with one of their daughters or sisters for a wife. I had concealed from myself the corrupt use I had made of a spirit so

173

loving that she had asked for nothing except to be allowed to love and to be liked and treated kindly in return.

And I had never been more faithless than in my failure to answer her letter waiting for me in Capetown three months before, and reply to which I could have had in her hand within less than four weeks by hand of one of the officers on a fine new steam-packet bound for Southampton, and which would have reached England while I completed some new business over in Argentina which I had discovered was there to be had for the taking because it had never occurred to anybody to look at it before.

The man to whom I could have sent her reply and assurance was one to whom I had once done a favour when he was young and foolish and like to be disgraced forever because of a trifling error committed in his first responsibility.

It had seemed a small, albeit necessary, act of compassion on my part at the time—although I will not pretend that the weight of William Hogarth's brief, almost casual assessment in the wretched man's favour, sinking the sentence of dismissal already agreed upon by a whole court of inquiry, did not fill me with a pride close to vanity . . . But the young man had made much of it at the time; and wherever I met him after, he would refer to it in terms that near embarrassed me.

A letter to Eliza, by his hand, and any confidential message to her from me, would have been as speedily carried as his ship could be coaxed and as faithfully delivered as by a priest.

But I did not send her the letter. Nor did I go to her after my ship was warped up the Thames in late October, and I sent Harry Llewellyn the sort of message I had now earned the privilege to send, that I was home, with a cargo greater than I had promised him—and that I was off to Germany on urgent personal business but would attend in the boardroom of Llewellyn and Oates within the fortnight to discuss matters I believed they wished to put to me.

I am not a man of much imagination, but I think I can reconstruct the sort of exchange that must have taken place between Harry and Oswald as they speculated on the nature of my *"urgent personal business"* and laughingly, enviously, *approvingly,* damned me for a hot-blooded hound of a sailor who had been doubtless summoned imperiously to assignation with some fine French or German trollop who hadn't had her skirts lifted in eight months and who had, as doubtless, insinuated that if I didn't show immediate, I might have to put myself to the labour of lifting some young Hussar or fat Swiss banker from between her legs before I could drop anchor in my rightful berth again.

4

Caer Farm
Malyn Combe
Hereford
July 7, 1850

My dearest William,

I would not, for all the world, write you this except I am in great trouble which could be a shame to my dear parents who have used me so lovingly and with such pride in me since I was born that my trouble is to me a trifle against the shame I must cause them if you do not help me. As I am certain you will help me, William, for you are the dearest, most loving and honourable man who ever stepped since the world began, and even were you not the great gentleman by birth you affect to make such teasing mock of when we are together and I remind you of it, you would be a greater gentleman by Nature than by any patent or title a monarch could bestow on you.

The truth is, William, I am some two months with child—and even in my distress that this must soon be evident and the shame it will bring to those two whom I love only a little less than I love you, I cannot but feel a joy and pride, which I suppose only a woman can understand, that she is bearing a life given to her by a man such as you.

I feel no sin or guilt for what has taken place between us these five years since you passed us with such courteous words and respectful greeting on the road to the church. In a fashion I believe I could justify it before our Lord Himself. I did right to persuade you into possession of my body which was filled with such love and sweet anxiety for you on the moment you passed us trying to look so bold and masterful and strong on Mr Llewellyn's mare. And when I saw you in the church later

175

that morning, William, looking so content and *grateful*, like a man come home after having to live with strange manners, I knew that you would not be able to pass Eliza Manning with only a word of gentlemanly greeting and a lifting of your hat if Eliza Manning met you alone in the combe and demanded your attention. As Eliza Manning was determined to do from the moment she saw you again in Mr Llewellyn's pew in the church that morning looking so content at having come among your own people and with your air of being humble before God for having been made the great gentleman you are.

For you looked so frail, William, for all your fine set of body and strong, sweet face. Not sick, you understand, but as if you were in need of healing. And it was no surprise to me when I learned that you had indeed been close to death in those savage places in the East, after doing great service, and that Mr Llewellyn had insisted you come to rest in his house and be restored before venturing out again.

This need for your healing I saw as plain, and felt as tender for, as I remarked and admired your dark, commanding eyes; and I marvelled a little that my dear mother—who seldom misses such things—did not see it too.

And I am vain enough to suggest, William, that I played a great part in your healing that summer, and I daily thank God that he gave me the love, and body containing that love, to help bring you back to your full health.

Nor do I feel any shame or guilt for what transpired between us on your returns—except for the deceptions we were obliged to make to save my dear mother and good father from anger and concern.

I had no feeling or purpose, my dear, during those years than my love for you and my gratitude for the kindness of the finest man I had ever met—and who, let me confess, I had determined to bind to me.

For I cannot play the role of the gullible innocent seduced against her will—if that falsity is what would rouse you to pity for my condition and any sense of duty to be done by me. You were more virgin than I, William, when I first drew you down on me in the bracken of the combe—although I was truly a maid and you a travelled man of such handsomeness who must

176

have been brought to many a bed by many women of all degrees . . . But when you lay in my arms that day, sleeping with your face between my neck and breast, you looked so like a child that I cried a little and begged forgiveness of God that I had mayhap have corrupted an innocent.

My tears were dried, of course, before you woke, but I shall never forget the wonder and gratitude in your face when I smiled down at you. In that moment, I became a woman, as I grew into fuller and even more joyous womanhood with our brief times together between your voyages, in the combe, in Bristol, in Falmouth and in London.

Nor, let me assure you, on my most sacred word, did I ever think of asking you into marriage with me. My heart and head were too foolish with love for the noblest man the most foolish girl fed on foolish romances could ever have imagined coming into her silly, dull life.

I should have thought of marriage, I suppose, since such a man as William Hogarth could hardly fail to beget his kind on a healthy young woman who lay with him so often and with such pleasure. And I would have had marriage as the end of our loving embraces had you been other than you were. It is no uncommon thing, I need hardly say to you, in our country parts for such as I and a fine young farmer to prove that we can procreate before taking vows. There are long, disapproving faces at first, of course, from fathers, mothers, aunts and uncles when the maid has to confess that she has for a long time been no maid but is one month a mother. But so long as the intent has been to marry and the date of marriage is fixed early, those long faces soon grow round with satisfaction—as they do when a fine cow begins to swell with calf from being put to a bull from another farm.

But in this case, William, who would have thought of Thomas Manning's daughter, with the bastard child of a gentleman who merely passes by from year to year through our combe? What assurance would Jeremy Dodd, say, have that his fortunes would be advanced by such a connection, and what claim could my dear parents make on the father who does not own the land on which his child resides?

And even were I prepared to accept this, William—this thing

177

that has happened to so many girls with whom I grew—I could not live with myself or the child away from you.

I beg you to marry me, William. I will sail with you, if that is your wish, or await your return, for however long a time, between your voyages; and I will be a good wife to you and bring our child up in a fashion that will make him the gentleman you are as much as if you had begotten him on Mr Llewellyn's sister after proper ceremony.

I will be a good wife to you, William, because I love you more than I could ever have imagined any heart could feel love.

I know you like me and are fond of me and treat me in a manner such as I had read of but could not believe existed in true life; and in time, I think, your great heart will learn to love my poor one because the greater always takes nourishment from the lesser. Such is my love for you that I do believe I will capture you again with my spirit as I captured you that day, five years ago in the bracken, with a body that desired you, to be sure, but that desired most of all to nurse back to his full power the finest man I had ever seen ride the world with such grace while in patent pain.

Send for me, William! Or if that be not possible in your exacting business, marry me by proxy. I am advised by one who knows these matters that this is legal and frequently done and entitles a child to all his rights just as if the man stood in the church beside the woman and put his ring on her finger himself.

Oh, please write to me, William, and advise me, and tell me what you would wish me to do.

Even if there can be no immediate marriage, I will join you wherever you say (I have money for passage to whatever port or country you name) and I will be your wife, your loving wife, even if no priest reads a book over us.

> I love you so, William,
> and remain your friend,
> Eliza Manning

5

Had he replied to my letter. Had he told me of his return: for of course I knew within the day his ship signalled the Lizard.

(What sailor's woman does not get news of her man's vessel entering the Channel faster than do Lloyds or Trinity House?)

I found every excuse and explanation for him in my heart. My letter had not reached him in Capetown. (I dared not ask myself why, if this were so, there had been no letter from him from the Cape telling me what was to be his next port of call, for that had been our invariable custom: the letters sent between us through old Jessy Lake over in Bourne, who alone shared our secret and had from the beginning and kept it faithfully—although more than a little anxious for me, I think—because of a strange devotion she had conceived for me ever since I was a child and she one of my father's dairymaids). William left a generous purse for her, of course, whenever he came—for she had no kin, poor soul, and lived wretchedly in her old age now that she could not labour and had no provision save the little I had always brought her after she had to leave our service. But she would have done it for nothing, I swear, because of her love for me—and the importance of being the sole confidante in such a great romance as William and I were conducting.

Not that by now, in November, there was much need for a confidante and go-between. My condition was plain, and there was much whispering, and more than whispering, and not a few sly smiles—and many not so sly—of malice, and much tight-lipped, righteous sympathy for my poor father and mother. And I must always remember, even in my present bitterness and desolation—and I *do* try to remember in my prayers—that there was much kindness and understanding and comfort offered: much of it by those I would have least expected to contain such wells of generosity and compassion.

There was endless surmising and guessing, of course, but it was known that none of the young farmers in the combe or in the districts around had captured my steady affections. So the choice fell on some moment's wanton folly and weakness on my part; and preferably with a gentleman, for that would add a spice to the tale.

But *who*? William Hogarth was suspicioned, naturally. He was Mr Llewellyn's great friend and frequent guest when home from sea, and came much to the farm when staying at the Hall;

sitting with us even to supper sometimes and delighting us and
our friends with his stories of the wild coasts and green islands
and great rivers full of savages where much of his time was
spent . . . And he and I had been seen—meeting as if by chance
—he on Mr Llewellyn's mare, me walking up from Calcroft,
perhaps, or over from Bourne.

But we had been discreet, and after that first year many of
our meetings had been in Bristol or Southampton or Falmouth
or London. I was allowed much freedom for a young woman
and would tell my father that I wished to see some of the great
libraries and cathedrals and museums of which I had learned
at Miss Arboyne's. He would grumble a little about the expense,
and remind me that I was getting long past the age when a girl
should be thinking of such things but instead putting her mind
to marriage—with some steady young feller like Jeremy Dodd,
for example. My mother would hide a smile, for *she* thought I
was escaping for a day or two to see the new dresses and the
sights and the excitement such as I could only read of and
imagine in the combe, and she would slip half a sovereign to me
to add to the two guineas my father had passed me along with
his stern instruction not to waste it all on foolish diversions and
a reminder of how many quarts of milk a poor farmer had to
sell in order to send a great idle lump of a girl gallivanting off
as though she were some fine lady of fashion.

So if suspicion fell on William Hogarth, it was not strong
enough for more than that . . . and I would not reveal his name.
No. Not even to my dear mother when she held me close and
forgiving and tender against her in the privacy of my room and
begged for the name of my child's father.

What sealed my lips? Why would I have gone to the grave
rather than admit that I was bearing a child for William
Hogarth?

Pride, I suppose, for which I have been justly and mercifully
punished . . . But there was something more I cannot properly
name. Were I a man and not only a woman, I suppose I would
call it honour. A sense that as I had willingly shared so much
pleasure and happiness with him, I would not betray him to a
soul until he came to me, as I knew he would, to claim his share

180

in the consequences of what we had performed freely to-gether . . .

Had he but answered that letter he received at the Cape.

Had he but come to me on the instant of his return—if only to claim me and the child we had made and take me away with him to be the woman who kept his house against his returns.

Had he but come to me before the pain . . .

Oh God, I know that the pain you visited on me during those five days was the mark of your favour and of a mercy beyond my understanding. As you have visited pain and terror on others and delivered them from it so that they could be strong and resolute and devoted only to your Service . . .

But such pain! And I so unprepared for it!

I heard a woman screaming, and lay there wondering what poor creature was suffering so, and bewildered at my inability to get up and go to her and try to comfort her.

I heard a woman screaming until the whole world seemed disturbed me so I wished that she would die and let me sleep in peace.

I heard a woman screaming until the whole world seemed strangely silent, as though I had been deafened by her screams. And I hated her then and wished for her death, not because her screams kept me from my rightful sleep but because she had hurt me by rendering me deaf.

I heard a woman screaming until I despised her and and told myself I had seen mere animals, cows and horses and sheep, die in labour with more grace and dignity.

I heard a woman screaming until, one morning, the sound of her screams suddenly became sunlight in my room and my mother's face was looking down on me and smiling as tender as I had ever seen it smile even on the young ones when they were babes and I helping her to change and clean them.

"Eliza, you goose," she said, and it was only her voice that revealed the greatness that was put into her smile. "Eliza, how dare you fright me so? You all but went and died on me, you silly girl."

There were other faces in the room—Dr Tulloch from down Bourne way, and old Jessy Lake and Mrs Paley, the midwife who had seen me and all the others out of my mother—but I hardly saw their faces or even remembered them except as you might be troubled by familiar yet unformed faces in a dream.

It was only my mother's smiling face I saw and knew before I fell into the sleep that incessantly screaming woman had denied me for so long. Indeed, I was into sleep so quickly, as I afterwards learned, that I had no time to see my mother's smile become the tears she had held within her for five days.

Nor was she crying or reproachful or heavy with useless sorrow when she sat alone with me in the room, two days later, and I asked for the child.

"Born slow," she said, "and buried quick. I beg you to believe, my dearest child, that it was better so. I buried it myself. Would not let your father so much as touch the spade. When you are on your feet again, we will go together to where I have buried it. Just you and I; and we will pray for its little mercifully taken soul together."

"But—but it must have had to be buried in unconsecrated ground, mama," I whispered and almost could have wished the pain back; it would have been easier to bear than what I suddenly realized would be my heart's burden for the rest of my life.

"Eliza, Eliza!" my mother said. "D'you think that matters to Him who gave His whole kingdom to the little children? Oh, Eliza, don't look so. Do not be less merciful on yourself than He will be on you and that poor little mite I buried in full confidence of His infinite love."

But I had turned my face to the wall even as she spoke and would not speak to her, or anyone, for three days—until William Hogarth came riding up to our door . . .

6

The first thing a woman reaches for before or after any great event in her life is a mirror. It is a measure of what had happened to the woman I had heard screaming without let for five days, and whose unchristened child lay in unconsecrated ground, that I had not thought to look at myself. Even more measure, I suppose, that my mother or old Jessy Lake had not suggested I take a look at myself after they had washed and changed me and brushed my long yellow hair.

So when I heard William Hogarth's voice sounding up the stairs—quiet, steady and confidently commanding above my father's roaring anger—and felt strength return to me as from a potion, I was out of the bed and before my looking-glass at the dresser in less time than I now take to think of it.

What looked back from the glass more than shocked me, and now I understood why my mother and old Jessy had failed to do what should have occurred to any woman as natural as to see a child buttoned up straight before it goes out of the house or to clasp a new-baked loaf against the left breast for the cutting of the first slice.

It was not the paleness from the loss of blood, nor the bones emerged from the sweat of near a week's fever, nor that I was wan and poorly looking. We country people see that happen to healthy stock from accident, and the stock come back soon enough as fine as though they'd never suffered. (Indeed, my father used to enquire sometimes, when purchasing stock, as to whether there had been any history of illness in the breed and as to how many of the dams in particular had survived and calved well after. *You need the bull for the sinew*, he used to say, *but it's the cows that make the milk out of a season of dry grass*.)

No, it was not how I looked after a week, such as the screaming woman I had been had endured, begging for the false deliverance of death. Good food, my mother's care, a few walks and what I was made of would bring me back to the health to which I was accustomed.

But my face had changed. There was a purpose in it; a wonderment of recognition of new resolve such as Saul of Tarsus must have seen when the scales fell from his eyes in the house of Ananias in Damascus and he first saw his new face in the mirror and was baptized Paul.

I pulled the ribbons from my braided hair and put a heavy dressing-gown over my shift and my stoutest slippers on my feet, and was half-way down the stairs as my mother was ascending, with her face full of a sort of pleasure and pride such as I understood well afterwards.

183

"Eliza," she said in a frightened voice; for, of course, she had seen me so close to death, and could not begin to comprehend the Lord's strength and purpose that had raised me when I heard William Hogarth's voice below and seen the Lord's command staring at me from the looking-glass. "Eliza, my dear. Return to your bed this instant. Are you mad, girl? Captain Hogarth is below with us and has expressed contrition as sincere as any man of his rank could, and wishes to ask you in marriage if you will but forgive him and accept . . . But back to your bed, girl. He cannot propose to a creature fainted and unconscious at his feet."

"Indeed, mama," I said. "I heard Captain Hogarth's voice, although I did not know how honourably he had come to propose. I heard his voice and I am more than strong enough to look on his face and to hear what he has waited this long to say."

And with this I passed her on the stairs as though she had been old Jessy Lake or some frightened girl new come to light the morning fire for nine pence per week and a bit of the morning's bacon.

He stood before the fire in the parlour as though he was but lending it to my father (with my father pretending the fine, cold rage of one who has been wronged). But when he saw my face, and I his, I knew that his shock was as great as mine when my reflection had first confronted me from my looking-glass.

"Eliza," he said and came to me with his hands outstretched. "Eliza, I beg you to forgive me until death part us . . . But I beg you to add honour to your forgiveness and to be my wife . . . I have been a fool and a coward, Eliza, but a man can rise to love on his realization, his late realization, of his folly and cowardice . . . and I love you, Eliza. Will you marry me? I would say tonight, in this house could it be arranged, but that fool Blagrove tells me that even in such circumstances banns must be posted for three full weeks. I have your father's consent, Eliza, and I dare to hope I shall win your mother's blessing. And I only beg that you give me, from your great power to love, enough forgiveness for me to prove my love for you."

"A fine speech, William," I said, "but it comes late, don't you think? Our son lies buried in unconsecrated ground and from

184

what my mother tells me it is as well you never saw him . . . And Jessy Lake has advised me that should I ever attempt another, it could be my death also. Dr Tulloch disagrees with her opinion, and so does Mrs Paley, the midwife—but then they have not seen so many miscarried calves delivered dead as has old Jessy."

"Eliza," he said then—and was it the impatience I thought I heard in his voice then, the incredulity that he was being refused, that confirmed me in my reading of what the Lord had left on my face to see in my looking-glass?—"Eliza, my love! I cannot restore what might have survived had I not been a base fool and puffed with ambition. But I have come to my conscience, Eliza, late, perhaps, but come fully to it. I wish you to be my wife, and promise you such devotion as no woman has ever had from a man who has learned not only love but sacred duty . . . I . . . I have parted with Llewellyn on this issue. I told him and his Company that they took William and Eliza Hogarth together—as man and proudly presented wife—or could not have me. I will provide for you, Eliza, as well as I can labour for. And labour I will, believe me. I have some small savings, and Harry Llewellyn and his fellow directors very handsomely offered me a modest settlement for the past services when I told him I was not to be moved from my resolution to make you my wife . . . With what I have, I can purchase a vessel as will help us into a respectable fortune one day. And all that it earns, Eliza, will be yours to command, if you but ease my conscience by consenting to be the wife of one who delayed too long on the road to the salvation of your acceptance . . . Eliza, I love you. I must have loved you so deep and so long that my poor brain became distraught and I wandered into vain, empty distractions . . .

"Eliza, my dearest wife in fact, permit me to be your husband in God's sight!"

And I looked at him, then—so sure and proud, in his coat of a weave finer than any in the combe, even Mr Llewellyn's, and his fine, keen face so confident in the glow of my father's fire, and heard his words such as could never even have crossed the mind of a Jeremy Dodd, and the thought of my poor little midge laid beyond resurrection in unconsecrated ground, strangled

185

by its own mother's cord and broken in the breach, and of the face marked with the Lord's clear directives that I had observed a few minutes before in my looking-glass and I said: "I will marry you, Captain Hogarth. In Malyn Combe Church so that all can witness you have honoured my mother and my father, and grieve for our dead son ... I will marry you and sail with you wherever your enterprises may take you, for I do not intend to be left alone to wait on your return ever again. But neither will I again be your wife. I will marry you if that is what you offer me from your conscience, but I will never be your wife."

"I thank you, Eliza," he said, "from the bottom of my heart. It is far more than I had hoped to deserve."

I do not think he understood my purpose, nor believed that I would abide by it, as I have to this day. Neither did my father. What man would? There was a look passed between them then: satisfied, almost celebratory, as if an awkward business had come to an unexpectedly quick and agreeable resolution.

But there was consternation on my mother's sweet face; the beginnings of angry protest, even.

And before she could utter a word, old Jessy Lake spoke from the door to which she must have crept to eavesdrop unashamedly—after all she had earned and more than earned the right to listen in on what I purposed to do with the life she had done so much to save over the last five days.

"You bloody foolish bitch," said Jessy, standing in the suddenly opened doorway, her face red-brown as an old pippin with fury and contempt. "You foolish wicked bitch ... An' as for you," pointing at William Hogarth, "if you take her to the altar on those terms you ain't worth a yard of the many miles I've walked to post an' collect your precious letters these last five years ... Miss Eilza, I swear that unless you come to Bourne before your weddin' day an' tell me you spoke now from the heat an' shame of what you have just passed through then I shall not be in Malyn Combe Church to pray for you. God's pity on you both if you mean to wed on such an agreement."

And with that, she turned and left our house, with us all silent.

And I never saw her again, for she did not come to the marriage I made in Malyn Combe Church to William Hogarth . . .

But the thing I think I shall always remember most clearly of that day between William Hogarth and my father in my father's parlour were their two faces.

My father was in anger and outrage and threat, of course. What father would not have been? And William Hogarth was soothing and gentle and careful in his approach—as to a threatening animal.

But there was no *quarrel* between them.

William Hogarth had come into our house with no more sense of a *quarrel* to be settled than he would have gone into the kennel of a growling dog or the stable of an uncertain horse.

Part Nine

SEIZURES

CHAPTER FIFTEEN

There is a tremor that runs through a long-becalmed ship when the first breath of wind begins to swell the foreroyal, upper fore-topgallant, the main royal and swing the spanker on its boom. As there is a sudden toss and dip to the bow as the flying jib feels the first hint of freshening.

They need be no more than movements so slight that a glass of water balanced on the rail would remain steady, without the surface of the liquid even tilting.

But they are registered as surely in the body of an old sailor as the sound and the coursing of its mother's heart and blood are felt by a baby in the womb.

They will bring him from the deepest, most exhausted sleep, the most troubled dream, as if you had plucked him from his hammock to the deck at the end of a rope.

Old Calder was the first man out of the forecastle on that twenty-first morning in the middle watch, just before six bells, at three o'clock when sleep is heaviest.

He was dressed only in his drawers, and shouting exultantly to Mr Bullen and the men of the middle watch before even they, who had been awake and straining to discern any smallest sign of hope, realized what his sudden, extraordinary appearance meant.

But it was the boy Joshua who next appeared from among all off watch who were restoring themselves in their various sleeps.

Joshua was on deck, running towards Calder, his eyes alert and fierce as those of a rat, ready for any order from one who knew best what might ensure survival.

He was on deck and waiting beside Calder even before Reynolds, cursing and jumping into his trousers as he half-hopped, half-ran, appeared from the officers' cabins under the poop; and before Price seemed to materialize from his quarters like a *djinn* from the lamp, bawling for all hands on deck.

Joshua was out of his boy's sleep and his dream of the captain's lady, and standing beside old Calder in time to see Hogarth take over the wheel and hear Hogarth's voice, quietly, penetrate through even Price's roar, "Well done, Joshua. There's a sixpence on your smartness when we are set steady . . ." And then, as the breeze began to strengthen and the canvas above them began to assume its own undirected potential life, he began to call his orders down to the filled deck.

He did not roar like Price, nor even seem to have to rise to Reynolds' urgent, brusque shouts. He called, simply, on a note, in tones, that sounded with a curious, metallic clarity: peremptory, brief and decisive as the declarations of a bugle in the contending turmoil of noise during a battle.

And as most of the men began to vanish aloft into the rigging, and adjusted yards and halyards turned sails into their most advantageous set, Hogarth ceased to call any orders at all. There was no need for it. There were those who could speak for him as he had taught them. Through the spokes of the wheel (which he turned slightly from time to time as the complex and incredibly rapid labour above him was performed twenty, forty, sixty feet above his head by unlettered men to whose skill and courage the wealth of the world was entrusted) he could feel life and purpose returning to hs command. God's breath blown into a few square yards of dead cloth; his patiently learned knowledge, the craft of men he and others like him had nurtured—and this ship was no longer a useless box, however carefully designed and assembled: it was a creature more noble than any that had ever coursed these waters . . . Nobler because it could have life only when given into the care of those who understood how much it depended for its life on God's breath and had thanked Him for providing it.

"Mister Bullen," he called. Bullen on deck at the end of a calm—under his eye—was a safer proposition than Bullen aloft.

"Sir," Bullen called, and Hogarth watched with amusement the unnecessary, vigorous striding aft to the poop. He and Bullen could have quite easily conversed from where Bullen

190

stood by the midshiphouse; but on such a morning, with a steadily freshening wind beginning to push his ship out of the waste and despair which had been accumulating around it for twenty-one days, he could find no place for irritation in his heart.

"Mister Bullen," he said casually, "be good enough to summon that old feller, Calder, from aloft. I know he is the best fore-topgallant man we have, but I do not think he will be much needed there now. We would apear to have a steady, manageable wind on our south-east quarter now; and I would like to have him at the wheel to make the best advantage of it."

"By God," I think you're right, sir," Bullen said. "As soon as I felt this ship tremble—fast asleep as I was—and you know how a sailor can feel the difference between a catspaw and the start of something steady. I don't have to tell *you* that, sir, I'm sure . . . Well as soon as I felt it and was tumbling for the deck, I said to myself, I said: *Time enough's been wasted, Bullen. Three weeks of time, and we're going to need a man or two at the helm every hour of the day and night who knows how to coax every knot out of what has come to us. For I don't think it's going to be more than a fair, steady blowing and . . .*"

"Mister Bullen," Hogarth said gently, "your observations do you credit. You may wish to hear that they concur with mine . . . But, Mister Bullen . . . Calder, if you please. Call him down to me."

Perhaps, Hogarth thought, as Bulen made his clumsy salute and swung on his briskly tangled about-turn, it is because it is early morning and I can see him only by starlight and moonlight and the lanterns, that I can find him a source of amusement. Were it daylight, I have a feeling I would have struck him. But he is more like a creature in one of those dreams from which one wakes laughing helplessly, with no rational cause to attach to what has made us laugh.

From the shadow at the foot of the companion ladder below, Alex said: "You did right to send for Calder, Cap'n. That ol' man at a wheel will get an extra knot for you out of no more wind than a baby's belchin'."

"Alex," Hogarth said, "I didn't see you."

"How d'you expect to see me, cap'n, at this time of the middle watch, unless you got a lighthouse beam laid steady on the deck? I just come to tell you that I got some food preparin' against when the crew start comin' down off the yards. You goin' to have a happy crew, cap'n, for they was beginnin' to get frighted, an' there ain't nothin'll keep spirit stuck into the biggest man than a plate of good food after he's been lonely an' frighted. They'll be happy 'cause they're doin' some right smart work up there. An' I aim to see they get somethin' to fill out their happiness."

Hogarth looked down to the midshiphouse to where a plume of smoke was drifting north-west from under the little, cone-covered, cast-iron smokestack of the galley.

"I'll wager you had your fire lit before that breeze even stirred a ripple behind our stern quarter," he said.

"Well, you paint the fact a little, cap'n. But I had that stove gettin' red-hot, an' a few special victuals I'd been layin' by for this, pretty soon after I heard the crack in the flying jib."

"Oh, you heard that too, did you?"

"Of course! That's when I knew we were set with a steady wind behind us for the coast. A sigh into the main royal or the spanker movin' 'cause it's got tired standin' still can leave you becalmed a length of where you was, a minute later. But when you hear that flying jib raise a hoorah as it tries to pull the bowsprit clean out of the hull then you knows you're in for some long, close attention to your course."

"Alex, you should have been a captain. No, by God . . . an admiral."

"Why, Cap'n Hogarth? Ain't I a good enough cook?"

"You're an even better hypocrite, you sly dog . . . What, am I not to get my coffee while I keep my eye on this wind we've conjured up?"

"Now that's what I come to ask you about, Cap'n Hogarth— an' forget with all your talk of promotin' me to admiral—are you ready for your coffee?"

"What d'you think?"

"Mocha or the Jamaica Blue Mountain?"

"What d'you recommend?"

"The Blue Mountain. It don't stir you quick like the Mocha,

192

but the stir lasts longer an' surer . . . You want a couple spoons of brandy in it?"

"Yes! And none of that Spanish muck you and Reynolds fancy. Real cognac, y'understand?"

"I'll send Joshua along with it before you've had time to regret your unworthy thoughts, cap'n . . . Good night."

"Good night to you, Alex . . . and, Alex . . ."

"Yes, cap'n?"

"I am glad to have sailed with you . . . and proud that you have sailed with me during years when I know you could have found better fortune. Thank you, Alex."

"And I thank you, Cap'n Hogarth."

CHAPTER SIXTEEN

At the slaves' feeding time on the second day of the south-easter, Alexander Delfosse shot dead Boyo Dolan and the young Portuguese who together had charge of the culverin pointed into the slaves' hold.

He did it very quickly, with casual expertness, as he might have disposed of wounded animals, so that they were dead on the deck, under the poop and he on the poop with the muzzle of his second, fully loaded Navy Colt stuck under Hogarth's throat before the sailors around the opened hatch, waiting for the slaves to emerge, had realized that two of their fellows lay face-down with the tops of their spines shattered, and bleeding like cattle from their gaping mouths as Alex Delfosse looked down on them; and sounds such as they had never heard began to come from the hold.

So that when the dry, thin, oldish woman came onto the deck carrying Reynolds' severed head (with every feature of it broken horribly) and a young Baluba boy came next carrying the head of what must have been Price (although with features so smashed by chains that it could be recognized only from the fact that no white man on the ship had had a head as large as that), and when Dunn was flung through the opened hatch onto the deck before them, torn open from throat to groin but still making a strange sort of bubbling howl, there was nothing to do until the hold emptied itself of men unchained.

"Cap'n Hogarth," Alex said loudly, "tell 'em to lay them Springfields down real slow, an' all white men, except the helmsman an' a few aloft to furl sail, to gather up at the midship-house where I can keep an eye on them. But tell 'em to do everything quiet, cap'n. Quiet an' slow an' peaceful. Anything even looks as if it might happen to me an' terrible things is goin' to happen. I can just hold 'em as it is when they start

194

comin' from below. But God himself couldn't stop what'd follow
if me or one of 'em was to get hurt . . . Give the order, cap'n.
I beg you. I wouldn't want anything to happen to Mrs Hogarth
or Joshua or you, no matter what you may be thinkin' right now.
And that's God's truth. I swear it."

"You have all heard Alex," Hogarth said. His voice was
steady, remote, with no more modulation than the sounds made
when two large stones are clashed evenly together. "Consider
what you have heard him say as my orders. Gather by the midshiphouse. Mister Bullen send who you need aloft to furl sail.
Make sure the Portuguese understand fully, although I should
think they will require little translation to comprehend what has
occurred."

His face was remote, as unmoved as his words, but there was
a sudden greyness, more strange than any pallor, which seemed
not to lie beneath but to have been expertly applied to the
tanned skin.

From the moment that Alex had shot Dolan and the young
Portuguese and leapt up the companion ladder to Hogarth,
through the time that Tadene and the Baluba boy had brought
up the crushed heads from the suddenly clamorous hold and
Dunn had been flung onto the deck by unseen hands, to
Hogarth's last words, no more than three perhaps four minutes
had passed.

No man or woman aboard could tell. Nor would they ever
be able to tell in their later, measured times of recollection and
description.

For a ship is a world and who can tell how long it takes to
witness a world refashioned?

So that when Eliza Hogarth came from the cabin and stood
beside her husband, the men on the deck were still held in a
curious rigidity—almost as if they tranquilly contemplated
something of enormous significance being created in a space
and time that had little to do with the trivial ticking of a watch
recording the foolish, brief instant of passage between the first
protest against birth and the last protest against the end of the
life against which protest was lodged from the beginning.

"Oh, William," whispered Eliza Hogarth and held his arm
tightly. "William! William! I heard shots and—and—"

She looked down then and saw what Tadene and the Baluba boy had thrown among the sailors' feet, and saw what was the source of the bubbling growls that came from Dunn's ripped-open body which had been so roughly delivered from the hold. "God in heaven!" Eliza Hogarth screamed, and fainted.

She did not faint in the graceful, knee-bending tumble in which women are portrayed to faint. She pitched forward with the suddenness of a tree felled by the last stroke of the axe and with all the dead weight of her ten stone of flesh and additional stone of clothing. But for the railing, and Hogarth's quick clasp around her waist, she would have dived unconscious and head-first to the deck below and broken her neck.

"Now, cap'n," Alex said as Hogarth lifted her beneath her shoulders and knees, holding her against him. "Now, cap'n. You take her back into the cabin an' stay with her. I never wished for her to see what she's just done, but I always knew she'd have to ... You take her back to the cabin, y' hear me? An' neither of you come out unless I tell you. I know you've got your guns in there, an' I sure as hell can't leave this deck to come in an' take 'em off you. But don't think of usin' 'em on me, cap'n. An' I beg you don't think of usin' 'em on her to save her from what a man sometimes feels his lady ought to be saved from afore he comes out to do a little killin' and dyin' himself. I beg you don't even think of that, Cap'n Hogarth. Ain't a man on my ship, 'cept you, goin' to so much as touch your lady's hand. You got my word on that. An' there ain't a man on my ship goin' to lay a hand on you, cap'n, 'cept me when I help you down into the longboat to go your own ways when I get to where I'm takin' this ship."

For a moment, the grey, unnatural stillness of Hogarth's face quickened with the appetite of that curiosity which nothing can sicken in the superior mind. He held the inert weight of his wife against him with no more sign of strain than he might have held a child.

"And where are you taking my ship—I beg your pardon, *your* ship, Alex? Into what fortune do you propose to sail what you have taken from me—and from those you have murdered?"

"Cap'n Hogarth," Alex said, with a sudden anger—impersonal but as though driven by some greater force behind it, like a blast of sand in the desert. "Cap'n Hogarth take your lady to your cabin, an' leave me to achieve what I been purposin' for a lot longer than I've known you. Now get the hell off my deck, cap'n, an' try to gentle that good lady when she comes to, as best as you know how ... Get the hell off my deck, 'cause I've got a heap of work to do an' I can't get to it while you're here for all to see."

He watched as Hogarth carried the woman into the cabin on the poop. Then he watched as Bullen and the Portuguese on deck moved slowly forward and huddled against the bulkhead of the midshiphouse.

Then he muttered an order to the Portuguese at the wheel.

Then he stepped quickly down the companion ladder to where Dunn lay and babbled on a viscous, spreading stain larger than his own body.

"You poor son of a bitch," Alex said as he shot Dunn between the eyes, "I never intended to keep you waitin' so long."

And then he went to the edge of the opened hatch and shouted an order in pidgin Portuguese.

And after a minute, the first black man stepped onto the deck, carrying a doubled length of inch-link chain.

The man carried it awkwardly: as if it was a possession to which he had grown accustomed but now had to put to a new use for which he had not been trained and did not understand.

CHAPTER SEVENTEEN

1

At the taffrail, Hogarth stares at the star-drenched, receding horizon as the occasionally adjusted rudder leaves a scarcely curving wake astern under a deeply plunging stern. All the journeys of his life, the criss-crossing of the globe to which he has beaten with his cargo of invested ambitions, are now forging at twelve knots out of an ever-growing circle to a shore on which he will land with nothing but what he knows of how to use those stars to make ignorant rich men richer. He has sailed out of what could have been a grave into future, humble service to men, as yet unknown, who will be confident in his knowledge of the stars and the fortunes to which his knowledge of them can lead.

There is noise on the main and fore decks behind and below him: song; voices trying to establish the most elementary exchange in two dozen tongues; drums. How, in God's name, did drums come aboard, and why do they seem to speak to each other as diplomats might speak French to each other across a conference table?

He does not turn as Alex comes up behind him and leans against the taffrail.

"No cause to worry now, cap'n," Alex says. "I was a mite worried for a while this afternoon, 'specially after it began to grow duskish about three bells in the first dog watch. That kind of light is bad for near five hundred niggers who ain't seen it free for near three months. But I got 'em fed and singin' an' learnin' to talk to each other, an' I've told 'em them as wants to sleep on deck is welcome to do so. An' they's happy enough— as you can hear."

"And my crew? Are they safe?"

"Safer'n than they've been these last three weeks an' more cap'n. 'Cept for a couple of the younger Portugese boys may have to find themselves servicin' more of the young Angola women—the Angola gals like white men—than they can manage afore the night's through. For the most part, though, if they keep my ship handled right an' teach my people how to handle her until I put you off, any white man aboard's safe as if he was home with his own folks . . . In particular, your lady's safe. I command now, cap'n. For a spell there this afternoon after I brought 'em up an' tried to have it explained through that Angola boy, Kanuyi, I was a little tight in the stomach, but they took me. They don't understan' rightly where they're goin' yet or why—but I'm all they've got to go with, an' they're beginnin' to take it as better than where you were takin' them."

"And where are you taking them, Alex?"

"Up the Amazon, cap'n. You know we was goin' to have to transfer illegal off Canal do Sul—to all them agents the Emperor has to pretend don't buy since he stopped the trade . . . But there's a world inside that goddam river, cap'n. An empty world. Jesus, I've seen it! There's rivers feedin' into it bigger'n than the Mississippi, an' only a few Indians in there who don't know what they're livin' on, an' men on the coast—white an' black an' all colours in between—just waitin' for a man like me to start a kingdom up one of the rivers . . . Five years from now, cap'n, you'll be sittin' at my right hand at a table bigger than the maindeck . . . an' Alex Delfosse is goin' to be your host. The few hundred niggers you bought for me an' I took from you, an' this ship, is just the start. It was the start I needed; but what you goin' to see in five years, cap'n will be somethin' you won't believe."

"You are mad, Alex," Hogarth says, and his face in the glow of the taffrail lamp is now full and animated with concern. "You are quite mad. D'you think Dom Pedro will permit you to establish a separate, sovereign state in his Empire with a handful of savages and a ship like this? You will be hanged before you clear the Amazon estuary . . . How could you imagine? You—you—"

"You mean because I'm black, Cap'n Hogarth? You think a nigger shouldn't be considerin' such a venture?"

"You know I do not mean that. But the venture you propose is madness. For any man ... white or black. You propose to challenge an empire and establish yourself as a king within it ... They will destroy you as a common criminal, Alex, along with every poor ignorant heathen you gull into following you."

"It's been done before," Alex says, "an' not too long ago—by white men an' black, with less than what I'm takin' up the Amazon ... An' when they start seein' an' enjoyin' what I start sendin' them out of what I make from where I'm goin' to rule, they'll be happy I took it. They'll be sendin' big men up there to pin decorations on my chest ... an' there'll be those glad to come to me for *my* decorations ... All I needed was a start, cap'n, and you gave me that start."

"You're mad, Alex," Hogarth says. "They'll never permit you to fell a tree or clear an acre or—"

"So Cortez was mad, eh, cap'n? Takin' all of Mexico with one hundred an' fifty men. An' Pizarro in Peru and Emperor Christophe over in a little bit of place like Haiti who wrestled Napoleon to the floor seven times afore your great Duke of Wellington was much more than a sepoy general? An' look at what they did! Jesus Christ! If you wasn't such a goddam *good* man, cap'n. If you was like what Louis Delfosse was, what a kingdom I could make with you. You is better *quality* than Delfosse, but you don't have the meanness an' the hardness him an' me shared, so that's why I'm goin' to have to put you over the side to make your own way ... Reynolds, now, he was mean and hard enough for my purpose—but he didn't have your *quality*. I could never have put my hand in his an' turned my back on him, trustin', as I could with you—or as I could have with Louis Delfosse."

"This Delfosse?" asks Hogarth. "You share his name. Yet you have never mentioned him to me in the five years we have shared confidences on this deck. Who was he? Your brother— or one of your master's bastards?"

"We was closer than that, Cap'n Hogarth. He was Jean-Paul Delfosse's rightful son, as white as you, an' he was no kin to me ... But we was closer'n David an' Jonathan from the time we

200

was both little pieces of chaps bein' cleaned an' fed at the breast by the same ol' woman an' later learnin' to hunt deer an' raccoon an' bear in the same swamp . . ."

"And learning other things, I would suppose," Hogarth says. "Other things you may have related to Reynolds?"

"Yes, cap'n. Other things I would not have told you."

"And he is dead, I take it, from the way you speak of him?"

"Yes. He's dead."

"I am glad to hear that, Alex."

"I still grieve for him, cap'n."

"I have no doubt you do. But I am glad to hear that God rid us of him before you two were sufficient in your experience to practise your joint betrayal on the world . . . I can nearly find it in my heart to forgive you, Alex, for your betrayal of my trust. But I do not think I could have forgiven your brother —what was his name? Ah, yes, Louis. No, I could not have forgiven him had he shared in the betrayal you have faced me with."

"'Cause I'se black, cap'n? An' you expected nothin' else, but couldn't have taken it from a white man so much like me you couldn't have told us different save from his face 'gainst mine? Or 'cause it's me persuaded you gradual into slavin' from that day in Havana to now when I'm takin' from you what you never dare claim back?"

"You mistake me, Alex," says Hogarth, and turns his back on the face whose contours cannot be properly defined by the taffrail lamp. "I was coming to an understanding of . . . of brotherhood with all men, despite this trade, because of you. I was beginning to realize that men like you and I, despite our difference in appearance, truly belonged to a greater purpose than we could prove in an argument . . . And now you have betrayed me in a fashion for which I could never have forgiven one of my own race . . . In your betrayal, Alex, I discern an inevitability, a fixity of future if you like, against which I had begun to hope, foolishly, for equality and fraternity . . . I trust and hope that your race will serve mine to the end of time, Alex— as I trust and hope that there will be few of my race as foolish as I have been to take you into confidence. You could no more help your betrayal than an ape can help stealing fruit from the

house in which it has been taken as a privileged pet . . . Will
you leave me now?"

From the rail behind Hogarth, Alex Delfosse looks on the
straight, rigid back with a furious inarticulacy.

"Goddam your talk of betrayal, Hogarth," he says. "I never
betrayed you—not a piece . . . Betrayal was waitin' for us both
'out here, an' it was just who took hold of it first was all. You
know that! I never betrayed you. Betrayal was here to be
taken . . . An' you know that's how it's always been an' how
it always will be until God decides different."

2

When Hogarth returned to the cabin from the gold-fretted
night and moonlit deck, he found the dimmed radiance inside
disturbing—as though forcing him to make an adjustment of his
imagination and understanding to the reflections cast on the
wall of a *camera obscura* across which his now unpossessable
expectations passed, in image, upside-down.

He entered with no more sound than a young sailor learns
when coming off watch into the kennels of his youth—where he
must lie down beside desperately tired children asleep only
two inches from where he must settle himself.

He eased himself into the chair. The noises from the deck
had diminished, although the drums still sounded to each other
like heartbeats. Most of the freed slaves, he understood, had
decided to sleep on deck. But he had no fear of any of them
coming up to the cabin. Alex's pride would not permit that.
Nor—he smiled thinly as the thought flickered across a mind
too alert for true clarity at this hour—would Alex's life have
too certain a future if he did not establish what areas of Alex's
ship the freed slaves were allowed to roam and what areas were
to be entered only by Alex's permission.

"William," said Eliza Hogarth sitting up from under the
sheet, fully clothed, even to her shoes.

"Eliza, my dear." He was more than awake now. Bewilderment and attention quickened his mind like sheet lightning.
"I thought you were asleep. When I laid you down ten hours
ago I gave you laudanum enough to ensure rest until morning

202

at least. You were in a sad state, my dear, and I beg you not to think of what brought you to it, but to go to sleep again . . . and I removed your shoes before I covered you . . . Let me give you another glass of laudanum. I shall rest comfortable here, I assure you, until four bells when there are matters I shall have to see to. I have just spoken to Alex and, although he has betrayed us, he has assured me no harm will come to you. I do not fully understand yet what he intends, but no harm will come to you."

"William?" she asked, and swung herself out of the captain's bed and crossed to him in the diminishing light between the porthole and the chair from which he sat staring. "William? Have I been a wicked, cruel woman?"

"Eliza! Eliza!" He was stuttering, not from confusion but from foreknowledge—and from uncertainty as to whether he could, after ten years, arouse himself to console the body which she had begun suddenly (with demure wantonness, with all the artifice of insanity) to divest of its clothes.

If he could convince and console the body, he knew—as she turned her back for him to undo her buttons—her heart and mind might take care of themselves, after a fashion.

God send me strength, he said to himself as he rose from the chair.

CHAPTER EIGHTEEN

On the fourth day after the calm broke, just after three bells in the afternoon watch, H.M.S. *Beaver*, Lieutenant Michael Honeyball commanding, quartered down on the *Sure Salvation* as the barque was heeling sweetly to port at twelve knots before the south-easter, clearing the northern headland of Tocansa Island.

It was a smart capture. The *Beaver* had lain hidden in the cove, with its boilers damped and no steam coming from its stack, until the *Sure Salvation* had passed and was ahead of it on the wind.

Then Lieutenant Honeyball had spread all the thin sail he could cram onto his three masts and put the twin screws fed by his new boilers into full revolution.

Under sail alone, the *Sure Salvation* with the wind which she was filled from the south-east could have outrun the *Beaver* until dark: even beyond the range of the *Beaver*'s six-inch, Armstrong breech-loaders. But with the *Beaver*'s twin screws biting low into the water under the recently modified, narrowed stern, the assistance of her thin spread of sails and a following sea, there was no hope.

Within half an hour, Lieutenant Honeyball was able to hail the *Sure Salvation* across the water through his speaking horn. He kept his sail spread only to cut wind between him and his prize and prevent her from darting into a course that might yet make following and boarding difficult before dark or a sudden mist swallowed her in an immensity of ocean over which he might search for a year without ever finding even jettisoned evidence of her track.

Lieutenant Honeyball was a proud and dedicated man. He was proud of his astuteness in pressing for a command in steam at a time when the Sea Lords and the great captains tended to look on any officer who sought such commands as one who had formed a frivolous attachment to a useful novelty that could never really supplant sail. He was proud of the promotion that had come to him so quickly because he had accepted —nay, sought—position in the early steam vessels which his fellow officers had affected to despise, or had despised in imitation of those old boobies in the Admiralty who had posted them to great vessels built from a thousand oaks and more helpless than canoes manned by savages if the wind dropped on them. He was proud of the evidence he had given, against cautionary advice, ten years previous on the necessity of taking the entire Navy out of sail and wood and into steam and steel as speedily as was possible. He was proud of having overheard a man who, as a boy of twelve, had helped carry Nelson below to his death at Trafalgar say: *That damn Honeyball! He can't keep from makin' me life miserable with his damn steam. For God's sake give him one of those things he wants an' send him as far away as you can find on the damned map, for as long as you can. He means well, but he's drivin' me mad about the advantages of steam. Give him the best we've got, an' jus' make sure I don't see him again until he's Admiral of the Fleet and comes to pay his respects at my gravestone.*

Lieutenant Honeyball did not despise sail, since it had helped his new twin screws to ride out disadvantageous seas, or helped them to take fullest advantage of winds in the right quarter. And he knew that no man could ever understand the sea who had not had to learn how to live with the sea under sail alone. But the power he now had to command from his bridge with five hundred horsepower throbbing through the connection rod to his twin screws had made him a dedicated, almost obsessed, man. (When he made his last speech in the House of Lords, half a century after he boarded the *Sure Salvation*, it was on the greatness that more steam in ever-larger ships could bring to England.) And men listened with respect and attention to this old Admiral who had never fought a battle, but who had quartered down on the last of the slavers fifty years before and taken it as casually as a child might have lifted a toy boat from a bath, because he had learned how to use the sure power of steam against the immemorial energy of the sea that had now become random and helpless against the mind that could demand any direction or make any assertion with absolute assurance of the tireless, utterly obedient servant it was now able to command on a moment's decision.

Lieutenant Honeyball was, in his politics and social beliefs, more Tory than had been the great duke in whose death, seven years before, he had felt there was prefigured the death of an England that was all that a nation should be: a country to be envied, imitated, even reverenced by others less fortunate, but never to be equalled by any. He had read Mr Charles Darwin's *Origin of Species* on the day after its publication because a mischievous friend who liked him much had told him it was a diverting account of a voyage around the world. He had read it with a mounting detestation greater, perhaps, than he felt for those damned foreign pamphlets on socialism which sometimes came his way and which his too tolerant, too easy-going, too confident country actually allowed to be written, translated, printed and circulated within its own borders.

And yet Lieutenant Michael Honeyball, as he hailed his order to the wallowing *Sure Salvation* to heave to and prepared to board her, was more truly a revolutionary figure than any of the great scientific or political investigators whose existence he found so disagreeable and so damnably dangerous to all that he cherished.

In his early, passionate commitment to steam, in his fidelity to it at a time when such fidelity might have cost advancement in the career of a man who had little more on which to live than his pay, in his advocacy of it and untiring experiments with its uses—experiments sometimes paid for out of his own light purse—Lieutenant Honeyball was more than a conscientious professional in an old, exacting craft.

Lieutenant Honeyball, as he descended into his lowered cutter to board the *Sure Salvation*, was a new species—all the more terrible in his potential to alter the development of his kind for good or ill, because he was utterly unaware that his youthful understanding of the new power he had inherited, and found so congenial and tested with such scruple, made him as different a creature from the heroes of his boyhood (Nelson, Wellington, Rodney, Cook, Columbus, Drake and the great reformers of the Anglican Church) as they had been different from the apes to which that damned Darwin had recently suggested they were linked.

CHAPTER NINETEEN

"My God!" said Lieutenant Honeyball as he sat at the table in the midshiphouse he had commandeered after boarding the *Sure Salvation*.

He could, of course, have taken the captain's cabin on the poop deck; but the intimacy that a woman scatters in any place she occupies had made any idea of using it as a place of inquiry quite impossible. Short of ejecting the captain's wife, her clothing and other evidences of possession: short, indeed, of fumigating the little room in which she had breathed and had her being and in which her presence lingered as strong and disturbing as the smell from a mangrove swamp, there was no possibility of his making more than a hurried, embarrassed inspection of it, and leaving a marine on guard on the deck outside it.

Hogarth, too, was permitted to keep to the cabin with his wife. Not only because of his rank, but because Lieutenant Honeyball, after two seconds converse with him, had realized that here was a class which it would be as unthinkable, as indecent, to chain in the forecastle with the others as it would have been to confine the woman herself.

The officers' quarters—those of the dead one, which also contained a woman, black and naked, and the other living one —were too small for the purposes of interrogating the crew, particularly when he needed the black cook, Alex, to act, more or less competently, as a translator between him and the Portuguese. Besides, there should always be a distance between the examined and the examiner: a space which the examiner could fill with righteous anger, or could imply was necessary to protect him from possible contamination.

He was left with the midshiphouse, which had space enough for his witnesses to stand before a table, even if he had to allow for the presence of a nigger and his boy cooking at any hour for the five hundred bodies that had to be fed while he compiled his deposition from the various witnesses who were marched before him for question.

"My God!" Lieutenant Honeyball said.

It was the fifth or sixth time he had said so since he first came scrambling up the *Sure Salvation*'s ladder and smelled what hung above a slaver's decks and lay in its holds even after five days' of cleansing and the free movement of bodies.

Again he could not know, but what he smelled and saw and roused him to blasphemous utterance would not have distressed unduly the generation just before he was born, and would, again, be no surprise to the generation thirty years after he died (his grandson, for example) that marched into the camps in Treblinka, and Buchenwald, or were sent daily to work and die in the camps of Siberia.

"Now you," he said to Alex who stood before him on the other side of the table. "If I understand rightly, you are a free Negro. What were you doing on this wicked venture, eh? Taking your own people into slavery?"

"I'se a cook cap'n," Alex said. He was dressed in a fine, three-piece suit of white linen and held a broad-brimmed, black wide-awake hat with becoming deference across his stomach as he gazed with interest and calculation on the round, plain, red young English face sitting below him across the table. "I'se just a cook an' I signed on with Captain Hogarth to cook for a voyage an' didn' know nothin' of what the purpose of that voyage was all about until it was all too late an' I was in the middle of this ocean an'..."

"So it was like that, eh?" said Lieutenant Honeyball, but his voice was gentle and almost supportive. "Yet you are more than you suggest, my friend. Your name is entered in the manifest as cook, and your shares as signed by you with Captain Hogarth were to be considerable. And you speak a great deal higher up the scale of education than you're trying on me now ... What brought you to this, man? Why do I find a free Negro of your calibre in such company?"

"An' yet it was me that gave you a prize of already freed slaves, cap'n. You'll have heard that already—from Cap'n

Hogarth an' Mister Bullen an' that Angola boy, Kanuyi, I helped translate for you yesterday, an' that old woman, Tadene, who told you about me givin' the niggers the keys so'd they'd be free an' ready when the crew went down that mornin' to bring 'em up for feedin' an' exercise an' . . ."

"You expect me to believe that you did not understand what you were signing on for in Bristol six months ago?" Lieutenant Honeyball asked. His voice no longer coaxing, but harsh and cold. "You deny the paper of agreement signed between you and Hogarth which I found in his cabin?"

"I don' expect you to believe nothin', cap'n. An' I'm denyin' nothin'. You'll believe an' you'll accept what ever'n it is you want 'cause I'se black an' free an' you don' really like neither condition . . . But what I tell you is that you took near five hundred freed niggers as prize without trouble on this barque, an' it was me that set 'em free as was always my intention from the time we headed out from Africa . . . An' there's near five hundred witnesses willin' an' ready to swear on my behalf that all I ever done is feed 'em free until you jumped us right smart off that damn island. I was goin' to take 'em up the Amazon an' give 'em a kingdom . . ."

"You have committed murder," Lieutenant Honeyball said, and suddenly realized that it was he—in the chair on the other side of the table from the tall, coldly calculating black man in the elegant white suit—who must justify himself. "You shot two men, white men, in cold blood, and shot another as I have been told, and put a wounded Negro over the side while still alive to drown. And—"

"I shot two white men, cap'n, 'cause they'd have cut down near a hundred slaves with their culverin an' still left four hundred for illegal sale to the doms in Brazil. An' I shot another white man 'cause he was dyin' slower an' more painful from what had been done to him by the slaves than how any man ought to die. An' I put a poor broke-up nigger over the side without him even knowin' what I was doin' because he never would have lived it out even if that goddam calm hadn't broke an' I could have got him to Brazil with breath in his body. An' I was takin' near five hundred free niggers across to the Amazon, in my charge, cap'n, until you jumped me, an' I surrendered this ship an' its cargo to you without a fight."

"And you expect me to believe that tissue of lies from a slaver who was as ready to take his profit from his cargo as any of the white men whom I have already questioned?"

"No, Lieutenant Honeyball," Alex said, "I don't expect you to believe or accept a damn thing . . . except that you found me in command of a vessel of free souls, every one of which except the white men will stand witness for my action when you bring me to court. I did from inside what you would have done from outside, Lieutenant Honeyball, an' would have got a medal for it, as you probable will get. An' when you tell them about me in court, remember I'm goin' to play that side of it strong, an' that I've got near five hundred witnesses ready to swear that I was only waitin' on time an' a favourable breeze to bring 'em into freedom."

"You are monstrous," said Lieutenant Honeyball. "God knows what you would really have done with these poor Negroes had you succeeded in the execution of your plan."

Across the wide, thickly curled, back edges of the lips in the broad, flat planes of the face surveying him from across the table, Lieutenant Honeyball seemed to catch a smile so fleeting that it might have been a flake of light never quite reflected enough on the surface of a black pool to be more than a possibility of which one could be not sure.

"I ain't monstrous, cap'n," Alex said. "I just got a little unlucky . . . As for what I'd have done with those niggers? I'd have jus' put them to work."

He turned to go, as though it was he, not Honeyball, who must decide how much of the inquiry's time should be spent on each witness. He turned with such decisiveness, yet so casually, that he was almost at the door before the scarlet-jacketed marine guard presented his bayonted rifle at the advancing figure and said in a tone of sheerly disbelieving outrage: "'Ere you! 'Bout turn. Mister 'Oneyball never said nuffink 'bout you bein' dismissed."

"Oh let him go, Walsh," Lieutenant Honeyball said wearily.

He felt tired—as if a wickedness, a greed, a callousness older than time itself and as natural to man as his hands or eyes,

210

pervaded this ship like fever and had truly made him sick. And in none of those he had examined so far had he been made more aware of an illness, perhaps incurable, with which he himself might be infected, than in the tall black man who had just interviewed him.

The black man—who had scarcely glanced at the presented bayonet point, but had kept on walking as if knowing what Lieutenant Honeyball would say to the marine—turned in the doorway now.

"An' remember this, Lieutenant," he said, softly, almost compassionately, "you probably ain't never seen a slaver before— only heard about 'em or read about 'em—but how many slavers you ever heard of could bring near five hundred souls this far across the passage with no deaths among 'em, 'cept for that one we had to put out of his misery, same as you might have to shoot a horse that's broke its leg? I ain't denyin' that some of 'em ain't sickish an' all of 'em need perkin' up before they're strong . . . but there wasn't one death, Lieutenant, because we took real good care of 'em. I hope your conscience prompts you to remember that when you's givin' evidence against us in court."

"*Get out!*" Lieutenant Honeyball's red face was an alarming shade of burgundy as he jumped to his feet. "*Get out, you damned insolent*—" and stopped, and sat, as he realized how nearly he had come to uttering the word which the faintly smiling black man at the door had been waiting for him to say.

And then the tall black man, smiling faintly from such a distance of cynicism, stopped smiling and said something surprising, in a tone of unaffected kindness. What he said was to remain with Lieutenant Honeyball for the rest of his long life, and was sometimes to console him—with a curious assurance of self-esteem—in moments of guilt or doubt about his own worthiness.

"You're a good man, Lieutenant," Alex said. "You're a real good man. 'Least you try to be, 'an that's almost better. I give you my word of honour, I'll do anythin' I can to help you get this ship an' her crew an' the five hundred niggers you've become responsible for to wherever you're aimin' to take us. An' you're goin' to need help—if it's only keepin' the niggers fed an' not tryin' to do a mischief on the white men you got chained in the forecastle . . . You an' me could no more help meetin' up the way we done than we could help bein' born the way each of us was. It had to happen this way. But you're a good man, an' anyways I can help you 'tween here an' where you're takin' us, I will."

"I thank you," Lieutenant Honeyball found himself saying to a suddenly empty doorway, but nevertheless repeated: "I thank you and I believe you."

Part Ten

LANDFALL

CHAPTER TWENTY

1

It had been Lieutenant Honeyball's intention to take the *Sure Salvation* up the long haul to Georgetown in British Guiana—where there would be more resources to deal with the judicial procedures against Hogarth and his crew and to see the disposition of the five hundred newly freed people who must now be found shelter, work and clothing. Above all, clothing. The nakedness that paraded the decks every day when he was rowed across from the *Beaver* to inspect his capture and the prize crew he had left aboard under his senior midshipman, filled him with a sense of order overthrown, of blatant challenge to all proper and civilized progress, more serious than the smells and other evidences of slavery that still clung to the vessel he had seized.

But three days after he had boarded his capture, while they were still pressing steadily past Cabo Raso, under the finest south-easterly he had ever experienced, the connection rod of the *Beaver* began to wear a raggedly widening hole in the stern which a still sullen Admiralty had not yet conceded must be all iron, and not a foolish composition of wood and iron banding, if it were to contain the unremitting and remorseless spinning of the great rod that turned the twin screws which gave him such precise command of the oceans he patrolled and protected.

By five bells in the morning watch of the fourth day after capture, he had to order the fire in his boilers drawn and under full sail was barely able to keep within hailing distance of the *Sure Salvation* with more than half of her most important canvas furled.

"By God!" he said furiously to his senior midshipman—a brisk elder of seventeen who had come to sea only because he found life on land too full of boring decisions to be made about things in which he could take no interest—"By God, Mister Lowther, if I have to keep astern of you at this rate, and the wind drops three knots, it'll be a month before we cross the bar of the Demerara and drop anchor in Georgetown, eh!"

"I agree, sir," said Mr Midshipman Lowther. "I had to release the slavers, the white men, just to furl canvas enough to keep you in sight. I had 'em under guard, of course, and they performed obedient and docile as you please. But I don't like it, sir. You can keep up with us if the wind remains steady. But a couple of knots fall, sir, or a shift, and this craft could show you a pair of heels before you could even put a shell into a breech. Especially if such a fall or shift occurred just before dark. And I don't have enough men aboard, sir, to keep your prize steady if the wind starts playing me flirtations . . . Not without those slavers, I mean . . . and I don't have enough men to keep the Negroes we've freed and the slavers from each other's throats if the slavers decide to make a run for it and you not close enough to assist or drop a shell across our bows . . . That's about the size of it, sir, as I see it," Mr Midshipman Lowther finished cheerfully. The whole business, to him, did not involve making a complicated, infinitely tedious decision between a dozen contending possibilities . . . A man did what he ought to do, one way or t'other. What could be fairer or more satisfactory than that?

"Well then, Mister Lowther, since you have summed up your ticklish situation so neatly, what d'you recommend, eh?"

"Make for Abari, sir." Lowther pointed to the chart on the table before them: to the area where the larger but emptier and less important British colony of Abari lay five hundred miles east down the coast from British Guiana. "We can make landfall there in less than twenty-four hours if this wind don't drop . . . Is it possible for you to use your screws, sir? Not under full power, or course, but just turning over gentle like to give you an extra two knots? The sooner we can land this prize, the happier we'll all be."

"Yes," Lieutenant Honeyball said, with a sour face. "I'll have them put the screws to work again. But not one turn more than'll give me two knots, mark you, young Lowther. God knows what state my connection rod is in already, and I don't fancy having to explain to some damn fool court-martial of men who were old before Trafalgar what it means when you have five hundred horsepower hammering away inside a hull that's half wood. So keep this barque under close rein, y'understand! Don't suddenly get any ideas that you're in a tea-race home from China and go crowding canvas on me!"

"You may rely on me, sir," said Mr Midshipman Lowther, with the quietly happy satisfaction of a boy who has been growled at by a respected superior because he can be relied on to perform well.

2

In the cabin on the poop, Eliza Hogarth examined her face in the looking-glass of the little dressing-table.

"William," she said, in the casual yet demanding voice of a woman who has made up her mind and now expects confirmation on the wisdom of her choice. "William, I do believe I shall let my hair grow longer. It has been a deal too short these past few years."

Her grey, small eyes were happy and remote with the distance of insanity as she looked at her reflection in the glass and made little adjustments to the fading yellow of her severely trimmed hair.

"Yes," she said, "it is a deal too short for my face, which is too full, I must admit, for so short a cut. It needs a longer heavier fall of hair to fine it down, as it were. Don't you agree, William?"

"Yes," Hogarth said from his chair. His dark, dulled eyes looked at and through her with a kind of bewildered protectiveness.

She turned on the little stool, frowning and pouting fondly.

"Oh, so you agree that my face is too full and round, do you?" she scolded him. "Perhaps you would prefer one of those thin-boned ladies you can measure from cheek to cheek if you hold your thumb and middle finger this close."

She smiled and lifted her hand, placing the tips of her thumb

215

and middle finger about an inch apart. "Is *that* how you'd like to see me, William?"

"No, no, my dear," Hogarth said in a voice at once anxious and falsely bright: in the tone of one attending the bed of an incurable but courageously borne sickness. "You mistook me, my dear. I did not mean your face was too full or too round. You know how dull I find those narrow-cheeked women who look as though they've got space enough across their faces to hold no more than a nose. I meant that you should grow your hair again. Long hair becomes you so—whether piled high or brushed back in two full waves."

He smiled: a determined rictus of mock protest.

"Oh, William," she said, and came quickly from the stool to where she sat a few paces away across the little cabin. She sat in his lap, with the grace and lightness of a girl of twenty-three. "Oh, William, I *was* teasing, wasn't I? I know what you meant. *Really* . . ." She began to push the fingers of her left hand through his springy hair . . . "Am I forgiven?"

"Yes," Hogarth said as her fingers withdrew from his hair, passed gently down his cheek, over his chest and began to burrow between her broad bottom and his lap.

"By the time we get back to England, William, my hair will be near as long as even you could wish. I promise."

A few minutes later, the marine on guard outside the cabin heard, through the bulkhead, the muted sounds of a woman's unrestrained moaning of delight. The moaning persisted, rose in volume, became a plaintive and ecstatic command, and was suddenly, the beginnings of a triumphant shout: a shout suddenly stifled, as though by a bitten fist or by a hand laid across an opened mouth.

"My Gawd!" the marine thought, with generous envy and admiration. "At it again, eh, you old ram! Don't you ever get tired?"

3

On the yard of the upper fore-topgallant, old Calder peels and chews and digests the last artichoke leaf of his experience.

He is directing the furling of a spread of canvas so heavy

216

and so lively in the wind that fills it that the rapid, apparently unstrained movements of those he directs and assists seem almost like conjurers' illusions. Yet, for Calder the gathering in of those huge square yards of wind-swollen, coarse cloth presents no more of a conscious problem than the tying of a cravat represents to a valet.

He does what he has to do, because it has been ordered, and rightly ordered, by a young gentleman who knows his business.

Calder's ponderous ruminations are not really on the yard slanted sixty feet above the deck, and to which he adheres with no more thought than a monkey on a limb above a forest floor. He performs in the web of rope, blocks and tackle with a precision as nearly mechanical as what takes place between the boilers, connection rod and screws of the *Beaver* astern.

What Calder contemplated in the blue furnace of sky above him is his future and the dead.

The ship, he knows, is near the coast. For nearly ten hours now the grey-blue sea has been staining a deeper and deeper brown with the discharges from the huge rivers of the continent to which it is being taken.

Calder remembers Boyo and the Portuguese boy, lying face down, as if asleep, on the morning that he was brought up from the hold. He remembers what happened to Ned Dunn, in the hold, while he looked on, helpless, in the grip of suddenly freed black hands. He remembers Price's head in the scuppers, and that old black woman still holding Mr Reynolds' head and waving it around like a ball by its yellow hair. He remembers Captain Hogarth's face—blank, drained of all assurance and authority—as it looked down on them resting on the pivot of the revolver's muzzle thrust under its jaw. He remembers the captain's lady and how her face went suddenly wild and shocked —then curiously young—before she fainted. He remembers the confusion as the blacks came tumbling with ever-increasing energy of confidence from the hold. He remembers the shame and almost gratitude he felt as the sloop hailed them and the first bluejackets and marines climbed the ladder and fell to on the deck of the *Sure Salvation*.

He remembers all this as he directs the lowering of the fore-

217

topgallant—and he knows that he has come to the end of whatever was to be his end.

He does not know how old he is. He was a fair-grown enough lad at Copenhagen under Captain Colinton on the *Ominpotent*. Not a man grown yet, to be sure, but more than just a boy . . . And that was going on nearly sixty years ago.

In all his more than seventy years, old Calder has spent perhaps no more than twenty really inhabiting dry land.

But he has had free access to and walked the shores and banks of nearly every navigable port and river on earth.

He knows that when he has been landed at this last port and judged, rightly judged, he will be either hanged or confined for more years than he can hope to live . . . And he cannot be sure of the mercy of being sentenced to hang.

Old Calder jumps. He does not dive because he does not know how. Like many of his generation, has has refused to learn how to swim—feeling that the swift marriage of death by drowning is infinitely preferable to the slow hell of being able to keep afloat while waiting in vain to be rescued.

Old Calder jumps from the yard; and the warm brown waters of the ocean as he plunges towards it seem to open for him as welcome and comforting as the arms of a wife.

CHAPTER TWENTY-ONE

1

The *Sure Salvation*, with H.M.S. *Beaver* astern, came ghosting up the estuary of the great Abari, just after dawn on the first Sunday in June 1860.

Once this estuary and the mile-wide looping reaches of wine-dark water seeming to ascend forever into the recesses of the great land had spoken to the highest hopes, the most puissant aspirations, of men truly great in spirit, if not in knowledge. They had tacked their little vessels through shoals and sand-banks, without charts and with little provisions, up and up past savannah into rapids between great forests. They had been looking for the Golden Kingdom: for a place so rich that riches had relieved men of gross distress, of concern for tomorrow and tomorrow, of any material want; leaving them free to fulfil only the sacred, never-to-be-satisfied hunger of the spirit.

Most of them—Spaniards, Portuguese, Dutch, English, Africans—had died miserably enough, a few miles in from the coast: from fever, from malnutrition, from drowning, from the poisoned darts of the Indians who were the only people who understood that the relationship between the huge, nurturing land and those who lived on it was not one of possession but only of simple subsistence, of allowance made by the land to any men—red, white or black—against the day when the land would return to itself and its own purpose.

Now, after nearly four hundred years, the white men and their equally enthusiastic, although involuntary, black partners were no further into the land than a few hundred square miles of the sugar-cane between the coast and the rim of *kookorit* palms where the savannah gradually began to become forest.

The square, parallel-streeted town of mean houses and one

great cathedral, all built of trees painfully floated down-river from the interior, looked less solid, less likely to endure than the two vessels which Lieutenant Honeyball had ordered to be anchored in mid-stream until he could land the five hundred people he had salvaged with their private parts decently covered.

He was rowed ashore and returned shortly in a state that was dangerously choleric.

"Would you believe it?" he asked Mr Midshipman Lowther, flourishing his hand at the little, white-painted town where the smoke from the cooking of twenty thousand breakfasts still drifted in thin blue against the already hard white air. "Would you believe it? There isn't a damned person in that village they call a town?"

"I don't understand, sir," Mr Midshipman Lowther said. "I had a feller aboard while you were gone. Some sort of chandler's clerk or the like, welcoming us to Abari and offering us provisions at cut rates, and—"

"I mean," Lieutenant Honeyball snarled, "that the damned Governor, or whatever he calls himself, and his entire damned staff and every white man, woman and child have gone up-river from Friday afternoon on a picnic. Seems they had a holiday here every King's birthday. Don't ask me which king. This place has changed hands so often it could be any of 'em from William the Conqueror to the Grand Turk himself, but every first Friday in June they get rowed up to the falls and dance and drink, and fornicate for all I know, until Monday morning when they get their niggers to row 'em down again to start work—or what they call work. I tell 'ee, Lowther, there ain't a soul in that town you can talk to except a damned mulatto Clerk of the Courts from Barbados called Washington and a captain in the militia who don't look as if he knows which end of a musket the ball rams into . . . Oh yes, there's a Baptist preacher and his wife in their mission who'll take in Mrs Hogarth and the cook's boy—what's his name?—Joshua! But apart from that, there ain't a person in the town to pass our prize over to . . . and I'm five days anxious sailing from Georgetown where I can find a decent mastersmith and shipbuilder to look to my connection rod and that damned ugly rent in my stern."

By midday, every freed slave on the *Sure Salvation* had been respectably clothed: the men in drawers and the women in smocks. The black people of the town had contributed, stitched, cut and sewn, brought the material out to the anchored ships in skiffs, canoes and rowing-boats, been paid and had returned.

Shortly after noon, Lieutenant Honeyball had the *Sure Salvation* brought in and warped against the great *stelling* from which Abari shipped its sugar and on which it unloaded every material article by which it lived above the level of the savages in the forests ten miles behind it.

The freed slaves were let off the ship first. They looked around them—some with astonishment, some with contempt —at the town which was now theirs by right of Lieutenant Honeyball's gift.

The slavers, Captain Hogarth, Mr Bullen and the Portuguese, were delivered, handcuffed, into the charge of a peevish, middle-aged white man, an overseer on one of the adjacent plantations, in the red tunic of a captain of militia, who marched at the head of thirty exhilarated young black men in blue tunics who acted as if the public holiday had begun to have meaning but who treated their white prisoners with the greatest deference and cordiality as they marched them off up the broad, sandy street under the saman trees to the cathedral, which was the only building in the town large enough to contain forty men who had to be kept under guard.

"Now remember, William," Eliza Hogarth said gaily as she hugged and kissed her handcuffed husband, "we must be back in England before the end of August. Father'll be needing help with the harvest, and I don't know how we will manage without you to keep an eye on things. He just cannot *command* prompt obedience as you can, my dear."

She was helped into the buggy which had been driven down to the *stelling* by the pale and rather beautiful young Baptist minister and his sallow, very plain and even younger wife. The boy Joshua climbed in beside her without a glance at the handcuffed men on the *stelling*, or at the slaves, or at Alex, or at any person with whom he had shared contact until the moment

when these two strangers in a buggy drawn by a slight horse
had come to collect him. All his concentration was now fixed
on where he was being taken and how he was to use those who
had newly become responsible for him.

3

Half an hour after they had descended from the *Sure Salvation*,
the slaves began to dance on the great iron-heart stage of the
stelling beside the wide, wine-dark river.

They did not caper nor fling themselves about. Nor were all
their dances the same since they had been culled from such a
variety of tribes, nations and peoples.

But what they did—men, women and children, in their new
drawers and smocks—was dance. And the sound of their feet
—stamping into the planks of the landing tacked onto the edge
of this new land which they could not even begin to comprehend—made a curious harmony, as of different tongues trying
to discover the few important words by which they might
discover essential exchange.

The black people of Abari, all fifteen thousand of them,
gathered at the edge of the *stelling* and watched with incomprehension, resentment and visibly mounting interest the
dances that were being danced before them by people who
looked like them but with whom they could not exchange one
meaningful word.

Alex Delfosse sat on a bollard at the *stelling*'s edge above the
rush of the river.

He alone of the slavers had not been marched off under
militia guard, in handcuffs, to the great wooden cathedral.

"You'll need that chap," Lieutenant Honeyball had advised
the mulatto Barbadian Clerk of the Courts who was the only
officer of the judiciary left in Abari while the Governor and the
real people of the colony were on a picnic, two days up-river,
by the world-famous Abari Falls. "You'll need him, by God,
until your Governor and all the *sahibs* return. He'll have to
stand trial, of course, but he don't have any place to run off to,
and if I were in your place I'd let him roam free—under your

eye, naturally—until you've got enough help to keep this lot in order."

He gestured with great satisfaction at the five hundred black people dancing on the *stelling*—and at the fifteen thousand black people in white people's clothing and white people's expressions who were watching them with incomprehension, resentment and mounting interest from the green at the *stelling*'s edge.

"Yes, Mister Washington," Lieutenant Honeyball continued, his eyes fixed on where his wounded *Beaver* awaited him in the middle of the great river. "Yes, Mister Washington. If I were you, I would use this man as your *aide* until your . . . your . . . your real people come back from their holiday, what! He'll be invaluable."

"*Weddington*," said the Clerk of the Courts sulkily.

"Eh?" said Lieutenant Honeyball. "Who's this Weddington? Why didn't I meet him?"

"My name, sir," said the mulatto Barbadian Clerk of the Abari Court, "is *Weddington*—not Washington as you seem to believe."

"My dear fellow," Lieutenant Honeyball said in genuine embarrassment and contrition. "I do beg your pardon. Believe me, sir, I do most sincerely . . . *Weddington*, of course. How damned stupid of me . . . Been under a bit of a strain these past few days, y'know, and must have been listening with half an ear and all that. Could have sworn you said Washington when we first met this morning. Damned bad manners . . . Mister Weddington, of course . . . Well, sir, they're all yours now." Again he gestured expansively to the dancing blacks and their black spectators. "Sorry I can't wait until your Governor and Chief Justice get back. But that would take four days, y'know, for you to get word to them and for them to come back down from their picnic. And I must get my ship up to the yards in Georgetown. They have some first-rate fellows there y'know? Absolutely first-rate. Built the first railway in South America and they tell me it runs like clockwork . . . Good-day, sir, and I am deeply obliged to you for your courtesy and your service in helping me put a finish to this filthy, barbarous trade . . ."

But already he was making long, impatient strides across the

223

iron-heart planks of the *stelling* to where Mr Midshipman Lowther waited for him impatiently in the sternsheets of the *Beaver's* cutter.

"But, sir," Mr Weddington protested, "you have observed my situation here. Surely you do not propose to leave me like this with five hundred newly freed slaves and only thirty militia. At least, sir, you could remain until I send word to the Governor ... It would be two days at most."

"Can't afford it, my dear fellow. Believe me, Mister Wash— Mister Weddington, if it wasn't for my damned connection rod and the trouble it could cause if I delay fixing it another minute, I'd gladly stand by. But you'll manage. You'll manage, I assure you ... I must be away and up the coast to Georgetown or their Lords in the Admiralty'll have me shot on my own quarterdeck ... Good-bye, Mister Weddington, and thank you for your excellent services and reception. I have mentioned them, in full I promise you, in my letter of deposition and evidence you have in your pocket."

He turned again, and noticed with distaste that Mr Weddington's yellow-brown fingers were clutching at one of the buttons on the cuff of his tunic, smearing it.

"But Lieutenant Honeyball," Mr Weddington said despairingly as Lieutenant Honeyball began to descend to the cutter moored at the landing platform in the brown water that rushed past the *stelling*. "Mr Honeyball, sir, we have never had anything like this in Abari, sir. We are not prepared for what you have landed on us. You cannot leave like this without providing us with some protection ... It is your capture, your responsibility . . . *Lieutenant Honeyball!* he shouted to the back resolutely turned, already one hundred yards away from him in the sternsheets of the cutter being pulled to the *Beaver*. *"Lieutenant Honeyball! I say, sir! You can't leave me like this!"*

"Don't fret yourself, Mr Weddington," Alex said from where he sat on the bollard. "It's only five hundred niggers you got to worry 'bout ... I'll help you settle 'em in ... An' they sure as hell don't have no place else to go."